PRIMORDIAL ISLAND

RICK POLDARK

SEVERED PRESS
HOBART TASMANIA

PRIMORDIAL ISLAND

WWW.SEVEREDPRESS.COM

ISBN: 978-1-922323-18-7

PART I

CATALYST, REACTION

CHAPTER 1

Dr. Peter Albanese sat up on the stage at commencement in full academic dress next to Dr. Tracey Moran. He was sweating under his robe, but it wasn't from the weather. In fact, it was a cool, pleasant day in May, and the ventilation in the auditorium was thankfully working.

However, Peter hated crowds. They had always made him uncomfortable, and although he wasn't the focal point of this massive crowd of proud parents and bored siblings, he always found the occasion to be stifling and was appreciative it was only an annual tradition.

He looked over at Tracey, who was positively radiant, beaming as if she were graduating herself. Hers hadn't been that long ago, so the gravitas of the situation likely stirred happy memories for her. Peter's graduation was a bit further in the past, though not by much, and he felt the same way about it then as he did now.

After sitting through countless speeches from various university officers, guest speeches (this year from a local politician and a television actor he was unfamiliar with), the ceremony was wrapping up, and the Department of the Geosciences would be joining the other departments at the reception to follow.

When the graduates were applauded and the announcement of the reception made, Tracey turned to Peter. "Well, that was something."

Peter frowned. "Wanna blow off the reception?"

Tracey punched him in the arm and chuckled. "Aw, you know the dean would be displeased if we did that."

Peter stood up. "Time to meet the parents."

Tracey stood as well, and they followed the crowd of academics out of the auditorium. "Oh, it's not so bad."

Peter arched an eyebrow. "Not so bad? We are responsible for releasing their children, their pride and joy, the apples of their eye, into the world as doctors of paleontology."

Tracey hooked her arm in his. "Oh, come on. Stick with me and you'll be all right. Let's see our students off."

Peter, flushing a bit at Tracey's gesture, allowed himself to be led into the throng exiting the vast auditorium. His face felt hot, partially from his physical proximity to Tracey, but mostly from being shoulder-to-shoulder, bottlenecking like cattle being led to the slaughter, and wondering why there were those in civilized company that apparently didn't know the proper use of deodorant.

It wasn't that Peter didn't want to see his students off. He loved his students, and he loved teaching. It was the parents who didn't quite know what to say to him about their adult child who now had to struggle to obtain a decent-paying job in the narrow field of paleontology. He almost felt guilty about it. Fortunately, this year's class was only fourteen. There had been seventeen, but three had dropped out; one after the first year, and the other two after comps.

They entered the reception hall, and the place was filled with students, families, and faculty from the various departments on campus. He had planned on staying put in one spot and letting his students find him. Tracey had other plans.

She grabbed him by the arm again. "Come on. Let's go find them."

There was no arguing with her, so Peter let himself be ushered around the room.

Tracey pointed off to the right. "Look, it's Lucy. Let's go congratulate her."

They approached Lucy, who smiled when she saw them approaching and met them halfway. In tow were her parents and a bored adolescent brother who somehow deftly negotiated the crowded room with his face in his cellphone.

"Congratulations, Lucy!" beamed Tracey, hugging her.

This brought wide smiles to the parents' faces. The teenage brother glanced up at Peter and went right back to his phone. Peter stepped forward. "Congratulations, Lucy."

Lucy smiled and opened her arms to approach for a hug, but Peter awkwardly extended his hand for a handshake. Consequently, his hand touched one of her breasts.

He retracted his hand as if touching something extremely hot. "Oops! Sorry."

She, instead, extended her hand and shook his. Her father's smile waned a bit.

"Mom, dad…this is Tracey and Peter. Peter was my dissertation sponsor."

Lucy's father extended his hand first, and Peter shook it. Then he shook her mother's hand. "Pleasure to meet you, Mr. and Mrs. Gottesman."

Mrs. Gottesman drew her shoulders up to her ears, smiling a little too widely, looking unsure of what to say next. "Lucy's been obsessed with this dissertation for months. It looks like it was quite the project."

Peter nodded, smiling. "She was very brave, electing to study theropod tooth anatomy. She's devised the beginning of a feasible system of assigning specimens to their appropriate taxonomy based on total crown length, base length and width, base shape, squatness, apex location, and serration size."

Mrs. Gottesman's smile faded, her expression morphing to embarrassment and then possibly a hint of antipathy. She cleared her throat and placed her arm around Lucy. "Well, we're very proud of her."

"Yes," added Mr. Gottesman. "Now she can get a job as a dentist for dinosaurs." His tone was more sarcastic than humorous.

Peter managed a smile for Lucy. "Well, congrats. You worked very hard."

Tracey gave her one last hug. "Congrats!"

The group parted as gracelessly as it formed, and Peter and Tracey bounced around the room, engaging in similar interactions with their other students and their families. They were chatting it up with Mark Baker's parents when Peter noticed Petra Vasiliev milling around, apparently alone.

He didn't necessarily want to leave this conversation, as Mark's father seemed somewhat interested and enthusiastic about his son's dissertation, but seeing Petra wandering the crowd alone, looking sheepish, affected him. He knew how she must've felt.

Peter placed a hand on Tracey's shoulder, but he addressed Mark and his parents. "Excuse me for a moment."

He slipped away from the conversation, which Tracey continued alone, and he began to meander through the crowd towards Petra. Tall and thin, in a slightly short black dress and high heels, Petra played with her raven black hair, looking uncharacteristically uncomfortable.

When she saw Peter approaching, she flashed a dubious smile, shrugging her shoulders.

"Congratulations," Peter managed, not knowing what else to say.

"Thanks."

He looked around them. "Where are your parents?"

"They couldn't come."

"Really? I'm sorry."

"It's no biggie. It happens."

Peter felt bad for her. Petra was playing it off as no big deal, but it was a big deal. It wasn't every day one graduated with one's doctorate.

She glanced around the room. "Do you mind if we get out of here for a minute? This crowd is driving me nuts."

Peter couldn't have agreed more. He looked over his shoulder for Tracey, who had been swallowed whole by the crowd in the reception hall. "Yeah. Sure. Let's go."

As he followed Petra outside, he wondered where her parents were and why they didn't come. Petra never talked much about her family. She was an enigma. On the surface she looked like a Goth girl, but beneath the surface lay a keen analytical mind. She took particular interest in the predatory behavior of the Tyrannosaur, which made her the perfect match for Peter, academically speaking.

Once outside, Petra produced a cigarette, which she stuck between her lips, and then a lighter. She ignited a flame and placed it on the tip of her cigarette, shielding it from the wind with a cupped hand tipped with black fingernails.

Peter watched the quadrangle. It was nearly empty, except for some folks leaving the reception early. Everyone else was inside. "So, what's next? Looking for a job?"

"Nah. There's time for that."

"What are you going to do?"

"I dunno. Travel, maybe. Europe. I always wanted to go to Prague."

Peter wondered who was footing the bill for graduate school and Europe. Perhaps the absent parents were loaded. They had to be, which would explain Petra's general devil may care attitude towards life in general. "You know, there's a dig site out in Arizona. They've found some crushed Triceratops bones with trauma marks that need analysis."

Petra looked at Peter with those deep blue eyes. "Really?"

"I-I could pull a few strings and get you on the project."

She smiled. "You'd do that for me?"

Peter smiled back. "For my best student? Sure." It sounded like a flirtation, but Peter meant it. She was one of his best students, if not his best.

Petra turned up the corner of her mouth into her trademark smirk. "Pre- or post-mortem?"

"I believe Dr. Rathi said pre-."

"Any signs of healing?"

Now Peter was smirking. "Maybe." He was being playful, to lighten the mood and help her forget about her parents.

"Really? I just might have to take you up on that."

"I hope you do."

She took a drag of her cigarette. “So, what’s the story with you and Tracey?”

Peter was taken off-guard by the abrupt change in topic. “What do you mean?”

Petra grinned wickedly and bumped shoulders with him playfully. “You know what I mean.”

“We’re colleagues. Friends.”

“That’s all?”

“Yeah, not that it’s any of your business.”

Petra mulled this over for a minute. “Good.”

Peter was confused. “What’s that supposed to mean?”

She took another puff and leveled her gaze at him. “I don’t know. We can figure it out over a drink.”

Peter stepped back, placing his hands up, palms facing out in a defensive posture. “Petra, I think you’re misunderstanding this conversation. I just want to help you out with a job. Nothing more.”

Petra batted her eyelashes. On any other girl, it would look innocent, but Petra wasn’t innocent. She was a predator. “Oh, come on, Peter. I don’t see what the big deal is.”

“I’m your professor, your dissertation sponsor.”

Petra dropped her cigarette to the sidewalk and stepped on it, twisting her tattooed ankle to put it out. “Ex-professor. I graduated, if that’s what you’re worried about. I’m no longer your student.”

Peter had no answer to this. She was technically correct. “Where’s this coming from?”

Petra stepped forward, closing the gap between them, her confidence building. “I’ve always liked you.”

Peter took a step back. “Really?”

“Yeah. I just couldn’t show it. Because, you know, you were my professor, my dissertation sponsor.”

Her mockery of his words was playful, and it turned him on. “I don’t believe you.” His remark was more than self-effacing. It was the defense of a shy man who wasn’t used to female attention. Most guys with better social skills would’ve been on the attack, capitalizing on the vibes Petra was now putting out in waves. But not Peter.

His retreat appeared to embolden Petra. “Oh yeah?” She leaned in and kissed him on the mouth. It was a deep kiss, and when their lips parted, Peter’s face was hot. In a guilty reaction, he looked around. He felt a presence behind him, and he prayed it was anyone but the dean.

He turned to find Tracey standing there.

She gawked at them in disbelief. “I-I’m sorry. I didn’t mean to interrupt.”

"No," was all Peter could manage, but Tracey didn't stick around to hear an explanation. She made a hasty exit, disappearing back into the reception hall.

Peter turned to Petra. "Please excuse me."

Swearing profusely, he dashed back inside the hall, frantically scanning the crowd for Tracey. She was lost in the sea of people, swallowed whole. His mind raced, struggling to interpret her reaction. Was she upset? If so, why? Was it because she saw him kissing a student? Why would that matter to her? Ex-student, like Petra said. Was she disappointed? Jealous?

The true analyst, he began to question his own reaction. Why was *he* so upset? Any guy would've jumped at the opportunity with Petra. Was that what he wanted? What did he want? *Who* did he want? Did he have feelings for Tracey?

Peter ran into Nick Lyons, a fellow faculty member, nearly spilling his drink.

"Hey, Peter. Some crowd, huh?"

"Yeah. Nick, have you seen Tracey?"

"Yeah, she left with Joel."

"Left? With Joel?"

"Yeah."

"When?"

"A few minutes ago. You just missed them."

Peter pulled his cell phone out of his pants pocket and queued up Tracey's number, his thumb poised above the dial button.

Nick, oblivious to his predicament, decided to continue to mill around with his drink. Peter weighed his options in his mind. Did he dare call her? How would it look? Would it look desperate? Worse, would it look guilty? Guilty of what? Petra kissed *him*. But how could Tracey know that? How much did she see?

Peter cursed himself silently.

* * *

Noi Bai International Airport
Vietnam

Bill Gibson stowed his carry-on bag up top on the rack and plopped his carcass into the window seat over the wing of the airplane. He wanted the aisle seat, as his middle-aged bladder wouldn't allow him a non-stop back home, but he wasn't going to let that detract from his victory in Hanoi.

Construction on the new plant would begin within the month, which would make Alan happy. If Alan was happy, it would improve Bill's chances of landing the VP position up for grabs. Word around the watercooler was that the company was looking in-house. He would be able to deliver on that new kitchen he had been promising Trish.

An older Asian woman shuffled over to the aisle seat next to his. She smiled at him, and began to struggle stowing her carry-on up top. She grunted as she tried to heft her bag over her head, unsuccessfully.

Bill stood up, crouching a bit so as not to hit his head on the air vents above. "Let me help you with that."

The lady nodded and backed away a bit down the aisle to allow him out. Bill moved her black luggage bag out into the aisle to make way, and he maneuvered past the aisle seat. He grabbed her bag by the handle and lifted it up, shoving it into the overhead compartment with relative ease. He closed the hatch and nodded to the lady.

She smiled at him. "Thank you."

Great. She spoke English. Bill saw this as an opportunity, and one thing he was great at was capitalizing on opportunities. "Hey, would it be all right if we traded seats? You could have the window. I'm probably going to have to use the bathroom pretty frequently." He did his best to look sheepish.

"Oh, no," said the lady. "I'm terrified of flying. I don't like to look out the window. Too scary."

Negotiation time. "You can pull down the shade." Bill gestured to the window, pointing to the retractable shade, which was currently in the up position.

The lady looked agitated, waving her hands in front of her. "No, sir. Sorry. I like to stretch my feet out in the aisle. Poor circulation."

Bill saw that he wasn't going to win this negotiation. Being a gentleman, he let it go. He returned to his window seat and decided not to let his placement get him down. He was moving up in the world. Besides, he'd get his revenge by asking her to make way several times during the flight when his bladder would nag him.

Noi Bai was a busy airport, but after taxiing around a bit, the plane lined itself up on the runway for takeoff. The pilot's voice crackled over the intercom, relaying their flight time, weather conditions, etc. The flight attendants quickly finished their safety review, and Bill felt the engines revving up.

He looked out the window. It was pitch black, and rain droplets collected on the small portal. Lightning flashed up in the sky, above the clouds. That was what they were flying into.

Given his line of work, Bill was a seasoned flier. When the plane began to accelerate down the runway, he didn't bat an eye. The lady next to him, however, gripped the edges of her armrests until her knuckles turned white.

"It'll be okay," offered Bill. "This is safer than a car."

The lady, eyes wide, shot him a dubious look.

The plane lifted off the ground, bouncing around on the air, and outside Bill's window the flashes of light drew closer. They passed through the dark clouds, and within minutes, they reached cruising altitude. There was the occasional chop, which kept the seatbelt sign illuminated, but they were above the clouds.

The lady next to him seemed to relax a bit.

"The riskiest parts of air travel are during takeoff and landing."

She smirked at him. "What are you, a pilot?" She had an accent. He guessed she lived in Vietnam and was visiting relatives in Australia.

Bill smiled. "No, but I fly a lot for work. My name is Bill."

She smiled. "I'm Bian. Nice to meet you."

"Visiting relatives?"

"Yes. My daughter lives in Melbourne."

"Oh. That's where I'm returning to."

Bian loosened her grip on the armrests, but she startled when the plane jostled in the turbulence. "Nice city."

Bill smiled. "I like it." He looked out the window. "Nasty weather out there."

The plane shuddered again, suddenly dropping a bit, causing that unpleasant tickle in the pit of his stomach. Bian groaned. "I hate flying. Especially those quick drops."

"Just think of the air like a road. It's just as solid to a plane as pavement is to a car."

Bian frowned. "How can it be solid if it's air?"

The plane dipped again. "It's just turbulence. Like bumps in the road."

"You don't sound like you're from Melbourne," said Bian.

"That's because I'm originally from New York. I moved to Melbourne a few years ago when I took a job with my company."

Another abrupt drop in altitude. The lights on the plane flickered. Even the flight attendants looked flustered, as they smoothed out their outfits and regained their bearings.

Bian was watching them, concerned. "I'm thinking of moving to Melbourne myself, to be closer to my daughter. Do you have a family?"

Bill smiled. "A wife and two boys."

"How old?"

"Eight and ten. Real handfuls, the both of them."

Bian chuckled, but it was a nervous sound. "My daughter was, too. Still is. She hasn't settled down yet. I'm not getting any younger. I want some grandkids to play with."

Bill sneered. "Any time you want to borrow mine, I'd be happy to rent them out for a small fee."

"Are they house-broken?"

"Most of the time." Bill was pleased Bian was relaxed enough to quip with him.

The plane dipped again. This time, one of the flight attendants cried out.

"This isn't right," said Bill.

"Don't say that," snapped Bian. "You're supposed to be the voice of reason."

A mother coddled her young child, who clung to her, afraid. The other passengers were murmuring to each other in a mix of dissatisfaction and concern.

There was a clattering sound outside Bill's window and a loud bang. Before he could look outside, the plane dropped and angled downward. The passengers all cried out and screamed.

Bill clutched his stomach as it lurched up. The drop was so sudden, it felt as if he'd left his soul somewhere above him. Bian grabbed his arm and screamed. The pilot came on the intercom issuing instructions, but the tinny voice was drowned out by the din of panic in the cabin. Oxygen masks dropped down from the ceiling.

Bill snatched his out of the air and quickly strapped it to his face. He turned to his right to find Bian unconscious. He grabbed her mask and slipped it onto her face, securing it as best he could.

The plane lurched and bucked in the air, still dropping altitude rapidly. The flight attendants were shouting something about assuming the crash position, and then strapped in.

Bill leaned Bian forward, and he leaned forward himself. His mind raced with many horrible permutations of what was coming. If they were crashing into the ocean, he would grab the vest from under his seat cushion, and the cushion itself would serve as a flotation device. Once he was set, he would attend to Bian. If they were crashing on land, there was nothing he could do except hope he survived the impact.

All the times he flew a plane, and nothing like this had happened before. His mind succumbed to panic in concert with his stomach. He wanted to grab onto something to steady himself. Anything.

The plane leveled out a bit, preparing for landing. There was a loud bang as the ground rushed up to meet the descending metal cylinder.

Bill's mind jarred and everything went black. There was a flicker of the cabin being torn apart. He briefly felt rain on his face, and his eyes were bleached by a flashing light. Then blackness.

*

Bill awoke in his seat, and he hung sideways from his seatbelt, hovering over Bian. His vision was blurry, and his head thundered with pain. Actual thunder crashed above him as rain pelted the back of his head.

He reached to his left to feel for the side of the cabin, but it wasn't there. His window was gone. Instead, his fingers found the edge of jagged metal. As his vision cleared, he saw Bian hanging sideways beneath him, her limp legs dangling over the aisle.

Bill looked around and realized the cabin had been torn in two and exposed to the outside. He saw lush vegetation in the moonlight. He heard the pitter patter of the rain on large, tropical leaves. There were bodies strewn about, dangling from seats, lying on the muddy ground beneath them.

He reached out and shook Bian. "Bian, are you okay? Bian!"

She didn't move. He could only see the back of her head. There was no motion in the cabin. Was he the only survivor?

There was a thunderous, low-pitched sound in the distance. Bill knew it wasn't thunder. It had a low, growling quality to it, like a pack of lions roaring in unison, but muffled.

He looked at the tree line at the edge of the small clearing. The trees and vegetation were shifting about. Was the wind that strong? It wasn't the wind. Something was pushing its way through to the clearing. Something big.

He heard the sound of heavy footfalls as thin tree trunks were shoved away from each other at right angles. A large, dark shape loomed at the edge. There was a low growl, like that of a tiger. The low-pitched sound travelled across the clearing, triggering panic in Bill. He not only heard the growl…he felt it.

A large head poked into the clearing. It looked like a giant bird, its head and torso covered in white feathers, only the beak was too short and fat. That's because it wasn't a beak. It ambled out into the clearing, sniffing the air.

Bill wondered if he had died and gone to a worse place, because the thing hunched about a dozen meters off the ground. It had a long tail that was feathered at the tip. It moved its head from side to side, sizing up the wreckage of the machine that dropped out of the sky.

It approached cautiously, sniffing the air and grunting. It stomped over to the remnants of the plane, scanning the length of it with its eyes.

Bill remained absolutely still. It was on the other end of the wreckage, and he didn't want to draw attention to himself. He prayed it would investigate, lose interest, and vanish back into the trees from whence it came.

It nudged the broken fuselage with its snout, and the whole thing moved. Bill whimpered as he was tilted to his left. It let a burst of air out of its nostrils, emitting a high-pitched whine.

It nudged the fuselage again, and then a third time, pushing hard, until the body of the plane was righted. Bill felt the plane roll upright, and he was no longer hanging in the air. His hands drifted to his seatbelt buckle.

It fluffed its feathers on its head, like a parakeet, and it looked like it had a punk rocker hairdo. It sniffed the air a bit more and let out a loud roar, jumping backward away from the wreckage.

When there was no reaction from the wreckage, it crept forward, emboldened. It pushed its nose into the seats, sniffing loudly. It let out a low growl and opened its massive jaws, snatching a body from its seat with its front teeth. Still belted in, the lifeless torso tore away.

It tilted its head back as it tossed the morsel to its back teeth, and it bit down. Blood dripped past its lips, staining its white feathers, as it crunched bone and pulverized flesh. It swallowed the scrap, and thrust its nose back into the seat.

Jesus! It's eating the passengers. It's eating the damned passengers! Bill realized that he was a sitting duck in his seat. He slowly worked his hands, opening the belt buckle. He slid the two parts of his seatbelt off his body with a slow, deliberate movement.

It tore other bodies away from their seats, gripping them with its front teeth, and chewed and swallowed them. It was a disgusting sight. The passengers were already dead, or so Bill hoped, so they didn't feel anything, but it was horrific to watch this thing feed. It even lifted a huge, muscular hind leg and steadied the fuselage with its clawed foot as it pulled away pieces of meat.

Bill heard crying from up ahead of him. Someone else was alive! *Shush!* He thought to himself. Whoever it was, he or she was going to attract the thing's attention. Then he saw someone stand up.

It was a woman. He could tell in the moonlight it was a woman because of her long hair. She appeared woozy, swaying on her feet, holding her head.

Sit down! Don't you see it?

She screamed, answering his silent question.

The large, feathered beast tufted its feathers on its head, and it let out a deafening roar that sounded part freight train, part animal. The woman turned and began to limp down the aisle. She was heading right for Bill.

It took its foot off the fuselage, hunched over, and began to stomp alongside the plane, following her. Taking large strides, it was gaining on her fast.

Bill thought of that movie, the really popular one with the dinosaurs. "Stop!"

The woman, startled to hear another human voice, froze dead in her tracks.

"Don't move!" Bill called out. "It can't see you if you don't move!" At least he hoped that was the case. That movie was supposed to be thoroughly researched. Plus, the book it was based on was written by a physician.

Terrified, the woman stood rigid several rows from where Bill sat. Their eyes met, but their moment was interrupted when the large, thundering beast stopped short right next to the part of the plane where she stood.

It sniffed the air above her. Its racoon eyes, hidden in the shadow of sharp cranial ridges, were alert. Its teeth were long and sharp. They looked to be almost a foot long.

Bill silently mouthed the words, 'Don't move.'

The woman, shoulders raised up to her ears, froze, but she was sobbing softly. Her body trembled as rain matted her hair to her face. Her teeth were clenched as she stifled a scream.

The beast reached down and nudged her with its snout, its diminutive hands on short arms curling their two four-inch claws. She startled, staring straight ahead, shuddering from abject terror and the rain on her skin, but she stood her ground as it nudged her a couple more times, its nostrils drinking in her scent.

Oh crap.

She must've seen the look on Bill's face, because she crouched, ready to run, when the thing snatched her up in its jaws, spraying the seats with her blood, her cry stifled by foot-long teeth piercing her ribcage and crushing her lungs.

Bill wasn't going to stick around to be dessert. He jumped out of his seat and rolled off the left side of the fuselage, passing over where his window would've been, and he dropped to the mud below. He rolled under the curved edge of the fuselage and hid.

He heard crunching sounds as the poor woman he condemned to death with advice derived from popular culture was being devoured. The fuselage sank a bit, and he shifted away from it to avoid being pinned under the curvature of metal. The beast must've had its foot on the wreckage again, and it was bearing down on it with all its weight. Was it looking for him?

He heard more growling and sniffing, and the fuselage pressed down as the beast reached into the seats, no doubt picking more morsels to be eaten.

Bill didn't dare move. This thing had better eye sight than the movies had depicted. All he could do was wait, hidden in shadow under the curvature of the fuselage, until this thing had its fill and moved on.

Bian wasn't going to make it to her daughter's, and he prayed that he'd live to see his wife and two boys again.

* * *

Four Weeks Later

David Lennox slipped into the dark auditorium, careful to let the door close quietly, so as not to disturb the presentation. The auditorium was about three-quarters full, not bad for a paleontology symposium. Of course, having it center around the feeding behavior of the tyrannosaurus rex didn't hurt. He slid into a seat in the back row and watched the stage with great interest.

A short, olive-skinned, raven-haired man of medium build was talking. Dr. Peter Albanese was elaborating the findings of various digs. He pressed a clicker, and several pictures and bullet points popped up on a large screen behind him. "...as you see, in the vast majority of digs, solitary tyrannosaur skeletons were found by several triceratops skeletons that had suffered trauma inflicted by teeth mostly matching the dimensions of tyrannosaur teeth. One set of remains even included partially digested triceratops bones inside it."

There was a young woman standing at the opposite podium, waiting her turn, debate style. She had red hair, porcelain skin, and was quite attractive. David knew it was Dr. Tracey Moran.

Dr. Albanese pressed the clicker, and a bulleted list of conclusions appeared on the screen behind him. "Like most hunters, the tyrannosaur preferred a significant power differential, singling out a vastly weaker prey so as not to encounter much of a challenge.

"If you look at its anatomy, its front-facing eyes indicated an overlap in fields of vision, the degree of overlap determined by perimetry studies indicating a binocular range of approximately fifty-five degrees. Folks, that's better than the binocular range of a hawk. In fact, theropods in general appear to have had binocular ranges similar to many modern raptorial birds."

Dr. Moran jumped in. "Going back to remains, if you look at hadrosaur remains from a few digs, there were marks on bone that indicated trauma from what was likely a tyrannosaur tooth and healing, which means that the hadrosaur likely escaped an attack and lived to recuperate. If the tyrannosaur was a scavenger, there wouldn't be evidence of bone healing on the hadrosaur skeletons. There would only be trauma."

She clicked a button, and factoids about another dig appeared on screen. "However, there is always that one dig that contradicts the trend, calling into question the generalizations made. One dig found a collection of skeletons grouped together, as if they had all met their demise from a single, shared event, such as flooding. There are tyrannosaur bites on each of the skeletons, whether large or small, without evidence of healing, indicating indiscriminate feeding on carcasses. In other words, scavenger behavior. So, indeed, the tyrannosaur was likely both a hunter and scavenger."

Dr. Albanese picked up the discussion. "Some myths about the tyrannosaur propagated by popular culture and Hollywood…a big one from a popular movie—the tyrannosaur's vision was based on movement. Studies suggest that its vision possibly had visual clarity up to thirteen times greater than that of a human, with clarity extending out to five or six kilometers. They detected prey, whether it moved or not."

"Let's not forget their massive olfactory bulb," added Dr. Moran, which elicited some laughs from the students in the crowd. "They also had a more than adequate sense of smell."

Dr. Albanese smirked. "Then there's that scene where the tyrannosaur chased a car…because of its diminutive forelimbs, if it ever tripped and fell in hot pursuit, it was likely never to get back up. So, it was likely that the tyrannosaur didn't chase down prey in high speed pursuits. Instead it was a lumbering giant with powerful legs and jaws for rending flesh from bone."

Dr. Albanese and Dr. Moran continued down their list of myths about the T. rex and concluded their talk to enthusiastic applause. There was a brief question and answer period, during which David waited patiently. There were questions about something called closed mouth vocalization, where the T. rex might have emitted a low-pitch growl without ever opening its mouth. When the presentation concluded, Peter managed to escape the stage, but Tracey was still surrounded by a clinging throng of adoring graduate students and members of the public.

David decided to take the opportunity to introduce himself. He walked over to Peter, who was waiting patiently for Tracey to wrap things up, and stood next to him. “Excellent talk.”

“Thanks,” said Peter, regarding David momentarily.

David extended his hand. “David Lennox, Director of Personnel Recruitment at Poseidon Tech.”

Peter shook his hand. “Poseidon Tech? The Geophysics company that does those oceanic search and recovery operations?”

David grinned. “The very same.”

“What can I do for you?”

David arched an eyebrow. “Funny you should phrase it that way. I’d like to meet with both you and Dr. Moran.” They both looked over at her as she tore herself away from the last few straggling students.

“About what?” asked Peter.

Tracey walked over to Peter. “That was fun.” She looked over at David. “Who’s this?”

David extended his hand. “David Lennox from Poseidon Tech.”

She shook his hand, but her expression was tentative. “The Geophysics firm that does those salvage operations?”

David nodded. “There’s something I’d like to discuss with the both of you. Is there somewhere private we can talk?”

Peter and Tracey traded dubious looks.

“Sure,” said Peter. “We can use my office.”

*

Peter unlocked his office door and the three entered his office. David closed the door behind them, and Peter immediately started arranging his chairs. There were two side-by-side, next to his modest wooden desk. He faced them towards his chair and gestured to Tracey and David. “Please, have a seat.”

David nodded. “Thank you.” He sat down. He looked around the office, taking it all in. It was a small office covered in photographs of various dig sites and dinosaur skeletons. There weren’t any pictures of a wife or children. Although Dr. Albanese was in his thirties, he appeared to be unmarried and unattached. David wondered what Dr. Moran’s office looked like.

Tracey, making a sheepish face at Peter indicating that she had no idea what this was about, sat next to David. Peter sat in his chair. “So, what is this all about?”

David cleared his throat. “Are you familiar with Vietnamese Airlines Flight 207?”

Tracey nodded. "Yeah, the one that went missing in that storm. Are you guys involved in the search?"

"We think we've located the plane," said David.

"That's wonderful," said Peter. "Where?"

"On an uncharted island off the coast of Vietnam."

"Excuse me," said Tracey. "Did you say an uncharted island?"

David nodded. "Yes. That is correct."

"That's impossible," said Peter. "We have satellites. The globe has been scanned and imaged several times over."

"That's actually not entirely true," said David. "Cartography is fallible, and there are biases in how areas are mapped. The most mapped regions of the world have a lot to do with money, resources, etc. All of the attention goes there. There are, however, underdeveloped parts of the world that have been ignored."

"Hence organizations like Pan World," added Peter. "They're a non-profit group that collaborate with local governments in third-world countries to help update their mapping. But, how does an island get missed?"

"This island possesses certain electro-magnetic properties that interfere with survey and imaging equipment. The satellites have missed it," explained David.

"That would have to be one hell of an EMF," added Tracey.

"So, you found the island," said Peter. "From what you're saying, it sounds like surveying it is proving to be challenging due to EMI."

"Exactly."

"So, what does that have to do with us?"

David paused, choosing his next words very carefully. "There may be assets other than the plane wreckage on that island that may require expert handling."

"Assets?" asked Tracey. "What kind of assets?"

"I cannot go into detail at this juncture, but let me say that these kinds of assets would require your kind of expertise."

"What, fossils?" asked Peter.

David sighed and leveled his gaze at Peter, then at Tracey. "I am prepared to make you a generous offer for your expertise. I would like to arrange a meeting with you at Poseidon Tech to discuss the nature of the arrangement."

"Wait a minute," said Peter. "I'd like to know what this is all about before I go schlepping down to Poseidon Tech. I don't like entering into things blind."

"I understand," said David. "I cannot go into any further detail here. The meeting will be a proposal to you both. You, of course, are free to accept or decline. There is no commitment other than a non-disclosure agreement to be signed before entering the meeting."

"A gag order," said Peter.

"That pre-condition is non-negotiable," said David. "Please understand that there are proprietary rights involved. We have an exclusive contract with the Vietnamese government, and the operation is being overseen by two officers from the Vietnam People's Navy."

"I see," said Peter, sounding dubious.

"Oh, and you'll each be compensated thirty thousand dollars just for attending the meeting, even if you decline our proposal."

"Thirty thousand?" blurted Tracey, incredulous.

"Each," said David.

"Well, that's more than generous," said Peter, "but I'm still not comfortable with all this cloak-and-dagger stuff."

David chuckled. "You're used to working with the government through grants. This is the private sector, Dr. Albanese. We are a for profit company contracted to perform a salvage operation. However, these other assets that may be in play represent an unprecedented opportunity for you and Dr. Moran, as well as the field of paleontology, and time is a factor. We would like to fly you down to Florida tomorrow. If you decline the proposal, others in your field will be contacted. You two were our first choices. If I were you, I would at least hear what we have to say."

"It couldn't hurt to hear what they have to say," said Tracey. "I'm definitely intrigued."

David stood up. "Well, I'll leave you two to discuss it." He produced a business card from a silver metal holder in the right breast pocket of his suit. "You can contact me at this phone number. I need an answer on the meeting by eight o'clock tonight. After that, other parties will be approached."

Peter and Tracey both stood up. David shook hands with each of them and left Peter's office, closing the door behind him.

"What the heck was that all about?" asked Peter, plopping himself back down in his seat.

Tracey sat down as well. "Whatever it is, you better believe it has nothing to do with furthering paleontology."

"It has to be remains. They must've found something."

Tracey shook her head. "Yeah, well, I'm not sure what a salvage outfit wants with fossil remains."

"There's a big market for them in Europe and Asia," said Peter. "Museums over there aren't exactly finding many dinosaur bones in their backyard. A Japanese firm offered a museum in Montana three million for a T. rex skeleton recently."

"Holy smokes," gasped Tracey. "If Poseidon Tech is offering us thirty grand just to talk, imagine what they would offer us to excavate."

Peter frowned at her. "We're scholars, not profiteers."

"Think of what that kind of money can do to fund digs. Come on, Pete. Money has always been a factor. We've always complained that museums will only pay for intact skeletons, which don't tell us jack about theropod feeding behavior."

"We could fund digs for incomplete remains," said Peter, finishing her thought. "The information we would glean would be invaluable."

Tracey leaned forward in her chair, meeting his eyes. "I think we should talk to them. If we don't like what they have to say, we walk. Plain and simple."

Peter hesitated. He didn't like being a pawn in someone else's game, but being a paleontologist, it was unavoidable. Plus, he liked seeing Tracey all jazzed up. It turned him on, not that he'd ever tell her.

"Okay. We'll talk to them. See what they have to say."

Tracey grabbed his arm and squealed. "This is so exciting! Our first delve into the private sector."

Peter didn't like the sound of that. It made him feel like a mercenary. "We're just going to talk," he reminded her. "No promises."

She mock saluted him. "No promises."

Yet, he knew deep down that, against his better judgement, he would follow her wherever she dared to go.

CHAPTER 2

Peter and Tracey sat on a black leather sofa in a spartan waiting room inside Poseidon Tech. A secretary had offered them an espresso, but Peter had declined. Tracey was sipping hers. The furniture was modern, with clean lines and next to no adornment, and they were surrounded by television monitors depicting various past salvaging operations and use of geophysical data collection technology in the field.

Peter was watching the monitor depicting the use of drones and robotics. "Broad strokes."

Tracey looked at him, perplexed. "What?"

"Broad strokes. Robots are great for broad strokes."

"That's not true. They perform fine motor tasks in factories and labs all the time."

"Yeah, but can you picture them excavating a raptor skeleton? It takes a delicate touch."

Tracey placed her empty espresso cup on its saucer and back on the plain, black coffee table. "Why don't you relax? You're so tense."

Peter shrugged his shoulders. "I'm a paleontologist. I'm not used to having money being thrown at me like this. I've grown accustomed to an existence of begging and government grants."

Tracey placed a hand on his knee. "It's just a meeting. There's no commitment."

Peter grimaced. "The private sector makes my ass itch." He didn't mind her hand on his knee, though.

Tracey smiled, but it had nothing to do with his remark. She was excited, and it was obvious. "Aren't you the least bit intrigued? If they're throwing this kind of money at us, they must've found something significant."

Peter looked unconvinced.

Tracey switched gears. "Okay, say that this is a private excavation. It's going to go to a museum anyway. Maybe in Japan, like you said. It's not as if some fat cat is going to grind up the bones and snort them for fun."

Peter shook his head. "It's just that, this is an entirely different world. There are going to be demands, and they'll expect us to deliver results. It won't be on our terms."

"It's never been on our terms. The grants are pretty lax, but the specifications of the museums aren't. How many times have we had to abandon a dig because a skeleton was incomplete? How many times did they lose interest because there was trauma to the bone, broken teeth, crushed remains? They didn't care that it would've told us volumes about theropod feeding behavior."

Peter let out a long sigh. "I guess you're right. Besides, if we decline, they'll just go to someone else."

"Exactly. So, let's hear what they have to say with an open mind." She paused. "You know, you could've dressed up a little."

"They're not paying me for my wardrobe. They're paying me for my knowledge and expertise. Besides, it's a tech firm. It's probably a bunch of nerds in jeans and tee shirts." Peter's eyes shifted around the waiting room. "I bet they're monitoring us right now."

Tracey narrowed her eyes at him. "Now you're getting paranoid."

"I suppose so. Just take it easy when we get in there."

She frowned. "What do you mean?"

"I mean, work on your poker face. Don't seem so eager."

She elbowed him in the ribs. "Are you implying that I'm easy? Because I'm not."

David Lennox, dressed in a designer black suit, strolled into the waiting room. His face lit up when he saw the two paleontologists. "Ah, you're here. Excellent."

They both stood. David extended his hand to each of them, and they shook it. "I take it your flight was comfortable."

"I've never been on a private jet before," beamed Tracey.

Peter grimaced again. So much for poker faces. "Yes, it was quite comfortable."

David grinned. "Excellent. Thank you for making this on such short notice. If you would follow me to the conference room, the team is waiting."

"Of course," said Peter.

They followed David down a long corridor, around a corner, past a series of offices and a bullpen of cubicles until they reached the large wooden doors of the conference room. David got the door for them, and they stepped inside.

Seated around a long, mahogany conference table were three other men, all dressed in suits, and a woman in a pantsuit.

Tracey leaned in to Peter. "A bunch of nerds in jeans and tee shirts, huh?"

He wanted to respond that these were the executive, the grand poohbahs that oversaw operations from the top, the ones who made the decisions involving financing, but he didn't have the opportunity. He did, however, feel a bit underdressed in his golf shirt and khakis.

David gestured to a couple of empty chairs. "Please, have a seat."

Peter and Tracey did as they were instructed and took their places at the table. In front of each of them was a collated short stack of papers.

"What's this?" asked Peter, but he knew damned well what it was.

David took a seat next to him. "That, Dr. Albanese, is a non-disclosure agreement, as we discussed yesterday."

"I'd like to read it, of course, before I sign anything."

"Of course. Take all the time you need."

The suits around the table watched, waiting.

Peter made a face and leaned over to Tracey. "Are they going to stare at us while we read it?" It was a power move, a corporate pressure tactic, Peter was sure.

"Take all the time you need," prompted David. "But, we cannot continue until they have been signed."

Tracey looked at Peter and shrugged. They both began to read the agreement. The whole thing made Peter nervous. It wasn't just the legalese gibberish. The need for such secrecy concerned him.

He looked up from his contract. "We're not going to be asked to do anything illegal, are we? Because if that's the case, I don't care to hear what you have to say."

"No, nothing illegal, I assure you," said the woman from across from him.

"And who are you?" asked Tracey.

"I was going to wait for introductions until after you signed," said David. "But that's Maggie Schechter, Head of Legal."

Peter and Tracey looked at each other. Peter wanted to say that he wanted his attorney to review it before he signed, but Tracey picked up her pen and signed it. His face fell. She was moving too fast. It was just as well, as Peter didn't actually have an attorney.

He picked up his pen and signed it. He and Tracey slid the papers over to David, who graciously accepted them, stacking them in front of him.

"Excellent," said David. "Just to reiterate, nothing discussed here in this building today may be discussed outside of this building with other parties without severe legal repercussions."

"We get it," said Peter.

"Severe legal repercussions," repeated David.

"What's this all about?" asked Tracey, eager to begin talks about whatever they were summoned here for.

David pointed his right index finger into the air. "First, introductions." He gestured to the head of the table. "This is Brad Oster, our CEO." The man nodded. David gestured to the next man. "This is Fred Yates, our Director of Operations, and next to him is Ernest Preston, Chief Project Manager for Salvage Operations in the Pacific." He added as an afterthought, "and you've already met Maggie, our Head of Legal."

"You've found some remains," began Peter, anxious to get down to brass tax.

The executives all exchanged glances.

"Not quite," said Brad Oster.

Ernest Preston pressed a button on the table, and a monitor on the wall flashed a picture of the island. "This is the uncharted island we uncovered." Coordinates flashed up on the screen, superimposed over the images of the island.

"That's a large island to have been missed," remarked Tracey.

"It's 221,329 square miles, to be precise, located in the Western Pacific, in the South China Sea. It's roughly the size of Madagascar."

"Unbelievable," gasped Peter.

"Wait," said Ernest. "There's more." He queued up aerial pictures of the island. It was lush with vegetation, hilly and rocky in spots. "The island itself doesn't have coastal beaches. Instead, it is surrounded by sheer rock cliffs extending a few hundred feet from the water. So, we began initial reconnaissance with unmanned aerial drones, which provided us with these pictures."

Peter squinted, as the pictures were fuzzy. "I thought Poseidon Tech was famous for high resolution data gathering."

Ernest smiled. "We are. The electromagnetic properties of the island that shield it from satellite detection also interfere with our equipment, necessitating a land team to be dropped on the island to search for the remains of Flight 207."

"Have you confirmed that the plane is even on the island?" asked Tracey.

Ernest queued up another photo of what looked like a wreckage in a clearing, but the picture quality was poor. "We took this picture, which we believe to be the wreckage of Flight 207. If you look closely at the cylindrical shape, it resembles the fuselage of an airplane."

Peter squinted his eyes. "Okay…this is nice, but if you have us here, you must've found something else."

Ernest grinned and queued up three other pictures, arranged as tiles on the screen.

Tracey gasped. "Wh-what is that?"

They were aerial photos, this time of large shapes in various small clearings. The images were very fuzzy.

"We were hoping you could tell us," said Ernest.

"Those look like animals," said Tracey. "Large animals. Look at those dimensions compared to the surrounding trees."

"There's no scale to provide context," said Peter.

"Actually, there is," said Ernest. "Our estimates, based on our equipment, range from fifteen to twenty feet in height, approximately twenty-five to thirty feet in length."

"It has a tail," said Tracey, squinting. "At least I think it does."

"The region is known for having deer-like animals, and animals in the bovine subfamily. Tigers, crocodiles, and small reptiles," said Ernest. "These animals don't match any known species."

"You don't think they're dinosaurs," huffed Peter. Tracey joined in on the chuckle. However, no one else around the table was laughing.

Peter blushed with embarrassment. "Oh, come on! You can't be serious."

Brad shrugged his shoulders. "A moment ago, you didn't believe in uncharted islands."

"Good point," said Tracey, looking stunned. She stood up and approached the monitor. She stopped short of it and looked at Brad Oster. "May I?"

He nodded. "Be my guest."

Tracey placed her face right up to the screen, screwing her eyes to try and make out the animals captured in the images. "This is the cleanest resolution you could manage?"

"I'm afraid so," said Ernest.

"So, let me get this straight," said Peter, still seated. "You called us here to identify these animals in the pictures because you think they're dinosaurs?"

"We don't know what they are," said Ernest. "We were hoping you'd identify them in the flesh on the island."

"Look at their grouping," said Tracey, ignoring the exchange. "Look at the body lines. Either they have really short necks, or they're hunched over. They're situated in packs." She squinted at the third picture. "These are differently shaped. They appear squat, maybe horned. I can't tell."

Peter snorted. "Oh, come on, Tracey. These pictures are about the same quality as the Loch Ness Monster."

"They're herbivores," she continued, ignoring Peter's remark.

"How can you tell?" asked Ernest, intrigued by her statement.

"Larger theropods in that height range are solitary hunters. You'd only see one of them amongst prey. Maybe two. The carnivores that hunted in packs, such as velociraptors or deinonychuses, were smaller in height than whatever these are."

Brad Oster and David Lennox exchanged smiles.

"I see that you've chosen well," said Brad to David.

"These two are top in their field," said David, beaming.

"So, you may have found a bunch of undocumented herbivores," said Peter. "We specialize in carnivores, specifically theropod feeding behavior. We wouldn't be of much use."

"See, that's just it," said Ernest. "These are the only pictures we have of these animals on the island. It's only a sample, a snapshot in time. We don't know what other animals may be roaming around."

Tracey returned to her seat next to Peter. "Where there's prey, there are predators."

"Exactly," said Ernest, pleased that she was following his line of thought. "If we are to send a team of geophysicists onto the island, we want to be prepared if we do run into…what did you say…theropods, or the like."

"If your team runs into theropods, they're screwed," said Peter.

"I thought you didn't believe these were dinosaurs," said David.

This observation took Peter off guard. "Well, I-I-I don't," he stammered.

"But, let's say there are predators down there," said David. "Carnivores. Who better to advise our team than you two?"

Peter waved his hands in front of his face. "If there are carnivores down there, I don't want any part of this."

"There will be a fully armed security team accompanying the survey team," assured Ernest.

"Come on, Dr. Albanese," prodded David. "This is an opportunity to catalogue new species. If they are dinosaurs, or something like them, it's an unprecedented opportunity to catalogue and document them."

"Why is Poseidon Tech so interested in documenting new species?" asked Tracey.

Brad Oster leaned forward in his seat, "We aren't. We have a 'no-find, no-fee' agreement with the Vietnamese government, meaning if we don't recover the cockpit voice recorder or flight recorder, we don't get paid, and we'd stand to lose a significant amount of money. We are hiring consultants like yourself and a fully-armed security team to make sure our investment isn't placed in jeopardy."

Peter arched an eyebrow. "Consultants? What consultants?"

"Besides yourselves, two tropical biologists, a hunter-tracker, and of course, the armed security team. Ex-army. Very highly trained."

"Mercenaries," said Peter.

Tracey leaned forward in her seat. "What about us? What if we find new species?"

"Your first objective is to advise the survey team, so that they don't get killed trying to locate the wreckage," said Ernest.

"After that, whatever you find and document, you will receive full credit for," added Brad.

"If you stand to make so much money off of this, I would hope you have more to offer than credit," said Peter.

Brad Oster nodded to David, who slid over two envelopes to Peter and Tracey. "We are prepared to make a generous offer. The first check in the envelope is the thirty-thousand-dollar stipend we promised each of you for agreeing to meet with us today. The second is our offer for you to join the team on the island. That number doubles if we succeed in finding the wreckage and recover the flight recorder."

Peter stared down at his envelope as if it was going to jump up and bite him. Tracey, on the other hand, opened hers and looked at the first check. When she slid it behind the second check, she gasped.

Peter looked over at her, concerned. "What?"

"That's a mighty large number," she said.

"What?" Peter opened his envelope, quickly toggling to the second check. His eyes nearly bulged out of his head. "Ho-ly crap."

"I assume that means you're interested?" asked David.

"I-I-I..." Peter stammered.

"We'd like to discuss this," said Tracey.

"Be my guest, Dr. Moran, but that offer expires when you step out of this room."

"We have commitments," blurted Peter, flabbergasted, "to the university. We have an important dig scheduled."

"We've already spoken to your dean," said David. "She will cooperate fully with your decision, should you agree to join the expedition. It helped that we promised a generous donation to your paleontology program if you signed on."

Tracey squealed in delight. "Holy crap, Pete. It's win-win. We get paid, and more digs get funded."

"And we get eaten," added Peter. "You remember that movie."

David grinned. "Dr. Albanese, in your talk I attended, you yourself said that Hollywood propagated myths about dinosaurs. Between the security detail of heavily armed ex-army and your expertise, I'm guessing you won't be on the menu.

"Also, don't forget, there's the distinct possibility that there are no dinosaurs on that island, and you are along for the ride and get paid very generously for doing nothing." David's expression indicated that he knew he had Peter—hook, line, and sinker.

Peter and Tracey looked at each other like a couple about to get engaged, she staring at her checks as if they were a humongous diamond ring. They muttered and whispered to each other, and Tracey turned to David. "We're in."

Just like that, Peter and Tracey were married to Poseidon Tech.

* * *

Hawaii

In one of the biology labs, twenty or so undergraduates, sitting on lab stools, were poised over their disposable drinking cups filled with dirt, a tiny plant poking out. Each student had two cups, one labeled 'Experimental' and the other labeled 'Control.' Liquid droppers were positioned next to the cups. Some students were looking down at their seedlings, and others were looking at the front of the lab.

Dr. Allison McGary was up in front of the lab, addressing her class. "Okay, as we are about to introduce the gibberellin hormones, remember the three outcome measures we'll be watching…" She paused, waiting for one of the students to finish her thought.

"Germination, elongation, and flowering," volunteered a girl at the front of the room.

Allison smiled. "That's right. Remember to only administer the hormone to the cup labeled 'Experimental'." Something caught her eye in her peripheral vision. There was a man watching her through the small, square window in the door at the front of the lab to her left. She didn't recognize him.

Mark, her Teaching Assistant, approached her table. She handed him a bottle of the growth hormones. "Mark is going to bring the bottle around. After you've all administered the treatment, I'm going to send him around with the inhibitor for your cup labeled 'Control'." When she looked to her left, the dean was in the window, beckoning her with a curled finger.

Great. What did she do now that Dean Munoz was interrupting her lab? "Mark, take over."

*

Allison barely had enough time to call her husband, Patrick, before the flight to Vietnam. "Make sure you maintain the feeding log."

"I will," said Patrick on the other log.

"And make sure you sterilize the bottles and the nipples."

"Yes, honey."

"And her sleep log."

"Yes, I'll note everything down. Do you want me to weigh her bowel movements, too?"

"I'm serious, Pat."

"I know you are. Have a good meeting. I love you."

"Love you, too," said Allison. "I'll call you when it's over." She terminated the call.

She felt ill at ease, leaving her four-month-old. Returning to work after a couple of months was one thing. Flying to the South China Sea to join some kind of expedition was another thing.

Then there was the check. That humongous check. David Lennox had told her that was more money than she was going to see in her entire career as a botanist, and he was right. She hated to admit it, but it was college tuition for little Amber Rose. It was security.

Patrick had been laid off from his company, which was par for the course for a chemist these days. The generous check would prevent them from losing their townhouse. At least he would be home to watch their little Amber Rose. When Allison was hesitant, he was the one who nudged her to take Poseidon Tech's offer, even though he didn't know the specifics.

Her non-disclosure agreement even applied to spouses, so all he knew was that she was being paid a ton of money to go on a trip and catalogue plants. Dean Munoz had pushed on her end. The opportunity to catalogue new plant species was too hard to pass up. There was also the generous donation to the university.

Now, she waited at Daniel K. Inouye International Airport for Poseidon Tech's private jet. Her parents had always pushed science and math, as did Patrick's, but scientists didn't receive huge checks and fly in private jets. Not usually. No, she resolved to encourage Amber Rose to take up business, or something in health care. Something where she didn't have to worry about job security or the future.

Allison had to admit that she was curious about this uncharted island that had evaded detection. Given its location and geographic isolation, this place could be the new Galapagos. Besides, the fact that she was chosen would get Dean Munoz off her back.

The two had rubbed each other the wrong way from the get go. Truth be told, although she was tenured, Munoz had it in for her. It was a classic personality conflict (at least that was how Human Resources viewed it). Clashing egos and flame wars were not uncommon in academia, but Allison couldn't afford to lose her job. Not now.

Then came David Lennox, her knight in shining Armani, with his big checks and donation to the school. Poseidon Tech had stepped in at the right time. It was true deus ex machina, and for once, a heavy burden was lifted off of Allison's shoulders.

For the first time in a long time, she felt everything was going to be all right.

* * *

Baltra Island, Galapagos

Having just wrapped up her Biology of Neotropics Course, Mary Tambini was juggling a phone call with her mother while packing her bags for Vietnam.

"Where are you going now?" asked her mother.

"I can't tell you."

Her mother let out an exasperated sigh on the other end. "You've always been able to tell me before."

Mary placed rolled tee shirts into her luggage one-handed. "I signed a non-disclosure agreement. I can't say."

"Non-disclosure agreement? Is it government?"

"I can't say. And no, it's not government."

"Mary, what are you getting yourself into now?"

"I can't say, but it pays really well. *Really* well."

"The school is okay with this?"

Mary shoved socks into her luggage. "The school is okay with this. I have their full support."

"What about that nice young professor? I thought you had something going with him."

"Well, no I don't."

"Mary, you're not getting any younger. You're a smart girl. You need to meet someone nice. Your sister met someone nice…"

"Mom, Fran hasn't gone anywhere or done anything with her life."

It was going to be another one of those conversations. It wasn't enough that Mary had obtained a doctorate and had a tenure track position at a major university. Her mother had a checklist. She was to meet a nice, young professional next and settle down, get married, and pop out a few children. What her mother didn't realize was that doing so would mean giving up on her career that she had worked so hard to establish.

"Mary, don't talk bad about your sister. She's done well for herself."

"Mom, I can't talk right now. I just wanted to tell you that I'm going to be incommunicado for a while, and not to worry."

"I just want you to have a good life, honey."

"I do have a good life, mom. I gotta go, or I'll be late for my flight."

"You be careful."

"I always am. Love you. Bye." She ended the call. These conversations were becoming more and more exhausting. Apparently, her mother thought she could wear her down with incessant nagging. Now she knew what her father put up with all these years.

However, she wasn't going to let that put a damper on her new adventure. In fact, she was looking forward to a break from her mother's overbearing expectations. If her mother had only seen the size of the check she just deposited into her savings account, she might feel differently about the direction of Mary's life.

David Lennox had hopped from the Galapagos to Mindo to Tiputini, and had finally intercepted her back in the Galapagos. Now, she was to fly to Vietnam to catch a helicopter for on shore transport to one of Vietnam Petrocorps' off shore oil rigs for expedition debriefing. Then, she was to catch another helicopter to some uncharted island to help catalogue animal species that have apparently existed in geographical isolation.

This was her life, jetting from one location to another, and now, she was off to another location. Poseidon Tech had provided a sizable enough donation to CSUN to excuse her from her obligations to go on this expedition, which was apparently urgent.

Her phone rang. She took the call. "Hello? ...yeah…okay, I'll be right down."

Her driver was waiting downstairs. She zipped up her luggage and wheeled it across the room. When she opened the door, Lyle was waiting there, standing in his tight black v-neck, biceps bulging out of their sleeves. His shirt clung to his torso, revealing is six-pack abs.

When he saw Mary, his face lit up. He bit his bottom lip. "Hi, Mary."

"I can't talk now, Lyle. I've got to go, or I'll miss my flight."

"I-I just wanted to say goodbye."

She managed a polite smile. "Goodbye, Lyle. Good luck."

He nodded, but that wasn't all. He had something else to say. It was in his eyes. "I was hoping we could reconnect when you returned from your trip."

"I don't know how long I'm going to be gone for."

"It doesn't matter. I'll wait."

Mary frowned. She had tried sending him subtle hints, and then, when that didn't work, not so subtle hints. Lyle was dense. She gave him a quick hug. "Take care, Lyle. Have a great life."

He hugged her back, but it was awkward. He stepped aside and let her pass.

As she walked down the hotel corridor to the lobby, she couldn't help but feel a little guilty. The time they shared was fun, but her career didn't allow for much in the way of permanence. That was perfectly okay with her. She wouldn't have it any other way.

CHAPTER 3

Bill Gibson sat, crouched inside a small cave, his shirt and pants torn and saturated with sweat. He reeked of urine. His stomach lurched, partially in anticipation of the fifteen-foot lizard chasing him, and partially because he had consumed some wild fruit unfamiliar to him. In fact, his diet on this God forsaken island had consisted mainly of fruit.

He had caught some small animals with a spear he had fashioned and had managed to eat them raw. It made him nauseous, but it was protein. Besides, the fruit mostly gave him diarrhea, which only dehydrated him. He had found a small cascade of fresh water, but he was chased away by what looked to be a great feathered tyrannosaurus rex.

Of course, he told himself that was impossible. There were no such things as tyrannosaurs. At least, not anymore. Yet, here he was on this island, the only survivor, completely alone, being hunted by what could only be a T. rex.

The cave was dark and cool, providing some relief from the relentless sun. He wondered why no one came looking for the downed plane. He knew a bit about emergency locator transmitters. He knew they activated upon impact via a G switch. He also knew they were unreliable as hell.

Something stirred off in the vegetation about fifty feet away from the mouth of his cave. Bill pressed himself low to the ground, eyes ahead, hoping he'd blend into the shadows.

A three-foot tall bipedal lizard romped out into the clearing. It looked like a mini T. rex to Bill, or one of those velociraptors, only much smaller than the ones in Hollywood. It shook its head like a wet dog and sniffed the air. It sniffed the ground, stepping closer and closer to the mouth of the cave.

When it was twenty-five or so feet away, it stopped and turned its head up, barking into the air. After a brief moment, it was joined by two others in the clearing that were sniffing the ground.

Bill commando-crawled away from the mouth of the cave, careful to remain quiet. He knew his stench gave him away. When he was far enough away from the cave opening, he pushed himself to a crouching position, ears pricked for any sound.

There was none. He let out a slow sigh, hoping the raptors had lost his scent and moved on. There was a scratching on the ground up ahead, followed by snorts.

Damn. Bill knew they found him. He turned to run deeper into the cave as he heard grunts and growls at his back. The scratching of claws grew closer as they quickly closed the distance.

Bill ran headlong into the darkness of the cave as he heard the snapping of jaws behind him. He had no idea where he was going. All he knew was that he had to run for his life.

His flight was cut short as the ground dropped beneath him, and Bill found himself in freefall. He plunged into icy water some feet below, and there were splashes around him as his three pursuers fell into the water all around him.

They whined in panic as they reached out with their tiny arms, thrashing about, their tails whipping at his legs under the water. Bill kicked at them, crying out as they bounced off each other in the dark, splashing.

After a moment, the lizards' cries vanished as they sank beneath the water. Bill tread water, listening for sounds and kicking his legs. Satisfied they had drowned, he began to swim around, groping in the dark to assess the topography around him.

He felt a hard, vertical rock cliff in front of him. He figured he must've fallen from up top. There had to be another way out of the pool he was in.

He decided to swim laterally, to his right, and follow the cliff until it led to some kind of opening or platform. He followed it around, feeling it curve, until it opened almost directly opposite where he was before. At least that was what it felt like to him. In the darkness, it was difficult to know for sure.

He swam into the opening and forward, reaching out in front of him. The space in front of him appeared to extend on into infinity, a gaping void. Having no other choice, he pressed on, kicking his legs. The water was very cold, making breathing laborious as his diaphragm struggled.

At last, his hands felt a wall close in on his left, and then his right. The cavern was narrowing around him as he swam forward. The sound of his splashing changed, and the top of his head began to scrape on a low ceiling.

Bill wasn't claustrophobic, but he began to feel uncomfortable with the dropping ceiling. He reached a point where his nose was barely above water and the ceiling was right above him. It reminded him of the cenotes in Xcaret, Mexico, where he had gone on his honeymoon.

He knew those underground caves in Mexico ran on for miles, and many were completely submerged. There were all kinds of signs posted warning divers not to proceed past a certain point, and more than a few foolhardy adventurers had gone on, never to return.

He and Trish had gone on a guided tour, only they had life jackets and head lamps, as well as a guide who knew where the hell he was going. Down here, right now, he had no such luxuries.

Bill knew he had to press on, even if it meant holding his breath and going under. If he remained by the rock cliff, treading water, he would fatigue and eventually drown.

It was a leap of faith, but he had to push forward, praying that it opened up into another cavern. Bill was raised Catholic but hadn't been to Mass in ages. He wasn't an atheist. He was just lazy.

He said a silent prayer and took a deep breath. He dipped under the water and kicked at regular intervals, pushing forward. Every few strokes, he reached up only to find the ceiling now extended beneath the water's surface.

He kicked some more, lurching forward under the water, running out of breath. Panic entered his mind in the dark, but he shoved it back, willing himself to remain calm. His heartbeat quickened until his heart felt like it was beating out of his chest. Running out of breath, he began to wag his head from side to side under the water as he felt himself begin to lose consciousness.

One more kick of his legs and Bill reached up with the last of his strength, only this time his hands broke the surface of the water. He popped up, filling his lungs with air, moaning in more darkness.

He breathed in the cool air, shivering in the water, partially from the temperature and partially from nerves. He had almost drowned in the dark after nearly being eaten by carnivorous reptiles.

His heart rate slowing to normal and his breathing equalized, he pushed forward, kicking his legs and pumping his arms until he saw a crescent of light. He swam towards it, and the cavern opened into a grotto.

Exhausted, Bill swam up to the beach and rolled onto his back as he breathed heavily from exertion. His eyes felt heavy, and within minutes, Bill fell asleep on his back, oblivious to his location or surroundings.

*

Shivering, Bill opened his eyes, the sunlight shining bright, hurting his eyes. He rolled over to his side and felt the sand between his fingers. He knelt and cupped his hands, filling them with cool, fresh water. He splashed his face and looked around. The grotto appeared empty. He cupped his hands again, scooped up some water, and drank from it, hydrating himself. His stomach growled, startling him.

He pushed himself to standing and staggered to the entrance of the grotto, shielding his eyes with his right hand. He wondered how long he slept. Was it a couple of hours later or the next day? Judging from the rumbling of his empty stomach, he likely passed the night in the cave, fortunately without incident.

He checked the surroundings outside the cave, and he nearly froze when he saw a herd of large animals milling about outside. They didn't seem to pay him any mind. They grazed on the grass and vegetation on the ground.

Encouraged by their lack of response, Bill crept out of the cave to get a closer look. There was at least a dozen of them. They had fat bodies and short legs. Their head had a bony plate, and two larger horns above one smaller horn protruded from their faces. 'Triceratops,' he thought to himself. 'No way.'

He wondered if he had died in the crash, and maybe this was some kind of fresh hell, but he'd led a mostly good life, careful not to commit any major wrongdoings, so hell seemed unlikely. Did he go back in time? Was that even possible? Was this some Bermuda Triangle type stuff?

Bill stepped away from the cave, giving these creatures a wide berth, and they just continued to graze, occasionally snorting, but ignoring him completely. His stomach growled, but these creatures were too large to tangle with and their horns too foreboding, so he trekked through the underbrush into the jungle in search of more manageable game.

After walking for what must've been an hour or so, something shiny up ahead caught his attention. It gleamed, metallic, in the sun. He quickened his pace, momentarily forgetting he was starving, until he saw what it was. Up in a tree, flipped upside down, was the tail of the plane.

'Exactly,' he thought to himself. 'Often, if ELT units were upside down, they'd fail to transmit.' He wondered if the Emergency Locator Transmitter was intact. There was only one way to find out.

He approached the tree carefully, pricking his ears to any heavy footfalls or low-pitched growls coming from the surrounding jungle.

Satisfied he was alone, except for smaller animals, he walked up to the tree. The plane tail hung precariously above in the heavy vines.

The trunk of the tree was massive, the lowest branches tens of feet above the ground. However, next to the colossal tree was a smaller tree with what looked like red spines sticking out of its trunk. He followed the spines up to where the branches hung, one making contact with the branch of the more massive tree.

Bill walked up to the spiny tree, gently touching the point of a spine with the palm of his right hand. It was sharp, but the shaft of the spine wasn't. He grabbed a hold of one of the spines, protruding out half a foot, and pulled himself up, finding a footfall on another spine. His body was sore, and his muscles ached, but reaching the plane's ELT was his best hope for being found and the only idea he had at the moment.

He carefully selected hand-holds and foot-holds, climbing up the tree. It reminded him of one of those rock walls on a cruise ship he and Trish took last year. *Trish.* Bolstered by the desire to see his wife and children again, he ascended the tree, spine by spine. The sight of the plane's tail next door comforted him. It was a relic from his past life on this bizarre island. It was real to him, which drew him to it.

When he reached the lowest branch of his tree, he hoisted himself up onto it. *There you go, Bill. Easy does it.* Sweat dripped down his brow and made his hands slick, but the bark of the branch was rough, providing a solid grip. He inched across the bough until he was able to reach up to another above it. He found a large insect clinging to the bark. Without hesitation, he snatched it and shoved it into his mouth. It crunched as he chewed it, fighting back the waves of nausea. He felt its legs and antennae twitch against his tongue until he ground it up into a crunchy paste. He forced himself to swallow, and it scratched his throat, but it felt good hitting his stomach.

Jesus, what did I just eat? Doesn't matter. It's protein, and that's what you need right now. He pulled himself up, balancing on the branch beneath him. This branch made contact with one from the larger tree. He inched his way out across the branch. It dipped a bit under his weight, but it felt solid.

He made it out to where it touched with the other branch. He carefully transitioned to the branch of the other tree, the muscles in his arms straining. He crawled across the new branch, back towards the trunk. He rested a moment, catching his breath. He had to urinate, so he just went. His crotch grew warm and wet, and it trickled down his right leg.

The jungle was alive with squawks and chirps. Brightly feathered birds flew from branch to branch, carefully watching this intruder in their midst. Bill eyed how far away the plane tail was and estimated how many branches it would take to get to it.

He snatched another of those large bugs from the bark in front of him. It went down easier this time. He wasn't sure if it was the food or that he actually had a purpose at this moment, but he was starting to feel better, a bit more energetic.

He made his way from branch to branch in a methodical fashion, taking his time, careful not to fall to the ground, now fifty feet or so below. He couldn't believe he had made it so high, but he was determined to reach the tail, as if it represented grasping onto the familiar in this alien world.

He froze as he heard heavy footfalls, but they were a pack of those triceratops rumbling through in some kind of hurry. He wondered why they moved with such urgency. If there was a tyrannosaurus rex chasing them, Bill was well above its head. All he had to do was cling to the tree and wait for it to pass.

He waited, but nothing else came. So, he figured he'd continue over to the tail of the plane. He made it over to the tail hung up in the vines, balancing his feet on the branch.

There was a strange sound in the distance. It sounded to Bill like a long, continuous belch. What was worse was that it sounded as if it was in the trees. He froze, scanning the branches and treetops, but he didn't see anything. What nasty surprise did this nightmare cook up for him now?

He decided to investigate the tail section. It dangled above the jungle floor, its weight straining the thick vines, causing them to creak. Bill took a chance and grabbed one of the load-bearing vines. It groaned, but it held his weight. He slid down to the top of the tail section.

He nearly lost his grip when he heard that low, belching sound in the treetops. This time it was closer. He knew he didn't have much time. He slid on top of the tail section, straddling it, as it gently swayed in the cradle of vines.

It was torn at the end, leaving a space for him to crawl into. He swung his feet over, gripping the jagged top metal edge and swinging his feet inside the cavity. He slid himself inside on his back. Once inside, he shimmied and turned himself so that he was facing forward, and he crawled as far back as he could.

He saw it. The ELT, a bright orange box, was affixed to the inside of the plane, the antenna meshed with the outer skin. He crawled over to it to inspect it more closely. It appeared intact, and the co-axial antenna cable unbroken. It had a big label saying, 'WARNING: For Aviation Emergency Use Only,' a label listing part and serial numbers, and one with instructions reading, 'ARM: Switch in the "ARM" Position' and 'MANUAL ON: Switch in "ON" Position.' Then beneath that, 'RESET: Switch to "ON" position and back to "ARM".'

Normally, the aural and visual monitors in the cockpit would indicate if the module was transmitting, but the cockpit was nowhere to be found. The good news was, if it hadn't activated and he could somehow activate it, it would transmit continuously for approximately two days, if the battery was fully charged.

On the side of the box was a "female" antenna connector; remote switch plug-in; the reset and "on position" light; the activation switch with on, arm, and off positions. The light wasn't lit, so the transponder wasn't transmitting. He switched the activation switch into the on position, and the light illuminated.

Bill couldn't believe it. *Well, that was easy.* Only, it wasn't so easy. He had to scale a spined tree and go from branch to branch like a damned monkey. He wiped his brow and sat there for a moment, listening to the creaking of the vines.

Satisfied that he accomplished his objective, all there was left to do was find a safe hiding spot close by and wait. He turned inside the tail section and crawled right back out to the jagged opening. There was that horrible belching sound, close this time, and there was a thump on the roof of the fuselage.

Bill froze as he heard scratching along the top, moving in his direction. He rolled over onto his back, grabbed the top jagged edge of the opening, and pulled himself out and up.

He was face-to-face with a sizeable monkey. It opened its mouth, brandishing long, sharp fangs. Bill panicked and let go of the top edge of the opening as it rushed him, landing on his chest. The weight of the monkeys landing caused him to fall out of the fuselage. He grabbed onto a vine on the way down, and the monkey grabbed a higher vine, swinging away.

Bill clung to his vine, swinging above the jungle floor, his eyes squeezed shut. He heard the belching, now all around him. It was a horrible sound. When he opened his eyes, he was surrounded by monkeys. Big, brown monkeys. "Great, just great," he said out loud.

As if in response, the belching intensified in unison, as they shouted him down, a sign of dominance. They sprung at him, swinging from branch and vine, striking him as they swept past. Bill waved an arm to swat them away, causing him to lose his grip. He slid down the vine as they swarmed him, taking passing shots as they swung around.

Bill panicked and lost his grip, falling down to another branch, hitting his back, and rolling onto another branch. The monkeys followed him down, belching and growling, swiping at him, and poor Bill slid from branch to branch, falling onto a vine, catching it under his armpits as he fell.

He grabbed onto it with his hands, holding on tight as his antagonists swept down, striking him and swiping at the vine. At last, the vine snapped, and Bill swung down toward the ground. As he fell, his hands slid, reaching the end of the vine. He dropped the rest of the way, landing on the ground face down.

The wind knocked out of him, he groaned, trying to fill his lungs with air. It was one of the worst sensations he'd ever felt, and he couldn't inflate his lungs fast enough to end the agony. At last, he began to breathe, and he rolled onto his back. His vision was blurred, but he was surrounded by people. Naked people, save for crude animal skin loin cloths, and they pointed spears at him. Their faces were painted stark white, lending them a shocking appearance.

Bill's vision faded to black as he succumbed to unconsciousness.

* * *

Peter and Tracey found themselves aboard the offshore oil rig in the South China Sea. It was a noisy place, as they strolled past pumps, fuel tanks, and air tanks, led by the project manager from Poseidon Tech. Engines worked and intercoms blared. Employees manned computer stations and switches adorned with pressure gauges. As they navigated the platform, away from the helicopter landing pad, Peter couldn't help but notice they were completely surrounded by ocean.

"It's beautiful," gasped Tracey.

Peter looked a bit green from the helicopter flight over, but Tracey was chatting it up with the rest of the team. She was surrounded by Dr. Allison McGary and Dr. Mary Tambini, both tropical biologists specializing in plants and animals, respectively; Jason Barret, hunter/tracker; Poseidon Tech Project Manager, Susan Kinney.

"This is a nifty rig," remarked Tracey.

"The Vietnamese government let us use it for debriefing before transport to the island," said Susan.

"So, we're all going to the island by helicopter?" asked Peter. He wasn't thrilled about riding in a helicopter again. "Whatever happened to boats?"

"There's no beach head. The sheer cliffs surrounding the island necessitate it," explained Susan. "It'll be your only way on and off the island, but, don't worry. I'll be right there with you. One of our survey vessels will be in the vicinity. The helicopters will drop us right where we think we've located part of the wreckage. Then we'll assess the situation and decide how to proceed from there."

Allison, the botanist, beamed. "It's amazing, finding this uncharted island. Imagine the undiscovered flora waiting for us."

"Remember, our first objective is to locate the flight recorder safely," said Susan. "Your job is to make sure our team isn't in any danger from poisonous plants. Once we've achieved the objective, you'll have time to explore and catalogue."

Peter gestured to Jason. "What's he here for?"

"In case you, Dr. Moran, and Dr. Tambini find evidence of predators, large or small."

"I've hunted tigers, lions, you name it," winked Jason.

"That sounds very illegal," groused Mary with obvious disapproval.

"He wouldn't do much against a T. rex," said Peter.

"I can track and kill almost anything," said Jason. "It's a gift."

Peter snapped his fingers. "Now I recognize you. You're that guide who took that plastic surgeon on that lion hunt. It was all over the news. You were eviscerated on social media."

Jason frowned. "Yeah, well, let's just say I have some legal bills to pay off now."

Susan smiled, but it was joyless. "Jason, here, is necessary as part of our escort through the jungle. We also have our team of ex-military as backup in case things start do go sideways with the wildlife."

Peter groaned. "This is sounding worse by the minute." He turned away, his stomach lurching, as he struggled to keep down its contents.

Jason nudged Tracey. "Someone's a little too delicate for this kind of expedition."

Tracey smiled. "He's never liked helicopters. Or the ocean. I'm pretty sure he won't like the jungle either."

"I'm also not a fan of people talking about me as if I'm not here," added Peter.

Jason regarded Peter with a mix of pity and amusement. "So, what's the deal with you two?"

"What do you mean?" asked Tracey.

"Are you two, like, together?"

Tracey chortled. "Me and Pete. Nah, not like that."

"Good," said Jason, being bold.

"You're very forward," blushed Tracey.

Jason shrugged his shoulders. "I'm a hunter. When I want something, I go right after it."

"Oh, brother," groaned Tracey. "That was awful."

Jason shrugged, looking sheepish. "What? What'd I say?"

Allison rolled her eyes. Mary slapped Jason on the back, winking at him. "Looks like that one got away."

Jason smirked. "Not yet. Sometimes you have to pursue, wear the prey down."

"I can still hear you," said Tracey, standing by Peter, whose face was literally green.

Jason and Mary shared a laugh. Allison dreaded her little Amber Rose growing up and running into guys like this. She decided that, when she got home, Patrick had to get to work procuring a gun collection.

Susan checked her watch. "We meet in the debriefing room as soon as the security detail gets here. Then we take off and hit the island."

A soldier dressed in jungle camouflage fatigues entered the room, followed by eight others. "Security has arrived. Mario Torres, at your service."

"Excellent," said Susan. "The gang's all here. Follow me to the mess hall for debriefing."

The laughter died down, and there were nods all around. While the biologists and Tracey appeared excited about the expedition, Peter was weary.

Jason looked bored. Peter thought he was just playing it cool for Tracey's benefit. He wondered what each of the others were being paid, but more importantly, he wondered if anyone else felt anxious.

They followed Susan to the mess hall, where there was quite the spread furnished for them, no doubt by Poseidon Tech. "Grab some food and have a seat," announced Susan. As the team lined up, grabbing plates and trays, Susan reviewed some files and checked notifications on her tablet.

"This looks great," said Allison, gawking, taking it all in.

"I'm starved," chimed in Mary.

Tracey nudged Peter. "This looks good."

"I'm not very hungry."

"Have something," she insisted. "It'll settle your stomach."

Peter reluctantly took a plate and tray, and he settled on a bagel with cream cheese. The grumbling in his stomach overcame his malaise, and he added a small Danish to his tray.

Tracey stuck to the fresh fruit. She pointed to a tray of fish with her fruit tongs. "What's that?"

"Whitefish," said Mary. "Great for breakfast."

Tracey smiled and took some.

Jason, the hunter/tracker, loaded his plate up with bacon, eggs, and sausage, as did his team. Jason looked over at Susan. "You're not eating?"

She looked up from her tablet. "I ate already, thanks."

Peter sat next to Tracey at a table, eying what appeared to be two Vietnamese naval officers already seated. They weren't eating. They sized up the team. A third officer accompanied them, whispering to them as they nodded.

When everyone settled at the tables in front of their breakfasts and began to dig in, Susan looked up from her tablet and addressed the group. "Thank you all for coming. There's been a new development. As of six thirty-two am, Cospas-Sarsat relayed a signal sent from an aviation ELT unit on our uncharted island to the Air Force Rescue Coordination Center at Tyndall Air Force Base in Florida."

There were murmurs of excitement and celebration in between chews and sips of coffee.

"The registration data confirms that it is Vietnamese Flight 207."

"I thought you said that EMI was shielding the island from satellite view," said Peter between chews of his bagel.

Susan smiled, impressed that he caught that detail. "You're correct, Dr. Albanese. EMI would interfere with radio transmissions. It would appear some other, unknown factor is shielding the island."

"So, what's the plan?" asked Jason.

Susan placed her tablet on the table by her side. "We are going to arrive on the island by helicopter, as close to the coordinates sent by the ELT as possible, and we will attempt to locate the ELT unit."

"What are we taking?" asked Torres.

"Bell 412 Twin Turbines. A small team of technicians will be joining us to help us track the wreckage. We likely won't find the entire wreckage in one location but finding the ELT unit will be a good start. Based on the location and arrangement of what we find, we can extrapolate the trajectory of the crash and estimate the location of the rest of the plane.

"Consultants, we will need you to be alert, assessing possible threats from indigenous flora and fauna. As you all know, aerial pics and videos indicate that there are large animals on the island, some of which might be predators."

"What exactly is our protection?" asked Allison, looking concerned.

Susan gestured to Torres, "Mario."

Torres nodded, taking the ball and running with it. "The mobile team is armed with .338 Iapuas. Base camp will have mounted guard sites with M-2 .50 caliber machine guns and MK-19 grenade launchers."

Jason snorted. "Jesus, that's heavy artillery. Isn't that a bit of overkill?"

Peter noticed the third Vietnamese officer murmuring to the other two, translating the conversation.

Torres nodded, acknowledging Jason's observation. "If there are large predators down there," he shot a look in Peter and Tracey's direction, "then we need something heavy. M4's wouldn't suffice."

"Base camp?" asked Mary. "I thought we were going to be in and out."

"We have to establish a base camp as a staging base," said Susan. "We don't know how much of the plane we'll find at the ELT coordinates. Don't worry, we have plans for rapid extraction should things go sideways. Our main objective is to locate the flight data recorder, which is combined with the ELT unit. Anything else is gravy."

"We won't let anything happen to you," reassured Torres. "Poseidon Tech hired us because we're the best at what we do."

Susan nodded. "Consultants, your continuous assessment and input will help direct our activities and keep us safe."

Tracey shot Peter a nervous look, and Mary and Allison had both stopped eating their breakfast. Susan had their undivided attention as she laid out the rest of the plan for the recovery operation.

*

Peter and Tracey waited by the helipad with the other consultants, Susan, and four technicians with mobile computer equipment for their copter. Peter hoped it would be a short hop to the island, and he started to regret stuffing himself with a bagel.

Allison also appeared to be a bit uneasy, but Tracey and Mary grinned from ear to ear, chatting it up, excited by the adventure.

Their helicopter landed, and Susan led them over to it. They hopped inside, the engine whined, and the helicopter took off and away from the offshore oil rig.

Peter looked out the window as they flew, watching the water beneath skim by. He clutched his seatbelt with his left hand, his right finding Tracey's. She looked over at him and smiled, holding his hand. Peter flushed.

Jason shot him a sideways glance, smiling. It was a mixture of pity and derision. Peter ignored him and watched the other helicopters glide over the ocean.

After some time, Mary pointed out the window. When Peter looked, he saw it. The island was large, surrounded by steep vertical cliffs all around, just as Susan said. It was lush and beautiful, with a mountainous region in the center.

Within minutes, the helicopter was hovering over an area covered with a dense canopy. The pilot consulted with Susan up front and searched for the closest clearing, which seemed further away from the original spot than Peter would've liked.

After hovering for a bit, no doubt surveying the clearing and surrounding area, the pilot began to land the helicopter.

PART II
FIRST CONTACT

CHAPTER 4

When Peter, Tracey, and others exited their helicopter, Susan ducked and led them away from the spinning blades. They each followed suit, hunching over as they cleared the blades. The pilot cut the engine, and the blades began to slow.

Peter saw that the other helicopters had arrived first, and Torres and his team were already setting up basecamp, setting up the tents and machine guns around the landing site.

"They're moving quickly," said Peter.

Jason stood next to him, elbowing him. "Check out those Iapuas."

Peter squinted, straining his eyes to see. "Those are the guns, right?"

"Yeah. Those are modified to be portable. These guys are pros."

Peter smirked. "Oh, don't worry. It's not the size that counts. It's how you use it."

Jason smiled, slapping him on the back. "Keep telling yourself that, buddy."

Within minutes, the four technicians were set up.

"We have GPS," said one of them, a man in his early thirties with scruffy blond hair. Susan hadn't introduced them, so Peter didn't know any of their names. He figured that was on purpose. She wanted them separate from the others, so they could focus on their jobs.

"Ho-ly crap," said Mary, walking off to a spot to the right."

"What's she doing?" asked Susan, annoyed that one of the consultants had already become distracted.

Peter saw what she was investigating. "Her job." He followed Mary.

Tracey shrugged her shoulders, and she and Susan followed after him. They stopped in front of what appeared to be a sizeable pile of feces.

"That's some BM," said Susan. "Can you tell what kind of animal it fell out of?"

Mary slid off her backpack and pulled out a pair of latex gloves.

"Give me a pair," said Tracey.

Mary nodded and handed her a pair. The ladies slipped on their gloves and started picking through the feces.

Jason moseyed over, grimacing. "That's disgusting."

Tracey looked up at him and winked.

"There's no trace of undigested plant material," said Mary.

Tracey picked out a small shard of something hard. She wiped it off with gloved fingers and held it up for closer inspection. "Bone fragment. This here pile of poop is from a predator."

Peter turned to Jason. "What can I say? The woman knows her shit."

Susan crossed her arms, smiling. She was impressed. "How long ago?"

"Not long," said Mary. "Maybe a few hours or so."

Jason stepped past the dung pile and scanned the ground. "I've got prints here. About two feet long, coming from the other side of the clearing." He waved an arm off to his left. He squatted down on his haunches, following the tracks with his eyes. "They appear to go off in that direction." He pointed in the other direction.

"Two feet long. What do we think that is?" asked Susan.

"There's a drag mark on the ground," added Jason. "It had a tail, and judging from the tracks, it was bipedal."

Peter and Tracey exchanged looks.

Susan noticed. "What? What is it?"

"These look like theropods," said Peter. He pointed to the tracks. "Look at the stride. We're talking around fifteen feet. The tyrannosaurus rex had a stride like that. Also, notice the depth of the footprints. The T. rex was also a toe walker."

"So, you're telling me these were made by a damned T. rex?" said Jason.

"Something like a T. rex," said Tracey. "Probably not an actual T. rex." She pulled a feather out of the poop. "Look, Pete."

Peter hunched down next to her and took a gander. "No way."

Susan leaned in. "What's that? A feather?"

"Great," said Jason. "So now we're looking for Big Bird."

"Excellent work," said Susan. "Perhaps we shouldn't set up camp in this clearing."

Torres strolled up to where they were standing. "We'll be set up shortly."

"We need to move base camp," said Susan.

"What? Why?"

Tracey stood up and slid off her gloves. "Because an awfully large predator came through here a couple of hours ago."

"Large? How large? What predator?"

Peter placed his hands on his hips. "A fifteen-footer bipedal creature with a large tail."

Torres looked at Susan. "You've got to be kidding me."

She shook her head.

Torres sighed. "Okay, I suppose we could move into the trees, but we'll be leaving the choppers in the clearing. I can establish overwatch from a high position in the trees."

"Do it," said Susan.

Torres nodded and went back to give his men new instructions.

"He doesn't like taking orders from civilians," said Allison.

"Technically, he is one now," said Susan. "Okay, let's get the team together. We're going into the jungle."

Within twenty minutes, Susan had rounded up the team. A communications engineer was remaining behind at base camp, while the other three mobilized their GPS trackers.

"There's a problem," said one of them. A different man in his thirties, this one with brown hair, taller and filled out.

"What is it?"

"We've lost the signal."

Susan checked her watch. "It hasn't been forty-eight hours yet." She looked annoyed. "Doesn't matter. We have the coordinates."

The engineer nodded.

Torres walked over with four men. "We're ready when you are."

Allison looked concerned. "Only five of you?"

Torres winked at her. "It'll be enough. We'll provide bounding overwatch and handle fire and movement."

Allison turned to Mary. "I have no idea what he just said."

Torres smiled. "We're going to move up ahead and make sure the coast is clear. If we encounter problems, we'll provide cover."

"Ah, I see."

Susan waved an arm. "Okay, let's move out."

Torres took his fire team ahead, moving in bounding overwatch formation, leapfrogging from spot to spot. Susan then led the three engineers and the team of consultants after them.

They walked for a while, the consultants assessing their surroundings, and Jason looking for any indicators of large predators in the vicinity.

Allison was looking around, occasionally stopping and touching plants. "I'm seeing seed ferns that are unfamiliar to me. Some strange trees, too. I've read about ferns like these in…"

"Fossils," said Tracey, finishing her thought.

"Yeah. What does that mean?"

"Anything poisonous or dangerous to people?" asked Susan, refocusing the conversation.

Allison shook her head. "I wouldn't eat any of this. Other than that, no apparent danger."

Susan nodded. "Good."

There were strange sounds all around them—squawks, chirps, high-pitched squeals, and low belching sounds. The jungle was alive.

"Look at that," said Mary, pointing to a colorful bird perched up on a branch ahead. It chirped down at them as they passed underneath.

"Pretty," said Tracey. "What is it?"

Mary scrunched her nose. "I…don't know."

"Susan is going to ask if it's dangerous," quipped Peter.

Susan smirked. "That's right, Dr. Albanese. So, is it?"

Mary shot an 'Are you kidding?' look, but Susan pressed forward. Allison winked at Mary as she passed her. "Focused like a laser."

"Yeah," said Mary. "You can say that again. When are we going to get to observe and catalogue?"

"After we get the flight data recorder," said Susan, "and I deem the site to be safe."

"Well, I'm getting some pictures," said Mary, producing a digital camera. She snapped some shots of some birds and a monkey perched up high on a branch eating insects off the bark. She switched to her viewer to check out her shots. She shook her camera. "Dammit."

"It's probably the humidity," offered Allison.

"It's the island," said Susan from up ahead, without looking back.

"So, you're telling me I can't take photos," snapped Mary, growing impatient.

"Once we have the flight data recorder, you can take samples on our return to base camp."

The walk was arduous in the heat as the party navigated tree roots and became entangled in underbrush. Peter produced a small cloth and wiped his brow, pulling it away and looking at the resultant sweat stain.

Allison grimaced. "Gross."

Peter smirked. "I'm a little out of shape."

"Tell me about it," said Allison. "I'm still trying to lose the baby weight."

"How old?" asked Tracey.

"Four months. Amber Rose. My Amber Rose."

"You left a four-month-old to come here?" asked Mary.

Allison shrugged. "My husband lost his job, and we needed the money."

No one dared ask how much. Such topics were off limits in polite company.

"Yeah, that money sure will come in handy," said Mary. "I'm going to use it to travel the world. I mean, besides the university sanctioned trips. I'm tired of the tropics. I want to go to Italy or France."

"That's an odd sentiment coming from a tropical biologist," said Jason.

Allison shook her head. "No, it's not. The tropics are work. Europe would be recreation."

"I guess you're right," said Jason.

Mary turned to Tracey. "What are you going to do with your money?"

"Pete wants to fund digs for incomplete finds."

Jason arched an eyebrow at Peter. "You're a lot of fun."

Peter didn't appreciate his sarcasm.

Mary cocked her head. "That's oddly specific."

Peter cleared his throat. "Tracey and I are theropod feeding specialists. Museums only want intact skeletons, which tell us nothing about feeding behavior."

"Okay, that's what you're going to do with *your* money," said Mary. "I assume Tracey is allowed to spend hers as she wants?"

"Are you sure you two aren't a couple?" pressed Allison, relishing Peter's blushing response.

"How about you?" blurted Peter at Mary, hoping to redirect the conversation as he hopped over a fallen tree trunk. "Anyone special in your life?"

"There was this professor in Ecuador..."

"And? What happened?" asked Tracey, sensing a juicy story.

"It was just a fling," explained Mary. "He was there. He was cute. I was there. I was available."

"Nice," said Allison. "Was he upset when you left?"

Mary chuckled. "Confused, I think. You know how men are. He gave me those sad puppy dog eyes."

"You mean the ones Pete gives Tracey, here," teased Jason, stirring up trouble.

"Dr. Albanese to you," snapped Peter, "and, I have no idea what you're talking about." He tucked his head down in embarrassment.

When he snuck a peek at Tracey, she didn't seem embarrassed at all. She was smiling.

"No, I suppose you don't," remarked Jason.

"Are we keeping an eye out for threats?" prompted Susan, growing weary of the conversation.

"How about you, Susan?" asked Allison, shooting conspiratorial looks at the others.

"I have a husband, an eleven-year-old son, and a thirteen-year-old daughter."

"Do they have any idea where you are?" asked Mary, amused.

Susan shook her head. "No. Not even my husband."

"Did he give you any sad puppy dog eyes before you left?" teased Mary.

"Let's focus on our surroundings, Dr. Tambini."

The scientists all made furtive faces at each other, chuckling awkwardly, like children scolded by the teacher.

Mary held her hand up to the side of her mouth. "Seems I've struck a nerve."

The others shared a chuckle, except for Peter. His face was still hot. The gang was quiet for a while as they pressed on, scanning their surroundings, each looking for anything significant according to his or her specialty.

Allison would point out interesting vegetation, and Mary colorful birds. Peter and Tracey found some interesting tracks, most likely belonging to large herbivores.

"So, what if we run into a dinosaur?" asked Jason, needling Peter. "You don't look like you're very fast."

"I don't need to be fast," said Peter. "I just need to be faster than you."

Jason smirked at the barb. "Not likely, pal."

Torres came bounding out of the underbrush. "We've found something!"

Susan turned and addressed the group. "Let's go, folks."

They followed Torres, Susan walking beside him and the rest trailing behind. She was panting in the heat. "Where are the other men?"

"Establishing 360 security."

After a bit of a hike, Torres pointed up at a large tree. "Look. There."

They all followed where he was pointing, and they saw the wreckage of Flight 207.

"Whoa," gasped Allison.

"Is that it?" asked Mary.

Susan put her hands on her hips. "Yeah, that's it. Look, the tail is on the ground. That's fortuitous."

Peter leaned into Jason. "That means lucky."

Jason curled his lip into a mock snarl.

Susan interrupted them. "Mr. Barrett, any threats in the immediate area?"

Jason separated from the group, scanning the area, then the ground. He squinted his eyes and squatted, tracing the ground with his right index finger. "I've found prints. Lots of them."

"What type of animal?" asked Susan.

Jason narrowed his eyes. "Human."

"That's probably me and my men," said Torres.

"No," said Jason, shaking his head. "These were made by bare feet."

Susan looked surprised. "What? That's impossible."

"Is it?" asked Peter. "We're on an uncharted island keeping an eye out for carnivorous dinosaurs."

Torres got on his radio. "Alpha squad, check in."

Four other voices came on the radio, one after the other, each giving the all clear.

"That's weird," said the technician, looking at his own equipment. "No interference here."

Susan frowned. "So, that's a good thing. Right?"

"It's mighty inconsistent," said the technician. "It doesn't add up."

"Why don't you go check out the tail?" she instructed.

The technician nodded and walked over to the torn-off tail of the plane sitting on the ground.

"Look at the spines on that tree," marveled Allison, pointing to the tree next to the one holding the wreckage.

"Doesn't look like the whole wreckage is here," said Susan, looking up at the treetop as her technician crawled inside the tail compartment. "It was probably torn apart as it landed. I don't see the main fuselage."

Jason walked over to the tail of the plane, following the tracks. He looked off to the left. "There were at least a dozen people here. They all went off that way. They were dragging something. Or someone."

"Survivors?" asked Tracey. "Maybe there were survivors."

Susan shook her head. "One, maybe. Two, unlikely. Dozens, impossible. And, they wouldn't all be barefoot."

"So, what are you saying?" asked Mary. "There are indigenous people on this island?"

"Why not?" said Peter. "It would explain them all being barefoot. Geographic isolation through recorded history on this island. It's possible."

"Do you think they're friendly?" asked Allison, concerned, thinking of her husband and baby.

"My men are here in case they're not," said Torres. "I doubt they have full auto assault rifles. You know, geographic isolation and all."

"What's this?" Jason crouched down and picked up a small wooden shard. He sniffed the tip.

"What is it?" asked Susan.

"It's a dart," said Jason. "With something on it."

The technician came out of the plane empty-handed.

Susan looked disappointed. "Well?"

"The ELT unit is missing."

Susan shook her head. "It has to be close by. Everybody, fan out."

"Is she kidding?" asked Mary. "I don't even know what an 'ELT' looks like."

Susan called up a picture on her pad and showed it to them. "It's a bright orange box. If I find it, I get paid. If I get paid, you get paid."

Jason shoved past the technician. "Let me have a look." He disappeared inside the tail section.

"It's placed inside the tail section because it's the part of the plane that statistically sustains the least amount of damage in a crash," said Susan. "It *has* to be close by."

Peter shook his head. "The tail compartment doesn't look damaged to me, except the part that tore off from the rest of the plane. How could it have become dislodged?"

Jason emerged from the tail compartment. He held up tiny screws. "Because someone unscrewed the brackets lashing it to the inside wall."

"Unscrewed?" asked Susan. "That's impossible."

"There she goes with that word again," said Peter.

"So, now we're talking about a bunch of barefoot natives with screwdrivers?" asked Mary.

"None of this adds up," said Susan.

There were gun shots in the distance, startling the group.

"What was that?" asked Tracey.

"Automatic gunfire," said Torres, as his radio crackled. 'We're under attack! Repeat! The staging base is under attack!'

Torres got on his radio. "By who?"

They waited, listening to the response, wondering if it was the barefoot natives.

'Dinosaurs! Big ones! T. rexes!'

They all gawked at each other as more gunfire erupted in the distance followed by a thunderous roar. That last sound sent shivers down their collective spines.

"How many?" asked Torres into his radio.

'Three, and they're pissed!'

"We have to return to the choppers," said Torres.

"Not without the ELT," insisted Susan.

"It's not here," pressed Torres. "We have to return to the choppers. It's not safe."

"We're right here," she demanded. "It's around here somewhere." She turned to her technician, who was checking his GPS locator.

"There's no signal," he said.

"Is running *towards* the direction of that horrible roar the safest thing?" asked Mary. "I don't know about you, but I don't want to see any T. rexes."

"I'll go," volunteered Peter. "I have to see this."

Tracey gaped at him, obviously impressed. "Then I'm going, too."

"We're all going," said Torres. "The worst thing we can do now is split up the party."

Suddenly, his men emerged from the jungle around them.

"Did you hear that?" asked one of them.

Torres nodded. "We're heading back to the choppers, but we're not running headlong into a bunch of T. rexes."

"What are you saying?" demanded Susan.

"I'm saying, we're going to approach carefully and cautiously. I'm here to keep you all safe, and I'm going to do just that." He turned to his men. "I want a scout up ahead. You. Go."

One of his men dashed off into the jungle back towards the staging base. Torres turned to his remaining two men. "I don't want to get flanked." The other two men ran off, each to either side of the party.

Torres turned to the group. "I've got the rear. Ms. Kinney, if you would."

Susan nodded, swallowing hard. "Okay, gang. Follow me." She began to walk in the direction of the scout, her technician alongside her, consulting his navigation.

The rest of the group traded uncertain looks.

"Well, I'm not staying here alone in the jungle," declared Allison, and she marched after Susan. The rest followed.

Peter stayed behind, looking around. Torres walked up to him. "That means you, too, Dr. Albanese."

Peter looked at Torres. "Where's Jason?"

CHAPTER 5

Jason tracked the multiple footprints all leading away from the crash site where the plane's tail lay on the ground. He wasn't getting paid until Susan took possession of the ELT device, and someone purposely removed it. His legal bills weren't paying themselves, so he figured he'd take matters into his own hands and apologize later.

He felt a little guilty leaving the salvage team, but they had Torres and his men to protect them. He ignored the thunderous roars and popping of automatic gunfire in the distance, off in the direction of where the helicopters sat. He reminded himself that the others would thank him once he recovered the ELT.

The hunter stopped short, catching movement in a small clearing up ahead. He crouched down in the underbrush, careful not to make a sound.

In the clearing, a bovine animal milled about. Jason knew it wasn't a predator, but that wasn't why he stopped short. It was alone.

As a hunter, he knew that prey that wandered alone, away from its herd, wore a bullseye on its back. He scanned the rest of the area, and he found the rest of the group a hundred or so feet off to the left.

Jason shook his head, silently chastising the lone animal blissfully unaware of its vulnerability. Some movement off to the right of the clearing caught Jason's attention.

Large leaves and massive fronds shifted about and parted. The lone animal had also noticed the movement, and it shifted about nervously. However, it was still too stupid to rejoin the herd. "C'mon, stupid," Jason muttered under his breath, a hunter rooting for the prey.

Three large lizards walking upright burst into the clearing, quickly surrounding the animal, snarling and whining at it. The bovine prey shifted around, crying out to the herd, but it was already too late. The herd was too far away, and the reptilian hunters quickly surrounded it.

Jason, his hand resting on his rifle, marveled at the hunters. They moved like birds, light on their feet. They looked like velociraptors from that movie, but they were too small. They were about the size of large German Shepherds.

With closed mouths, they forced air out, communicating with each other as their prey appealed to deaf ears. The raptors exploded into movement, pouncing on the terrified animal, ripping at its hide with razor sharp teeth.

The bovine victim cried out as it bled, trying to shove its way through, but one of the raptors sunk its teeth into its neck, holding the animal fast.

Like Jason had seen so many times on the African plains, when a lion grabbed its prey by the neck, the animal, fully conscious, would just give up and allow itself to be dragged away like a ragdoll to be eaten alive.

In this case, the animal just hung there while the other two tore into it, with little to no protest. It was a horrible sight, but Jason gazed in awe at the spectacle. The raptor holding its neck released it, and the animal dropped to the ground on its side. The raptor joined the others in the feast.

Jason took this opportunity to back away and circumvent the area, giving it a wide berth. These hunters would be preoccupied with their kill. He would pick up the human tracks on the other side of the clearing, quietly and with his eyes peeled.

As he made his way around to the other side, he chuckled to himself as he realized one ironic fact—*he* had separated from *his* herd. He was the lone animal, until this moment blissfully unaware of his own vulnerability.

*

Susan led her group through the jungle, following the directions of her technician, who was consulting his GPS. When she looked ahead, one of the scouts had stopped.

"What's he doing?" she asked. "I don't think he's just supposed to stop."

The technician shrugged his shoulders.

"What's going on?" asked Tracey.

"I don't know," said Peter, furrowing his brow.

"Maybe they've found something," offered Allison.

Susan caught up with the scout. "What is it?"

The scout pointed off to the left. "That looks like the fuselage."

Susan followed where he was pointing, and her eyes lit up. "Do you see that?"

The technician nodded. "That's it. That's the fuselage."

The scout's radio crackled. It was Torres. 'What's going on? Why did you stop?'

The scout got on the radio. "We've located the fuselage, LT."

'That's nice, but it's not our objective.'

The scout frowned. "Yes, sir." He turned to Susan. "We can come back to this site." The roars and popping of gunfire drew noticeably closer.

"I want to see it," demanded Susan.

"Negative," insisted the scout. "We can return to the site once the staging base is secure."

Susan huffed and darted off in the direction of the fuselage. The technician, clutching his portable equipment, decided to remain with the scout.

"Ma'am!" called the scout after her, but she ignored him. He got on his com, notifying Torres.

"What's she doing?" asked Mary.

"She's going to get herself killed," said Peter.

Tracey took off after Susan.

Peter looked flummoxed. "Tracey? Tracey, what are you doing?" He looked at Allison and Mary, who both shrugged their shoulders.

"Ah, Christ," muttered Peter to himself, and he took off after Tracey.

Susan stopped short in front of the large fuselage, which rested on its belly, but the top was missing. There was a horrible stench in the air.

Tracey caught up with her. "Susan, do you really think it wise to separate from the group?"

Susan took in the wreckage. "Jesus. Think of how many died."

"That's what the smell is," said Tracey. "Maybe we should rejoin the group."

Susan ignored the advice, gawking at the wreckage. "It looks like it's been torn up."

Tracey stared at the ground in front of the torn metal tube. "We need to rejoin the group. Now."

Susan noticed her abrupt change of tone. When she turned to look at Tracey, she saw the paleontologist looking at the ground, eyes bulging in terror.

Peter caught up to them, panting. "What are you two doing?"

Tracey pointed at the ground. "Peter, look."

Susan saw what she was looking at. Her shoulders raised up and her body went rigid.

Peter stepped forward to glean a closer look. "Those are tracks."

Tracey nodded. "Theropod tracks."

"They were here," added Peter. He looked up at the fuselage. "No way. No. Way." Now his curiosity overtook his common sense, and he began to climb the wreckage to get a closer look.

Tracey made to join him, but she saw Susan walking with her. She turned to Susan. "Wait here."

Susan snapped out of her shock. "Why?" Her tone indicated that she didn't like being bossed around.

"Trust me," said Tracey. "If it's what I think it is, you don't want to see this."

"I'm not afraid of dead bodies," said Susan. "I've seen them before. It comes with the territory in salvage operations." She shoved past Tracey, bumping the paleontologist's shoulder.

Tracey raised her eyebrows, looking miffed. "Okay," she mumbled under her breath. She climbed the fuselage to find Peter there at the top. Susan was bent at the waist, her body contracting, emptying the contents of her stomach.

Seats were strewn about, filled with blood and flesh, flies hovering over the piles of gore.

Susan wiped her mouth with her forearm, the vomit on her breath drowned out by the stench of hot, rotting flesh. "Is that from the accident?" But she already knew the answer.

"No," said Peter, shaking his head. He covered his mouth with a handkerchief he produced from his pocket.

"These are the remains of theropod feeding," said Tracey, finishing his thought.

"So, they do scavenge," said Peter, more fascinated with the scene than repulsed.

Susan gulped, forcing down rising vomit. "So, you're telling me that a T. rex came and ate these people?"

"They were already dead," said Peter. "It was an easy meal."

Torres climbed up to join them. "What the hell are you guys doing?" He paused, taking in the horror. "Jesus Christ."

"There was a T. rex here," announced Susan.

Torres nodded. "Yeah, I saw the tracks. It's not safe here. We need to rejoin the group and continue to our objective." By perfect timing, there were loud roars followed by growls in the near distance. The gunfire sounded less coordinated and more sporadic.

Susan pointed an accusatory finger at Torres. "You think this spot is dangerous, yet you want to run headlong into whatever is going on over there?"

"Ma'am, I know you're scared. We all are, but we have to return to the staging base, and if possible, leave."

Susan stomped her foot. "I'm not leaving. Not when we're so close."

"We're not close to recovering anything," said Torres.

Susan narrowed her eyes. "We found the tail. The ELT device was removed by someone. Someone human. They have to be in the vicinity."

Peter and Tracey watched the argument in silence, not sure of what to do. They knew what happened here, but it wasn't their call to make.

"The situation has become unstable," said Torres.

"I'm in charge of this operation," declared Susan. "I say we go back, away from those roars and gunfire, and search for the ELT."

Torres shook his head. "I'm in charge of security, and I'm declaring this operation unsafe."

"Do you hear that?" asked Peter during a lull in the argument.

Torres and Susan both rounded on him, shouting in unison, "What?"

"The shooting's stopped," said Tracey.

*

Bill Gibson rubbed his eyes, waking from what felt like a deep sleep. His face felt numb, and when he reached a hand up to rub it, his fingers felt like pins and needles. As he touched his face, rubbing his eyes, he felt a fine powder. As his vision began to clear, he realized he was outside. The sun momentarily white washed his vision, but he felt as if he wasn't alone.

He startled as he saw silhouettes against the sun standing around him. They were diminutive, but numerous, and crowding around him. As his vision cleared, he realized he was surrounded by people.

They pointed spears at him, watching him, muscles tensed. One wrong move, and he was sure he'd become a human shish kabob. He placed two defensive hands up, palms out, bowing his head but keeping his eyes on his captors.

They tensed up, inching forward with their spear tips, which glistened as if painted with something wet and sticky—a poison, no doubt.

"Hi," began Bill, as the short men around him gasped in reaction. "My name is Bill." He swallowed hard. "I am your friend." He added that last part rather dubiously, according the tone of his voice. He hoped they didn't interpret it as disingenuous.

As he got a better look at them, they were short men, about five feet tall or slightly less, naked except for loincloths, with body paint. Most of the men donned various colors painted under their eyes in rows of two, as if applied by two fingers smeared across the face. They had long, black hair that was straight and shoulder-length. These were warriors.

They remained silent, pointing their spears. Bill figured that if they wanted him dead, he'd have been skewered by now. No, they were waiting.

Suddenly, a klatch of equally diminutive women barged into the circle, shoving their way past the warrior men. They wore smiles and were talking to Bill, though he didn't understand their language. He didn't even recognize it.

They approached him, touching his shoulders and squeezing his arms. They spoke to him and to each other, nodding and smiling. They grabbed him under his armpits and pulled him up. He struggled to his feet. The short warriors backed off, spear tips dropping, and the women surrounded him. They ushered him off to a spot where there sat a chair, crudely fashioned from bamboo shafts lashed together with vines.

They sat him down, and several continued to pat him on the head and shoulders, reassuring him. Others ran off with urgency, smiling and gesticulating wildly.

Bill was relieved. He appeared to be welcomed, at least for the moment, and the warrior men dispersed, leaving the women to their task of apparent hospitality. A couple retuned, one carrying a large basin of water, the vessel honed from what appeared to be a tree burl. Another carried what looked like a large sea sponge.

The women began to take off his shoes and roll up his sleeves. "Hey, wait a minute…" Bill sat up, protesting, but they shoved him back into his seat, reassuring him in their native tongue. They now began to unbutton his shirt, which was so tattered at this point, it practically disintegrated in their hands. Bill squirmed under their touch. "Please…stop…you don't have to…"

One woman dipped the sponge into the water and began scrubbing his feet. It tickled, and Bill pulled his feet up, but the woman with the sponge continued to scrub. She then washed his hands.

When she dipped the sponge back into the water, Bill took the opportunity to sniff his hand. There was a eucalyptus-like odor, potent but pleasing. He saw the dirt and sweat from his time on the island begin to wash away, and he realized how truly filthy he had been.

He decided to sit back and allow the woman to scrub his head, neck, and chest—not that he had much choice. The women noticed the change in his demeanor, and they patted his head in encouragement, smiling and talking to him. Their tones sounded friendly, and Bill didn't want to insult them. However, he was going to stop them if they pulled at his pants.

Fortunately, they stopped at his waist and didn't venture further south. The woman with the sponge tossed it into the filthy water and ushered the bowl away.

The women backed off, and Bill took a moment to examine his surroundings. He was sitting in the middle of what must've been their village. Small, tee pee-like structures sat, scattered around him as women scraped animal skins, tanning them in the sun. Off to his right, a more permanent wigwam type of building stood, like one he saw in a Native American museum once in America.

The village was surrounded by a crude perimeter fence fashioned from bamboo, but upon closer inspection, Bill realized the fence wasn't constructed at all. Rather, the people had cultivated a naturally-growing fence surrounding the small village.

Children hauled large fish over to waiting mothers to be cleaned and prepared. Women held woven baskets containing large, colorful fruits. The entire village was busy, each individual carrying out a task that contributed to the whole, and Bill took it all in as the women now hugged him and spoke softly into his ear.

The woman with the sponge returned, this time with a large basket. Inside was a large fish, cleaned and cooked, and a large melon. Bill's eyes widened in ravenous hunger as he saw the food. Truth be told, he was famished, having subsisted on insects and fruit that caused diarrhea.

He reached out and snatched the fish in his hands. The women chittered in delight as he sunk his teeth into the fish, chewing eagerly, and swallowing, only mildly careful to avoid bones. Another woman brought over a smaller bowl filled with water. It looked clean, so Bill grabbed it in his right hand and washed some of the fish down. It wasn't bad. In fact, it was actually quite tasty.

Bill grunted his gratitude between bites and chomping. He quickly devoured the fish as a woman took out one of the melons and chopped it in half on a large, flat stone. Juice poured out, and its sweetness reached Bill's nostrils.

He grabbed one half of the melon and shoved it into his face, his teeth scraping off chunks from the rind. It was sweet and juicy, a welcome chaser to the fish dinner. Was it even dinner? Or was it lunch? He had lost complete track of time.

After gorging on the provided feast, Bill sat back, drowsy, patting his belly. One of the women, a slender woman in her twenties (although it was tough to tell with all of the face paint), strode up to him, a dreamy look in her eyes. She had long, straight, raven black hair that fell down her back, practically to her waist. She was thin, but her build was athletic. Bill, nervous, sat up at attention, unsure of her intentions.

He was full, he was hydrated, and that was plenty. He didn't need any other needs met, and if offered, he would refuse.

The young woman stopped in front of him and bent at the waist so that she was face-to-face with him.

"Uh…hi." He blushed, unsure of what to say.

The woman raised a hand in front of her face, palm up, as if she was going to blow him a kiss. Bill noticed a small pile of white powder sitting in the palm of her hand. It looked like the powder he wiped off his face when he came-to earlier.

"Hey, wait a minute…"

She blew hard, and the powder became airborne. Bill's face was covered in a white cloud and the jungle around him went black.

CHAPTER 6

Shortly after the gunfire at the staging base ceased, the party felt a thumping on the ground. The beat was irregular, but it shook the ground and quickly grew louder.

"What's that?" asked Susan.

Allison spread her stance and placed her hands out, as if to balance herself. "Earthquake?"

Peter shook his head. "Footprints."

"Two sets," added Tracey, looking at Peter.

Torres got on his com. "Scout, report."

There was no answer.

Torres traded looks with Susan. "Scout, report…" No response. "Alvarez, report…Alvarez!"

A low growl emanated from the vegetation in front of them. Torres raised his rifle. "Everyone, take cover!"

Peter placed a hand on Torres' shoulder. "You too. Trust me."

Torres shot Peter a look, mulled it over, and then nodded.

"Why? What's happening?" asked Allison, panicking.

Tracey grabbed her arm. "Allison, we have to hide. Now."

"Hide?" asked Susan's technician, still holding his GPS equipment. "Where?" He turned to Susan for direction, but she had already dashed into the trees behind the wrecked fuselage.

"Our fearless leader," said Mary, her tone dripping with sarcasm.

The group scattered as a large, thunderous lizard burst through the tree line in front of them. It sniffed the air and swung its head from side to side, tracking the fleeing prey before it.

Peter and Torres took cover behind the fuselage, following Tracey and Allison. Mary took a moment to gaze at the bipedal horror standing before her, the expression on her face one of admiration. She shouted at the Poseidon Tech technician, "Hide, stupid!" She began climbing the fuselage.

The tech, named Barry, stood there, grasping his GPS equipment like a frightened child clutching his favorite toy for comfort.

The tyrannosaurus stepped forward, first eyeing Mary climbing up onto the twisted metal carcass of the plane, and then down at Barry, whose body went from trembling to shuddering. He dropped his equipment at his feet and turned to run, but the tyrannosaurus bolted forward after him.

Barry tried to climb the fuselage as Mary dashed in between seats, crouching down. The enormous lizard reached down and snatched Barry up in its jaws. Barry's lungs collapsed under the sudden pressure, and he was unable to scream. The T. rex tipped its head back, tossing Barry further into its mouth. Its muscular jaws worked, its teeth tearing Barry to shreds, snapping his bones.

Mary averted her gaze in disgust as Barry's blood dripped down its mouth. The T. rex swallowed the poor man's mangled body down in one gulp and turned its attention to the fuselage.

Mary heard the thunderous footsteps grow closer as she hid her face, unable to look at the approaching horror. It growled at her through closed teeth, the low grumble causing the fuselage to vibrate. It sounded like the low rumble of the movie theater next door during a loud scene.

Suddenly, the popping of automatic gunfire erupted from either side. Mary looked up to find the T. rex shaking its head as bullets barraged it. She stood up, looking down to her right, seeing one of Torres' flanks shooting at the monstrous lizard. When she looked down to her left, she saw the other flank.

However, the brush behind him shuffled about, and the feathered head of a second T. rex reached out and snatched him up, crunching through the Kevlar and camo. The original T. rex turned its attention to the remaining flank, bounding towards the shooter.

Mary turned and jumped behind the fuselage as she heard the mercenary cry out in pain and terror. She had heard that sound before. It was the pathetic bleating of prey that knew, in its last fraction of a second on Earth, that it was going to be eaten.

She fell in front of Peter, Tracey, and the others, huddled under the curved metal shell. Torres and Tracey pulled her to her feet and dragged her against the fuselage.

"The gunfire stopped," whispered Torres to Mary. "Did you see what happened?"

Mary's eyes welled up, her mouth contorted, stifling a cry, and she nodded, indicating the fate of his men.

"Dammit," he muttered.

"I told you," whispered Peter.

Their whispering was interrupted by a pair of low growls. They startled when the fuselage next to them began to roll away from them.

The group looked up in horror to find the feathered T. rex looking down at them, its leg up on the fuselage, pressing down on it. It roared at them in ferocious hunger.

Peter saw Torres mouth the word, 'Run,' his volume drowned out by the roaring of the feathered beast. He bolted forward with the group, feeling the ground tremble as the other T. rex rounded the fuselage after them. He figured they had a head start on it, though a slim one.

It lumbered after them as they scattered into the jungle. They dodged low hanging vines, occasionally getting caught up for a moment. Being the most out-of-shape, Peter lagged behind. Tracey slowed her pace, shouting at him. "C'mon, Pete! Hurry!"

He looked over his shoulder to see both tyrannosaurs bumbling through the underbrush, slowing so as not to trip on vines or uneven terrain. Its caution was their only chance.

He turned back around to find Torres, Allison, and Mary all tumble forward and down. He stopped short next to Tracey, as she watched them tumble down a ravine and into a creek.

"Pete, we have to follow them."

He looked down. "There's no way I'm rolling down this hill."

Twin roars erupted behind them, as they felt the heavy footfalls of approaching certain death. They turned to see both tyrannosaurs gaining on them, coming from each side, navigating the tricky terrain.

Tracey gave Peter a hard shove, and he went tumbling, head over heels, into the ravine. She ran down, trying her best to maintain her footing, but the grade was too steep and the vegetation too obstructive. She tripped and fell forward, rolling down the hill after him.

When they crashed into the creek below, Allison and Mary helped them to their feet as Torres looked at the middle part of the hill. "Dammit, I lost my rifle."

"Are you okay?" Allison asked Tracey. Tracey nodded, catching her breath.

Peter stepped in front of Tracey, looking outraged. "You pushed me."

"She saved your life," snapped Mary in Tracey's defense.

Tracey hugged Peter, and he melted, his protest evaporating. "I'm sorry," she said. She released him. "I knew you wouldn't jump on your own."

Peter looked up at their two pursuers, who gazed down at them from the top of the hill. They paced back and forth, sniffing the air and growling.

"They won't follow us," said Peter. "If they fall over, they're toast."

"Thank God for tiny arms," quipped Mary, wiping the tears from her eyes.

"I thought they were supposed to be fast," said Mary.

"That's only in the movies," said Tracey. "Once again, they don't want to fall over and not be able to get up."

"Their muscular legs are meant for attacking and pinning prey," added Peter, "not sprinting."

The two tyrannosaurs appeared to lose interest, splitting up, one going left and the other right. The thumping of the footsteps grew distant.

"I have to find my rifle," said Torres. "It's somewhere up on that hill. We're defenseless without it."

"It didn't do your men a lot of good," said Mary.

Torres frowned. "It's better than nothing." He climbed the steep incline.

"I'm glad we have dinosaur experts," said Allison.

Mary nodded. "Yeah, I'm way out of my depth here. But, it's got to be kind of cool, seeing what they were really like. Now you know tyrannosaurs really don't run fast, and apparently some of them did have feathers."

Peter shook his head. "They're not really dinosaurs."

Allison and Mary looked stunned.

Mary smirked. "I dunno. They looked pretty damned real to me."

Tracey shook her head in agreement with Peter. "What Pete means is that these animals have been geographically isolated for millennia on this island, subject to different selection pressures than in pre-historic times. These are different creatures than the ones that roamed the Earth in the Jurassic Period."

Mary understood their point. "So, it's like the Galapagos Islands. They were home to a unique variety of species."

"Exactly," said Tracey. "So, that tyrannosaur with the feathers may be an artifact of the selection pressures unique to this island and may not be representative of what they looked like before."

"Or, the one without feathers may be the artifact," added Mary, finishing Tracey's thought. "So, this really isn't confirming or refuting anything."

"Exactly," said Peter, wiping the sweat off of his brow.

Allison looked confused. "So, these aren't dinosaurs?"

"They're technically the descendants of dinosaurs," said Peter.

*

Torres saw his rifle caught up in some low-hanging vines. He grunted, as he struggled up the incline in the oppressive heat, swatting bugs off his neck.

When he reached the rifle, he snatched it up, grabbing onto a vine for balance. Something caught his eye through the vegetation. It looked like a wooden crate with odd markings on it. "Guys! I think I found something up here!"

"What is it?" called Peter from below.

"It's a crate! I think it's a wooden crate!" He shouldered his rifle and began pulling away vines and branches. As he worked, he exposed more of what was definitely a wooden crate.

"I'm coming up!" called Peter from below, but Torres ignored him. He was curious about the existence of a wooden crate on an uncharted island filled with dinosaurs. He grabbed it by the edges and began to pull it out, pulling his end from side-to-side to wiggle it out.

He nearly fell backwards, down the hill, but Peter came up behind him and caught him. Torres' rifle dug into his torso. "Are you all right, LT?"

Torres regained his footing. "Yeah, thanks." He pointed down at the crate. "Look what I found."

Peter looked down at the crate and at the markings. "It's Japanese, if I'm not mistaken. That's impossible."

Torres laughed and slapped Peter on the shoulder. "After today, that's no longer a word in my vocabulary."

"What's in it?"

Torres inspected the box's dimensions. "A weapon." He reached down, his fingers finding the edges of the lid of the crate. "Help me out."

Peter nodded and grabbed the top right corner of the crate, while Torres grabbed the top left.

"Okay, pull," said Torres.

"Don't we need a pry bar or something?"

"If it's what I think it is, it's got to be around eighty years old. You pull, I'll pry with my knife." Torres unsheathed a rather large hunting knife and began wedging the tip under the crate lid and pulling up.

Peter groaned as he pulled upward on the lid. After a few minutes, the lid began to give. Torres re-sheathed his knife and helped Peter pull up.

"What are you two doing up there?" called Tracey from below.

Mary had climbed the hill and was beside Peter. "Need help?"

Peter was grunting, sweat dripping down his brow. "Yeah, grab an edge and pull."

With the extra set of hands, Torres was free to pry some more with his knife, and after another moment, the lid was off.

"Oh my God," gasped Torres.

"It's a gun," said Mary.

"That's a Japanese rifle," said Torres, eyes bright like a child who just opened an impressive Christmas present. "From World War II."

Mary looked dumbfounded. "What? That's impossible."

Peter and Torres traded smiles.

Torres began to lift it up out of the crate. "It's a Type 97 automatic cannon."

"Do you think it still works?" asked Mary.

"Probably not," said Peter. "Not anymore."

"Well, hold your horses," said Torres. "This thing was packed correctly." He ran his hand over it. "I can still feel the grease."

Mary leaned forward, looking into the crate. "Is there any ammunition?"

Peter leaned over the crate, looking inside. "I see some ammo."

Torres turned the dial for the sight. He nearly squealed with glee as it clicked with each turn. "I can still read the range indicators." His hands found their way to the stock. He pressed a button and rotated the stock inward. "This is the position if this rifle was inside a tank. The stock goes out if it's up on the turret."

"So, this is a tank gun," said Peter. "Do you think there's a Japanese tank around here?"

"If the Japanese were here in World War II, how was this island kept a secret all this time? Do you think we knew about it?"

"Doubtful," said Torres. "This weapon is in its original packing, never opened or fired."

"They never had to," said Peter. "We were never here."

Torres nodded. "This doesn't add up."

Peter shot him a sideways glance. "Come on. Does any of this add up?"

Torres studied the weapon. "No, I mean what are the odds?"

"I don't follow."

"Come on, Dr. Albanese! What are the odds of finding this intact? Not just intact, but in practically mint condition?"

There was a low growl coming from down the hill, but off in the distance, in the trees. The ground shook with the percussion of heavy footfalls on the jungle floor.

Peter and Torres traded terrified looks, and simultaneously shouted, "Get up here! Now!"

Down below, milling around, Tracey and Allison looked up at Peter and Torres, squinting. They saw Mary up the hill with them, looking around, scanning the trees and underbrush. They couldn't make out what she said, but Tracey grabbed Allison by the arm and yanked her towards the hill. Allison gaped in horror as the two tyrannosaurs came crashing through the vegetation, stomping after them.

"Hurry!" cried Peter. He turned to Torres. "We have to help them!"

However, Torres began fiddling with the Japanese relic.

With no time to waste, Peter went charging down the steep embankment, his feet moving faster than his brain controlling them. He nearly lost his balance a couple of times, but he steadied himself on nearby branches and hanging vines. He slammed chest-first into a small tree, the impact nearly knocking the wind out of him, as thorny underbrush tore at his pants, scratching up his legs.

He met Tracey and Allison halfway.

Allison looked up at him in horror. "They're back!"

Peter reached out hands for Tracey and Allison. Tracey declined it, placing a hand on his shoulder. "I'm fine. Help Allison."

Peter nodded as Tracey raced up the incline, the thunderous footfalls growing louder. Peter grabbed Allison by the hand and began pulling them up the embankment with all of his might.

Allison looked over her shoulder as the two tyrannosaurs closed the distance. The one with scales let out an ear-splitting roar, while the feathered one stepped onto the hill, leaning forward.

It lowered its head over the sloped earth, clawing at the underbrush and dirt with its tiny arms, scrambling up the embankment, its snapping jaws only ten feet away from Allison and Peter.

Peter felt his hand snag on Allison's dead weight as she froze in terror. Grunting from exertion and pulled on by Allison's inertia, Peter spun around as Allison released his hand. Allison froze in her tracks. He looked past her and saw the feathered predator struggling, working its fore and hind limbs to ascend the hill, now only several feet behind them.

"What's wrong?" demanded Peter. "Are you stuck?" He looked down at the ground to inspect, but Allison's feet did not appear to be entangled. He heard Tracey calling his name from the top of the hill.

"Allison, we have to keep going! Now!"

She shook her head as the tyrannosaur snapped its jaws, craning its neck and lunging. Peter felt its hot, pungent breath hit him in the face. He grabbed Allison by the arm and pulled her up the hill with all of his might. Allison tried to work her legs, but there was an apparent disconnect between her brain and muscles at the moment.

Both Tracey and Mary were crying out to them from up the hill, their words drowned out by the growls and snapping teeth of the feathered terror inching closer.

Peter's legs became entangled, he rolled his ankle, and he went crashing down on his side. He pulled Allison down on top of him.

The tyrannosaur struggled, emboldened by their folly, stretching, desperate to reach the tasty morsels. However, its weight worked against it. Its hind legs slid down the incline as its toes lost traction in the loose dirt. It clawed the ground with its arms. Whenever its feet found solid ground, it lunged forward, only to slide back down again.

Peter and Allison pulled their feet up, curling into fetal positions as nearly footlong, razor sharp teeth closed, just missing. Peter, in his struggles, gave it a swift kick in the snout, but frenzied with hunger, the tyrannosaur ignored the strike.

Peter turned to look up the hill at Tracey and Mary one last time when he saw Torres aiming the Japanese relic right at the feathered monstrosity. There was a loud bang as something whizzed over Peter and Allison. Peter looked down at the tyrannosaur.

They heard a dull, percussive thump as blood splashed from in between its eyes. Its fierce, narrowed eyes widened as it lost traction on the slope. Its frail forelimbs wavered, trembling under its own weight.

Peter pulled Allison close. "Now."

Together, they scrambled on all fours up the hill as the pursuing beast gazed at them with a vacant expression. There was the discharge of another round from up the hill. This time Peter didn't dare look back. He and Allison continued to climb, clawing at the ground and underbrush with their fingers.

*

Tracey looked down the hill as Peter and Allison were commando crawling up towards her. She and Mary jumped up and down, crying out to them as Torres fired a third round.

Tracey saw the monster's eyes glass over as it fell on its own arms. Its body slack, it rolled on its side and down the slope until it crashed down at the bottom. The other tyrannosaur paced back and forth at the bottom of the hill, watching the other tumble down. It sniffed its dead comrade's body and tipped its head back, letting out a roar that shook the jungle.

Tracey bounded down the hill, stepping sideways like a billy goat, Mary following right behind her. Hot tears streamed down Tracey's cheeks, the simultaneous expression of relief and shame. Relief that Peter was all right. Shame that she had left him behind.

CHAPTER 7

Susan wandered around the jungle, cursing herself under her breath. She had been so close. Why didn't Torres let her inspect the wreckage? Why did he undermine her authority over this operation? Her mind raced, vacillating between fear and task orientation. There was nothing to be done about it now. She had to keep moving to safety. Once in a safe location, she could run a task analysis and generate a decision tree.

When she believed she had put enough distance between herself and the tyrannosaurs, she slowed down in a clearing. She stopped, bending over and placing her hands on her knees as she caught her breath. She surveyed her surroundings, scanning for any immediate threats. To her right was a cluster of trees. In front of her was a tangle of underbrush and vines. Off to her left, movement in her periphery caught her attention.

She turned her head. In the distance, she saw what looked to be a herd of ostriches…on steroids. They appeared to be just milling around. They were tall and muscular-looking. As she looked at them longer, they came to resemble giant hawk chicks or hatchlings. They stood on thick legs leading up to a plump, brown feathered body.

Susan gasped at one peculiar feature that prevented them from looking like hawk hatchlings. Each bird possessed a large, bulbous, hooked beak. Although they looked relatively harmless, she began to back out of the clearing.

Each of the strange bird's heads perked up at her movement, and they screeched at her. The sound sent a chill down Susan's spine, as ostriches didn't screech like that. At least, she didn't think so.

They picked up their feet and began to glide towards her. As they picked up speed, they each lowered their heads and clicked their beaks in anticipation.

Susan knew she was in immediate danger, and having barely caught her breath, she sprinted off into the jungle. Her mind no longer preoccupied itself with decision trees, prioritizations, or cost-benefit analyses. Her reptilian brain took over, and it was screaming at her body to pump her legs and get the hell out of Dodge.

As she ran, meandering through the trees, she cast nervous glances over her shoulder. At each look, the strange, apparently flightless birds appeared closer. Their clicking sounds grew louder, as did the snapping of their beaks.

Realizing that she wasn't going to outrun these creatures, Susan dashed right at a ninety-degree angle and into a thick patch of bushes. She heard the large birds skid in the dirt behind her, their clawed feet scratching frantically, and turn to pursue.

She brushed branches aside, pushing her way into the thickets. Thorns brushed her arms and legs, cutting her skin. The lacerations burned like acid as she waved her arms out in front of her, doing her best to shield her face.

She turned to look behind her and saw the massive birds trying to push their way through the thickets, their feathered bodies cushioned from the thorns. Their eyes looked fierce as they snapped their beaks at her, advancing faster than her, using their size and weight to force their way through.

As her cuts burned and itched, a sensation of pins-and-needles began to spread through her limbs. She grunted and whined as she scraped her way through, her progress being slowed by thickening branches and increasingly uncooperative limbs. Panic set in when she realized she could no longer feel her feet.

The massive avian predators pushed inward, quickly gaining on her as she was no longer able to lift her arms. She staggered and dropped to one knee, dragging her other leg behind her as she lurched forward. At last, her progress was halted as the thorny branches and serpentine vines seemed to wrap around her, holding her fast.

She hung above the ground, her limp limbs dangling. She heard the scratching of claws in the dirt and chattering beaks behind her, anxious to tear into her flesh. Her face hung slack where it was scratched, as if the dentist had overdosed her on Novocain.

Susan closed her eyes, waiting for the death stroke to come, hoping it would be over quickly so she didn't have to witness being eaten alive.

*

"What do you mean, you're leaving me?" Susan was incredulous. She never expected this after fourteen years of marriage.

"You heard me," insisted her husband, Chris. "Frankly, the fact that you seem surprised by this just goes to show how out of touch with reality you are."

"Out of touch with reality? I'm the one, out of the both of us, who is most in touch with reality. Who do you think pays the mortgage, the car payments, and everything that makes this household run?"

Chris turned away from her, shaking his head in exasperation. "There you go again, throwing that in my face, as if I don't contribute to this household."

Susan wagged a finger at him. "I never said you didn't contribute. Don't you put words in my mouth."

"No, you just list all of your big-ticket items and happen to leave out what I contribute."

"Come on, Chris. You know I appreciate you watching the kids."

Chris pantomimed exaggerated gratitude. "Oh, well, how magnanimous of you. I had a career, too, you know, and I threw it all away so that you could pursue yours."

Susan shrugged. "It made logical sense. The money was there, as was the security. Someone had to be around for the kids."

Chris laughed, but it wasn't amusement. It was a bitter sound, and he choked on each guffaw. "Be around? I feel like I'm a damned single parent. Who gets them ready for school? Who picks them up? Who helps them with their homework and goes to parent-teacher conferences?"

"Exactly, and I love you for it. The kids love you for it."

"Love? Really? I haven't felt love from you for some time now."

That remark wounded her. "That's not fair. I do all of this for you. For our family."

"You're married to Poseidon Tech. Jesus, I think the kids see more of Marta than you at this point."

Susan pointed a finger at him. "I hired Marta to help you, because you felt overwhelmed. Now, you just want to cut and run. Is that it?"

"Susan, I lost you the moment your career started taking off. That took priority over everything."

"What was I supposed to do, Chris? Handicap myself so that you could be the alpha male?"

"Oh, come on. You know that's not it."

"I don't know. All I hear is you complaining that you had to sacrifice your career; that you have to be involved with the kids."

"I love being involved with the kids, and you know it. I'm a damned good father."

Now it was Susan's turn to chortle and huff. "Oh, what's that supposed to mean? I'm not a good mother?"

"The kids never see you. I never see you."

"I can't be everything to everyone! Just as you can't be the stay-at-home dad *and* the big corporate conqueror. We each have our roles, and each is important."

Chris turned back to her, leveling his gaze. "I'm having an affair."

Those words sucked all of the oxygen out of the room. "What?"

"You heard me."

"Who? Who is it?"

"Your sister."

"Patricia? You've got to be kidding me."

"She was around. You weren't."

This time, Susan turned away from Chris. "That bitch. That lousy bitch. She always wanted what she couldn't have. She was always jealous of what I had. My success."

Chris laughed. "Your success. Is that what this is?"

Susan shook her head, like one shakes an Etch-A-Sketch, as if she were wiping away the current argument and resetting. "I know I've been spending an inordinate time at work. You don't understand. We're on the verge of a breakthrough that, if we're successful, will change everything."

Chris leaned with his back to the wall, looking exasperated. "You're right. I don't understand. You never take the time to explain it to me."

"It's because I can't. Believe me. I want to, but Poseidon Tech is very strict about this stuff." Susan looked around the room. "I wouldn't be surprised if they've even bugged the house."

Chris threw his hands up. "Oh, great. Now you're paranoid."

"Honey, if you only knew..."

"You claim you love me."

"I do. You have no idea."

"Then tell me. Fill me in."

Susan looked around. "Not here."

Chris looked perplexed. "The kids are with my parents."

Susan looked around again, speaking, but not to her husband. "Let's go for a walk. Clear our heads. We're wasting time we have alone on bickering and fighting." She was saying this for someone else's benefit.

Chris gawked at her, confused. "Ah...okay. Let's go. I'll go get our jackets."

Susan nodded emphatically, and Chris disappeared from the kitchen, returning a few minutes later with their jackets. Susan grabbed hers, and they both slipped them on. She grabbed him by the arm and yanked him out the back door, locking it behind her.

They walked down the block, waving to neighbors, pretending like it was a normal stroll about the neighborhood. When they were far enough away from the house, Chris had the courage to speak. "Susan, what the hell is going on?"

"You want to know how much I love you? Here goes. I'm risking my career, a lawsuit, and maybe even more."

"What's with all the cloak and dagger stuff? You're acting as if Poseidon Tech is spying on us."

"Remember a little while ago there was something in the news about confirmation of the existence of gravitational waves?"

"Yeah, I guess. Vaguely."

"Our R&D has been working on a project for some time manipulating them when they come."

"Manipulating them? I don't understand."

"The universe is always expanding, right?"

"Yeah."

"Well, think of gravitational waves like waves on a beach. Whenever a wave reaches the sand, it wipes away all of the footprints. Smooths everything out."

"Okay."

"Well, gravitational waves do the same, only for the fabric of the universe. It smooths out any distortions."

Chris was intrigued. "Fabric of the universe?"

She nodded, her eyes darting around. They settled on an unmarked work van parked at the end of the block. At the intersection she pulled Chris right, away from where it sat.

She was quiet for a moment as her husband waited patiently. She scanned the block, her eyes searching between houses. "The space-time continuum. When gravitational waves encounter an object of a certain mass, like our planet, there's a distortion in the space-time continuum. At least that's my understanding from the physicist who explained it to me. I might be getting some of the small details wrong."

"Okay…"

"In that distortion lies the potential to breach the gap between…you're really going to think I'm crazy…"

"Probably, but continue." Chris was smiling.

Susan loved his smile, from the moment they met. She was encouraged by the small gesture; "…between our dimension and…well…others."

"What, like alternate realities?"

"Not just laterally alternate, but also forward and backward in time. Potentially all simultaneously."

"You're right. I do think you're crazy."

"But you don't look mad."

"No, I'm more confused."

"About what?"

"About how I should feel right now."

"I promise, we're on the cusp of something huge. When we make the breakthrough, we'll be set. There'll be much more to do, but I'll be able to set my own terms. They're not going to want to bring in new people, if they can help it."

"How do you know if there is going to be a breakthrough? It all sounds so…far-fetched."

"We've already had a glimpse. Suddenly, during one of the distortions, an island appeared in the South China Sea, not too far from Vietnam. Chris, it wasn't there before."

"Did anyone else see it?"

"No. The satellites are focusing on populated areas of interest, so they missed it. And it was only a flicker. Now that we know it is there, we're going to try and sustain the distortion. Something about quintessence fields, and such. I don't fully understand all of it."

"Holy smokes," Chris gasped. "You're not kidding."

Susan shook her head slowly. "No, I'm not. That's why I've been so busy at work. I signed a non-disclosure agreement."

"That's why you're so jumpy."

Susan stopped walking and leveled her gaze at her husband. "Chris, you cannot tell anyone."

"I won't."

"This is very dangerous information."

"Does the government know about it?"

"They're partially funding it, but they don't know the full extent of our findings yet. Chris, you can't tell anyone. I mean *anyone*."

"Who am I going to tell?"

"Good. You know that I love you, but I can't walk away from this."

"I think I understand."

"Do you?"

"Yes."

"This is not only an important scientific discovery. It's going to be good for us. It'll pay for college, retirement…we'll be set."

Chris suddenly looked stunned. "What about other governments? This could be very dangerous."

"That's why we need to keep this quiet. This is why I'm risking more than my career telling you this. Do you understand?"

Chris gulped, realizing he and she were now both in danger. His eyes began to dart around, scanning up and down the block. "Why *did* you tell me this?"

"You forced my hand. I don't want to lose you. Not when I'm so close…"

* * *

Bill Gibson woke, his vision blurry and his head pounding. As his vision cleared, he felt like he was experiencing a nasty hangover. The sun hung low in the sky. His arms felt like they had pins-and-needles. As his mind and vision cleared, he realized that his hands were tied behind his back. He pulled his arms, but he realized his hands were lashed to something behind him. He leaned backwards and felt a post press up against his spine.

Before him sat a crude, stone temple, overgrown with green vines and lush vegetation. The stone blocks appeared crumbled from age, and stray stones lay on the ground after having fallen. At the front was an entrance, what lay beyond was hidden in shadow. In front, skeletons and bones, green from mold, lay strewn about. Lit torches on long poles stuck into the ground surrounding him, offering some light in the darkening jungle.

Bill turned his head to the right, where he saw a grouping of skeletons in torn blue overalls. The bones were white, indicating a more recent demise, the flesh picked clean from the bone. They sat around an orange, metallic object, as if guarding it. It was the plane's ELT unit.

The area around him appeared deserted, but he heard footsteps off to the right. Branches moved as if something were brushing past them, and Bill prayed it wasn't one of those velociraptors.

A head poked out from the vegetation. Bill sighed, as it was a human head, wearing a hat. It wasn't one of the natives. The person eyed him cautiously, and scanned the area. Satisfied there was no immediate threat, the man crept out from the vegetation and into the clearing. He was wearing camouflage clothing, but he didn't look like a soldier. There were no insignias or patches, and the jacket rolled up at the sleeves was open, revealing a black tee shirt underneath.

"Oy. You alone, mate?"

Bill nodded. "Who are you?"

The man looked at the skeletons in the blue overalls arranged around the ELT device. His eyes widened when he must've recognized the device. “I’m looking for that, over there.” The man ran over to the device, inspecting it closely. “Yeah, that’s it.”

Bill was a bit annoyed that this man appeared more interested in the device than him. “A little help.”

The man was now looking over the skeletons. He appeared particularly interested in their blue overalls. He pinched off a piece of cloth from the breast area, inspecting it closely.

Bill saw a patch with lettering, but he was unable to make it out from his vantage point. Becoming inpatient, he cleared his throat loudly.

The man in the camos looked startled, as if he had forgotten Bill was even there. He came running over to Bill, took a knee, and slipped a rather large knife from his boot.

CHAPTER 8

"My name is Bill. Bill Gibson." He was mildly concerned about what this man was going to do with the massive hunting knife.

The man began to cut Bill's bindings behind his back. "I'm Jason. Are you a survivor? From the plane?"

Bill's hands were freed. He rubbed his wrists, which had red ligature marks from the bindings. "Yeah." He noticed the rifle on Jason's shoulder and the sidearm in its holster. "You have any water?"

Jason shed his pack, unzipped the top, and produced a canteen. He unscrewed the top and offered it to Bill.

Bill grabbed it and took a generous pull, dribbling water down his chin.

"Hey, easy," protested Jason. "We have to make that last."

Bill swallowed and handed it back, wiping his chin with the back of his hand. "Sorry."

"Who did this to you?" Jason inspected the bindings, which appeared to be made of intertwined vines.

Bill struggled to stand. His legs were numb. Jason helped him to his feet, Bill using the post for added support. "There's a local tribe. They fed me, bathed me, and knocked me out. I woke up here, just moments before you showed up."

Jason was inspecting the ground, probing the dirt with his fingers. "Lots of footsteps. The ones going toward this spot are deeper than the ones leaving. They carried you to this spot and left you here."

Bill looked weary. "What are you, some kind of tracker?"

"Something like that." Jason furrowed his brow as he detected other sets of footprints in front of Bill. "Well, these are strange."

"Everything here is strange."

"These tracks lead to the temple entrance. The strides are long…no, scratch that. These indicate dragging feet."

"How do you know it's a temple?" asked Bill.

The hunter-tracker frowned. "I've seen my fair share. The way those skeletons were arranged, the way you were tied up…looks to me like offerings." He looked around shiftily. "But, there are other things worse than natives around here."

"You ran into the dinosaurs, too?" asked Bill, now standing on his own. He stamped his feet and shook his hands to get the blood flowing again.

"Big ones. T. rexes. How about you?"

"Velociraptors."

"Great. Just great." Jason returned to the orange ELT device. "I'm here with a salvage operation looking for this here device." He picked it up, hefting it.

Bill looked around. "Where's the rest of your group?"

Jason stepped away from the skeletons in the overalls. "We were scattered when we were attacked by the T. rexes."

Both men's heads turned towards the temple when they heard sounds from inside. They sounded like groans.

"Maybe we should find your group," offered Bill.

"Excellent idea," said Jason.

They turned to run, but stopped dead in their tracks when they saw that they were surrounded by natives lining the tree line, armed with sharp spears pointed right at them.

"Oh, crap," said Bill.

"Are these your friends?" asked Jason.

"That's them."

Jason shoved the device into Bill's arms. "Here. Hold this." After unloading, he pulled his handgun. The noises from inside the temple grew louder—groans, grunts, and shuffling noises.

"Wait," said Bill. "They're not attacking us."

"They're not letting us leave either," said Jason, pointing his gun. "You were left here as a sacrifice."

"To what?" Bill sounded horrified.

"Let's not stick around to find out." Jason fired a warning shot into the air once.

*

The loud bang caused the line of natives to shrink back, but Jason noticed they weren't looking at his gun. They were looking past Bill and him.

Jason felt Bill tapping his shoulder. "Um. You should have a look at this."

Jason didn't want to take his eyes off the armed natives, but they were receding into the bush, and he didn't like the tremor in Bill's voice.

He turned to see humanoid figures lurching out of the temple entrance, eyes red in the firelight, in tattered rags. Their exposed flesh was stark white in color, and they staggered out like a bunch of drunkards on a pub crawl. When they caught sight of Bill and Jason, they cried out and snapped their jaws like wind-up chatterboxes.

Bill sighed. "Great. Zombies."

Jason hefted his handgun. "Nope. No such thing. Cannibals."

"No such thing? Really?"

"Can you run?"

"Yeah."

"Good. You run. I'll shoot. Don't drop the box."

Bill looked terrified. "Shouldn't I have a..." Jason had already taken off. Bill turned to find the cannibals had doubled their efforts and were closing in on him. He ran after Jason, who darted off from the direction he arrived, firing shots at the natives hiding in the bush.

He tagged one, who dropped to the ground, clutching his shoulder. Spears let fly from the bush at Jason. He instinctively turned away as a spear hit his pack. He turned and ducked and dodged as he ran, firing at anyone who was visible.

Bill followed behind him, clutching the ELT like a wide receiver running to the end zone. He dodged as spears flew past him, one bouncing off the orange metallic box he cradled.

Jason quickly ran out of ammunition, but he holstered his weapon rather than waste more bullets by firing blindly into the dark. Now in the thick of the bush, he ran ahead of Bill like a blocker, shoving any native that entered his path.

Spear tips jutted out as he and Bill ran the gauntlet, retreating from the bloodcurdling shrieks of the pursuing cannibals. Their clothing was torn and arms and legs jabbed, but the wounds were shallow as they were moving targets, and adrenaline masked any significant pain.

Jason looked around the tumult and noticed the natives were running with him, away from the cannibal onslaught. "Try to stay right behind me," he called back over his shoulder to Bill. "Stay in the middle of the pack."

The fleeing tribe, along with Jason and Bill, burst into a clearing of tall grass. They dashed through, running blindly, but Jason knew to follow the natives. They knew where they were going.

Jason heard rustling in the grass on both his flanks. A native on his right was snatched off his feet and disappeared into the thick cover. There was a growl, and one to his left was snatched in the same fashion.

Jason slowed his pace to slap a new clip into his handgun, when Bill plowed into him.

"What's going on?" asked Bill, now trotting alongside Jason.

"We seem to have run into your raptors. Stay in the middle of the pack and try to keep up."

Shrieks of terror and wails of pain erupted all around them as natives and cannibals alike were snatched by stealthy jaws hiding in the tall grass. Jason darted through, keeping in the center as his flanks and rear were picked off one-by-one.

His legs grew tired, and he noticed Bill was losing steam. He caught sight of reptilian eyes under sharp, scaly ridges watching him, appearing and vanishing in the tall grass, growing closer with each appearance.

A long snout lunged out at him, flashing sharp teeth, and he fired at it and ran past. He heard Bill cry out behind him, but when he looked over his shoulder, he saw Bill was still following. However, fatigue was setting in and Bill began to lag.

The clearing ended, and they dashed back into the tree line on the other side, tripping over vines. Jason grabbed Bill and threw him to the ground between two fallen tree trunks. Human footfalls and tribal hoots and yelps passed them on either side as Jason shed his pack, throwing it between the fallen trunks. He ducked down, lying next to Bill, face-to-face, as he pulled his pistol close to his chest. Bill panted in his face, struggling to catch his breath. They lay there, absolutely still, as fleeing tribesmen hurdled the trunks.

After a few moments, the jungle fell silent around them, but both men continued to lay still, waiting in the dark. Only one of them was afraid.

* * *

30 Years Ago

Jason stormed out of the kitchen where his mother was hysterical, crying out Joey's name between sobs. He had tried to console her, but he was in shock himself and barely keeping it together. A building, animalistic rage squelched any tears as he piled on layers for the Alaskan cold.

His father was on deployment, which made him the de facto man of the house. He decided he'd rather take action than sit around and listen to his mother's pitiful wails of grief. He strapped on his heavy-duty boots and grabbed his father's hunting rifle, a .308 Winchester, and plenty of ammunition. He slipped his father's hunting knife into his right boot and left the cabin without saying goodbye.

As he trudged through the knee-deep snow, the icy air stung his cheeks. He controlled his breathing, harnessing his bloodlust to push on, into the woods, in search of revenge.

He and his little brother had traversed these woods on many an occasion, both with their father and by themselves. They knew better than to travel alone, or at least Jason did. He couldn't have imagined what possessed Joey to go off on his own.

With their father gone, their mother became unbearable, hovering over them, berating them at every turn. She took her anxiety and resentment at their father's absence out on them, but was it enough this time to push Joey out into the woods alone?

When Jason had found his body, it had been ravaged by pack hunters…wolves. There were pawprints all around Joey's gored body. His coat and clothes were torn, and he lay face down in the snow, his neck broken.

He had no idea what he planned to do, if he found the pack. Wolf packs were territorial. There was a good chance they were still in the area, lurking around. He had to be careful.

Once, he had seen a pack rip apart one of their own, a juvenile who had apparently become injured, perhaps on a hunt. The ferocity with which they consumed one of their own was disturbing.

He crunched through the crusty snow for a few hours, the sun waning in the sky. Good sense told him to turn heel and return to his cabin as the temperature plummeted and the woods grew dark, but his wonton lust for revenge and his anger towards his mother told him otherwise. He heard howls in the distance, and as he pressed on, they grew closer.

Surrounded by towering peaks, he crested a hill dotted with evergreens when he first caught movement in his peripheral vision. He turned his head to the right and stopped dead in his tracks when he saw them in the moonlight. The large, silver alpha was standing next to his smaller black mate, and they nipped at each other affectionately, tipping their heads back to howl. They had four juveniles with them, wrestling and pinning each other down, grabbing each other by the throat in playful practice for the real thing.

Jason knelt down on his left knee and unslung his rifle from his shoulder. He steadied himself, raising the rifle, closing his left eye and looking through the scope with his right.

He was no stranger to firearms. His father, an army sergeant, taught him and his brother to shoot when they were very young. He took a deep breath, sighting his targets, but realized he was probably too far away. At three hundred yards, his father would've taken the shot, but Jason knew his limits. He had to get closer.

He stood and crept amongst the trees, moving off to the right to flank them. The snow crunched beneath his feet, but he kept his distance. Snow began to fall, which hushed his surroundings into silence, buffering against ambient sounds. When he was alongside them, he took a knee and raised his rifle. He was close enough now, about a hundred and fifty yards or so, and felt comfortable attempting to set up a shot.

He slowed his breath and focused on the large alpha. If he took out the alpha, it would disorient the pack.

He heard the soft crunching of snow off to his right. He looked away from his scope to find a large female wolf who had gotten the drop on him. As his eyes focused, he saw one behind her and off to the right. Then another, and another. One-by-one, they appeared to materialize from the surrounding darkness, feral eyes glinting in the moonlight.

The wolf lowered its head and bared its teeth, and the others followed suit. Jason froze, terrified. The snowfall had masked their approach, and now he was taken off guard.

Not knowing what else to do, he thrust his rifle out in front of him, swinging wildly and yelling, "Yah! Yah! Git!"

The wolves recoiled with each swing, but they kept approaching. No matter how much he yelled and screamed, they seemed to come closer and closer. He fired a warning shot into the air. The wolves shrank back for a moment, but they advanced again.

Panicking, Jason ran through the snow, back from where he came, the wolves following him, flanking him. Every so many feet, a wolf darted in at him, snapping its jaws and missing. He swung his rifle at them, missing.

One lunged forward and gripped his left leg above his thigh. Jason cried out and brought the stock of his rifle down on its head, but another approached and clamped down on his forearm, sinking its teeth through his coat and into his flesh.

The two wolves began to play tug-of-war with their prey as others closed in. Jason was blinded by searing pain and terror as the wolves savaged him, taking him down, his rifle dropping to the snow stained with his blood and vanishing beneath it.

*

Jason caught glimpses in the darkness of a shadowy figure standing over him. He opened his eyes to see flickering lights, and his body ached. If his eyes were open long enough, he felt sharp, stabbing pains in different parts of his body. He slipped in and out of consciousness as this figure occasionally stood over him, dressing his wounds and speaking to him in a gravelly voice.

After an indeterminant period of time, Jason awoke. His vision clear, he looked up and saw the wooden roof above him. He looked to his right and saw a large pot-bellied stove. It felt warm on his face. He felt a pressure on his body. When he looked down, the motion causing searing pain in his neck and shoulders, he saw that he was under blankets made of animal fur.

"Don't try and move. You're banged up pretty good." The voice came from across the cabin to Jason's left.

Jason lay back and looked up at the ceiling. "Where am I? What happened?"

"You are in my home," answered the disembodied voice. Although it was coarse, it was as warm as the pot-bellied stove. It had a comforting, reassuring quality. "What happened? You underestimated the raw power of nature."

Jason tried to crane his neck, but the stabbing pain prohibited it. "How did I get here?"

"I found you, mangled in the snow. You tried to tangle with Tikaani."

"What?"

"Brother wolf and his pack."

"They killed my brother."

"And you thought you'd go and return the favor?"

"Something like that."

The rough voice laughed, but it was also a warm sound. "You are very brave…and also very stupid. How old are you?"

Jason had to mull the question over a minute as he struggled to get his bearings. "Sixteen."

"A little young to be hunting a wolf pack with the taste for man, all on your own."

"There's only me."

"Where are your parents?"

"It's just my mother."

"She approved of your hunt?"

"I didn't give her any choice."

"You almost lost your life to the very same pack. How would your mother have felt then?"

"I didn't do it for her." Jason sounded defiant, insolent, and every year of sixteen.

"I see. Do you wish to become a hunter?"

Jason hesitated. "I just want to kill the pack that murdered my brother."

"To hunt animals, other predators, to take their lives, you must become a hunter. A true hunter. Do you know what that means?"

"I don't want to hunt."

"You just want your revenge."

"I guess."

"What you ask is no light task. It's no…one-and-done. You must know everything about your opponent, because that is what they are. You must be prepared to hunt the hunters in their element. You must study and be able to track their movements. You must learn to travel light, silent, to mask your presence."

"You make it sound like being a hunter is like being some kind of ninja."

The laugh came again, amused without being derisive. "To hunt predators, there must be no hesitation. No attack of conscience. Animals, while beautiful, are dangerous. Predators kill. Your brother is not the only life claimed by this pack. Are you ready to kill something beautiful and dangerous?"

* * *

Jason pushed himself to standing, his ears and eyes peeled for any movement. It appeared quiet. A trail of ants in a perfectly straight line marched across one of the tree trunks, each carrying a leaf.

"Can I get up now?" asked Bill, face down in the dirt.

"Yeah. We're alone." He reached down and helped Bill up. Bill was still clutching the orange ELT unit. Jason smiled.

"You say you came here with a search and rescue party. I say it's high time we found them and got off this island."

"Search and retrieval," corrected Jason. "We camp for the night."

Bill's eyes widened. "Are you crazy? The sooner we get out of here, the better."

Jason looked up at the sky. "It's almost dark. In order to find my group, I need to track. It's much easier to track in daylight. Plus, in the dark, I won't be able to see who or what is tracking us."

Bill paused for a moment. As if on cue, there was a reptilian roar not too far off in the distance. "Maybe you're right."

"If you want to survive this, stick with me. Do what I do."

Bill nodded. "Where do we set up camp?"

Jason looked around, surveying the area. "Not here. We already know this is a raptor hunting ground."

"Okay, so where do we go? Up a tree?"

Jason shook his head. "The T. rexes will get us up there. We need a good cave. One with a mouth too small for the larger predators."

Bill knew what he meant by larger predators. "I know where there's a cave. It has a drop-off inside with deep water at the bottom. I used it to get away from some raptors."

"Is it close?"

"I think so."

"What happened to the raptors?"

"They fell in and drowned."

"Perfect. Lead the way."

* * *

Torres had led the group back to the extraction site, only to find both of the helicopters had been trashed by the tyrannosaurus attack on base camp. The tents were torn down, equipment scattered everywhere, and he spoke to what was left of his detail, assessing the situation.

"We're screwed," said Allison, standing in the moonlight, looking listless from terror and exhaustion. "We're really screwed."

Mary placed her arm around Allison's shoulder. "Don't say that."

"I'm never going to see my baby again. Coming here was a huge mistake."

Mary turned Allison to face her, and she looked her in the eye. "Don't say that. You're alive, and Torres is going to figure out how to get us out of this."

Allison shook her head. She looked down at her feet and back at Mary. "Look what they did to base camp. They took out our helicopters. You saw the sheer cliffs."

"They'll radio for more helicopters. It'll be fine."

"What if they come back? The T. rexes."

"Torres formed a perimeter around camp. They won't get through."

"A lot of good that perimeter did before."

Mary looked crestfallen. She knew Allison was right.

Off to the side, Peter looked up at the sky. Tracey strolled up next to him. He felt her looking at him. "It's getting dark. Something on your mind?" He turned to look at her. Her eyes, welling-up, shone like mirrors in the twilight. "What is it?"

Tracey swallowed hard and averted her gaze. "I-I…I should've helped you back there."

"Back where?"

Tracey shot him an *oh, come on* look. "You know what I'm talking about."

Peter sighed. "We were all scared. Terrified. It's a natural reaction."

Tracey shook her head emphatically. "No. Not you."

Peter chortled. "Are you kidding? I was terrified beyond all rational thought."

"But you did the right thing. You helped Allison."

"You're making too much of this."

"Pete, you almost died."

Peter was speechless. This wasn't just guilt over Allison. "We all almost died."

That simple fact did nothing to assuage her.

"Listen, I've been wanting to talk about what happened that night."

Tracey put her hands up, waving them in front of her face. "That requires no explanation."

Peter pressed the matter. "I believe it does."

She shook her head and took a step back. "What happened was between two consenting adults."

"That's just it, Tracey! Nothing happened. Nothing."

"I saw what I saw, and it's none of my business."

"I didn't care for Petra. Not like that."

"Oh, please. She was hot."

Peter paused a minute. "Yeah, she was, but I didn't want to be with her."

It took Tracey a moment to follow where he was going. Suddenly, her expression morphed from anguished to annoyed. She shook her head and stormed off.

Peter was left alone, more confused than ever. "What did I say?"

"Nothing," came a voice from behind him, "and everything."

He turned around to find Mary standing there. "Oh. Hey. How's Allison?"

Mary stepped forward. "Shaken but fine, thanks to you."

"I'm glad someone here isn't pissed at me."

"Why? I'm not pissed at you."

"I-I just can't figure her out."

"Tracey? She doesn't know what she wants."

"How do you know?"

"Because that's the way I am. I go from guy to guy, sucking them in and letting them go. Chewing them up and spitting them out."

"Man, you sound worse than the tyrannosaurs."

This made Mary laugh. "I've always gone after the hunky guy. The badass. All looks and no brains." She paused a minute and then locked eyes with Peter. "Maybe I've been looking for the wrong type."

A chill of realization shot down Peter's spine. He knew that look. Or, at least he'd seen it before, but it was usually directed at other guys. The type of guys Mary was describing.

"Uh…um…" His awkwardness was interrupted by an announcement from Torres. "We make camp within the tree line tonight. Let's get moving."

CHAPTER 9

Bill pointed across a clearing. "There! I see it!"

Jason stepped in front of him. "Stay put and be quiet." He crept out to the edge of the clearing and squatted on his haunches, scanning the ground, probing the dirt with his fingers. Satisfied, he waved Bill over. When Bill, cradling the ELT like a baby, reached where he was standing, Jason shouldered his rifle and pulled his hand gun. "Stay behind me, and don't drop the ELT."

Bill nodded, like a child being instructed by a parent or teacher.

The two men crept towards the mouth of the cave. Jason pulled a flashlight and swept the beam and the muzzle of his gun back and forth. "Let's go," he muttered.

They crept inside the cave, and it was silent except for their footsteps echoing off the cave walls. They pressed forward until they reached the drop that Bill mentioned earlier.

"That's it," whispered Bill.

Jason shined his beam of light down, illuminating a small stone shelf next to the water. "That's where we sleep tonight."

Jason shrugged off his pack and dug inside. He pulled out fifty feet of rope.

"What's that for?" asked Bill.

Jason answered by squatting down and tying the rope around the ELT device in a harness. "When you go down, I'll carefully lower this down to you. Then, I'll come down."

Bill nodded. He went first, climbing down carefully. The wall was jagged enough that he was able to find a couple of handholds and footholds as he descended what he estimated to be about fifteen to twenty feet. When he reached the bottom, Jason shined his light down on his face.

"Ready." Bill's voice echoed off the cavern walls.

Jason dangled the ELT over the edge and slowly lowered it down. It was light, around three to four pounds. He saw Bill grab the device, hugging the precious cargo. Jason shined the light on the jagged wall, planning his descent. Looking from side to side, listening for the scratching of claws on rock, he lowered himself down.

When he reached the bottom, he took the ELT from Bill and placed it on the far left of the shelf, in the corner between two rock walls. He placed his pack on top of it, and lay down on the shelf, using his pack as a pillow.

This didn't leave much room for Bill, who stood there awkwardly. "Where do I sleep?"

Jason curled his legs up, making a few extra inches of room. "Where there's room. Take off your pants and roll them up. It makes a handy pillow." Jason turned off his light.

Bill didn't know what to say.

"I'll take first watch," said Jason in the dark. "Get some shut eye. You're going to need it."

Bill curled almost into a fetal position, hugging the rock wall. He wedged himself into the corner opposite Jason's head, where the floor met the rock wall and side of the cavern. He decided against taking his pants off. "Something's eating you," he said, addressing the darkness. "Ever since you found me."

"It isn't you," replied Jason.

"Then, what is it?"

"Remember those skeletons in the blue jumpsuits?"

"Yeah."

"Those were Poseidon Tech."

"So?"

"So, that means we weren't the first salvage team on this island."

"You didn't know that? They didn't tell you?"

"No, they didn't. Susan and I are going to have a talk when we leave this cave."

"Who's Susan?"

"Our team leader, mate."

"Oh. Where are you from?"

Jason arched an eyebrow. "Why do you ask?"

"You sound like you might be from Australia. I'm from Australia, but not originally. I'm a transplant from New York."

Jason sighed. "I'm from all kinds of places. I was an army brat. I left home at a young age and travelled the world, on my own, honing my hunting skills, amongst other things."

Bill sat up. "Other things? Like what?"

"Nothing I want to talk about right now."
"I'm sorry. I-I didn't mean to…"
"Go to sleep, Bill."
"Okay."

*

When Jason awoke in the darkness of the cave, he heard murmuring. He lay still, till his eyes and ears adjusted, cursing himself for trusting Bill to have second watch. It was a necessary evil, as he was exhausted, both physically and mentally.

He slowly reached for his handgun in his right hand, and then the flashlight in his left, careful not to make a sound. There were definitely two voices in the dark, Bill's and another.

He flicked the flashlight on and pointed his gun. "Freeze!" To his surprise, Bill was conversing with an Asian man dressed in a blue jumpsuit. Next to the Asian man was one of the tribe members who had tied Bill up and left him for sacrifice. "What the hell is going on here?"

Bill put his hand out, palm facing downward. "It's okay. He's Poseidon Tech."

Jason didn't lower his weapon. Instead, he kept it trained on the Asian man, but he was watching the tribesman. "Why is he with this one?"

"My name is Mark Hong," said the man in the blue jumpsuit. Upon further inspection, his jumpsuit appeared tattered. He was smiling, but he looked nervous. He gestured to the indigenous man. "It's okay, he's with me."

"It's okay," said Bill. "He's a friend."

Jason sat up. He lowered his gun, but he studied Mark. He didn't recognize him from the current expedition. He turned on Bill. "I told you to wake me if you saw anyone."

Bill shrugged his shoulders. "You looked exhausted. He wasn't a threat, so I figured I'd let you sleep. You were right, by the way. He's from the original group."

"I know," said Jason. "I could tell by the condition of his jumpsuit."

"You're a part of the current group?" asked Mark.

Jason nodded.

"How many have there been after mine?"

"Good question," said Jason. "I wasn't aware of any others. Your masters kept that little part a secret."

"He's been here a long time," said Bill. "He's befriended the local tribal group."

"You mean the one that almost sacrificed you?" said Jason pointedly.

"I wasn't aware that there were other Poseidon Tech on the island," explained Mark. "And, I had no idea they were sacrificing anyone. If I had, I would've put a stop to it."

Jason narrowed his eyes. "How do we know you didn't order Bill, here, to be sacrificed?"

Mark shot him a sideways glance. "Come on. I would never do that. I want off this island. In fact, I have no idea how long I've actually been here."

"Enough to make friends with the locals," said Jason.

"He knows about the zombies," said Bill. "He said they're controlled by another Poseidon Tech team member."

Mark nodded. "He was our original project manager. Mike Deluca."

Jason leaned forward. "I'm going to need a full explanation, because none of this is making any sense. We were sent here with biologists and paleontologists to recover the ELT of a downed Malaysian flight on an uncharted island that has somehow remained hidden from satellites and cartographers; we were attacked by dinosaurs and cannibals; now I find out we're not the first team Poseidon Tech sent here. *And*, somehow I don't think this is about the crashed plane or the ELT."

Mark sat down in front of Jason. His tribal companion squatted next to him, looking uncertain of what was happening. Bill sat next to Mark, with his back against the cool, uneven stone wall.

"Okay," said Mark. "Here goes."

"The full story," insisted Jason. "I need to know what we're dealing with."

Mark nodded. "I assume Poseidon Tech had you sign a gag order. It's mandatory for all staff and consultants." Jason nodded, and Mark continued. "We've been experimenting with manipulation of quintessence fields."

"What, like magnetism?" asked Jason.

"Not exactly. Let's just say that time doesn't only exist in a linear fashion—as in past, present, and future. We've confirmed the existence of alternate, lateral realities."

"You've got to be kidding me," muttered Jason.

"Let him finish," insisted Bill. "It'll all make sense once he explains it."

"I get it," snapped Jason. "That's why this island isn't on any maps or satellite pictures."

"That's right," said Mark. "It doesn't exactly exist on our plane. That's why getting a signal on or off the island from our reality is sketchy. This island both does and doesn't exist on our natural plane simultaneously."

"The Malaysian flight?"

"An unfortunate coincidence," said Mark. "Poseidon Tech used the salvage operation as a cover to explore the island without interference. However, we weren't prepared for the fauna on the island."

"Okay, so I get the dinosaurs," said Jason. "But zombies?"

"This island has strange properties that defy the laws of physics as we know them," said Mark. "When our team was attacked and stranded on the island, we banded together with the indigenous people. They were friendly. They took us in, helped us to survive."

"So, what went wrong?" asked Bill.

"Our project manager, Mike, started acting strange. He wanted to set up rules, which quickly became laws. It became less of a democracy and more about power. His power. He became paranoid, saying we needed to take extreme measures to maintain our safety, even though the indigenous tribe was more than capable of keeping us safe. He began to treat them cruelly."

"Holy smokes," said Bill.

"Human nature," added Jason. "Crises bring out the very best or the very worst in people."

Mark nodded. "Some of us didn't like how he was treating the indigenous. Our group fractured in two. With the help of the tribe, we ousted them from our group. No longer welcome in the tribal village, Mike and his faction disappeared into the temple. The one the zombies came out of."

"What were they doing in there?" asked Bill.

Mark shook his head. "I don't know, but when he emerged, he was different. Transformed. Those from our team he entered the temple with never came out, and Mike suddenly commanded an army of the dead."

"You've got to be kidding me," said Jason.

"I wish I was. Every so often, mostly at night, he would emerge and slaughter members of the tribe, adding them to his undead ranks. My whole team was wiped out. I'm the only one left."

"They almost got us," said Bill.

Mark's eyes glinted in the illumination of the flashlight. "The only things they fear are the dinosaurs."

"So, they tried to sacrifice me to appease this Mike Deluca?" asked Bill.

"They're a superstitious people," said Mark. "They told me that the temple, which used to belong to them, sits on top of a cave system that runs deep underground. They told me stories of monsters and magic within those caves."

Jason shook his head in disbelief. "Wait a minute. How did you have time to learn this tribe's language to be able to communicate with them? And, this Mike...how did he accomplish all of this in such a short period of time?"

Mark looked perplexed at the question.

"It's only been a month since the Malaysian flight crashed," said Jason.

Bill and Mark exchanged stunned looks.

"It's only been a month?" asked Bill.

"It feels much longer," said Mark. "It must be the wrinkle in spacetime."

Jason sat up, dusting himself off. "Look, I don't know about all of this. All I know is that we have the ELT. I want off this island, and I want to get paid."

"I couldn't agree more," said Mark. "Where's the rest of your group?"

"We were attacked by dinosaurs," said Jason. "I split off from the group to track the ELT. Now that we have it, we can find the rest of the group and get off this island."

"There's one problem," said Mark.

"What's that?"

"Now that Mike knows there are others, others from our reality, he won't stop until he kills you all."

"Great," said Jason. "First the dinosaurs, and now this. The hits just keep on coming."

"Doesn't Mike want off the island, too?" asked Bill. "He can leave with us."

Mark shook his head. "Mike is no longer Mike."

"What do you mean?" asked Bill.

"He refers to himself as the Death Lord now. He's a different person, if he's even still human."

"You said he only comes out at night?" asked Jason.

"That's right," said Mark.

"Then, at first light we make for base camp. We have a security detail and choppers."

The tribesman, unsure of what was being discussed, stirred.

"What about your friend, here, and the others?" asked Bill.

"The hell with them," snapped Jason. "They're not our problem."

"Nor were we theirs," said Mark. "Yet, they took us in and helped us. Now, one of ours commands an undead army that routinely slaughters these poor people."

"Not our problem," pressed Jason.

"What can we do?" asked Bill. "We can't help them."

"If you have an armed security detail, maybe we can take care of Mike," suggested Mark.

"The squad escorting our group was wiped out by two T. rexes," said Jason, sounding more and more impatient. "What make you think they're equipped to handle the Death Lord and his loyal army of flesh-eating zombies?"

Mark looked at his tribal companion, who looked concerned at Jason's tone. "I feel bad. These poor people didn't ask for any of this."

"Neither did we," reminded Jason. "We leave at first light. When you and your friend arrived here, was it still dark?"

"The sun was beginning to rise," said Mark.

"Then we leave now," said Jason. "Tell your friend to go home."

*

They ventured out of the cave, careful to avoid roving packs of velociraptors or tyrannosaurs. When they reached the eastern flank of the tribal village without incident, Mark's companion was reluctant to leave him, shooting sideways glances at Jason and Bill.

"You have to go now," insisted Mark, waving his indigenous companion away.

The tribal man answered, but only Mark understood what he was saying.

"I don't like the way he's giving us the stink-eye," said Jason, hefting his rifle.

"He's only met two people like us," explained Jason. "One turned out to be an evil Death Lord of the underworld."

"I see your point," said Jason.

"You have to go," said Mark. "I'll be back. I have to talk to the others. They can help me."

The tribal man made a shrugging gesture and spoke, gesticulating with great emphasis. The tribal man gestured to Bill, who was cradling the ELT like it was a baby.

Mark shook his head. "No. You left it there before, and it didn't help."

The indigenous man emitted guttural sounds of protest.

"It won't make a difference if we take it."

It appeared as if the two were now arguing, but it was unclear how much the native man was understanding. While Mark knew some of his language, he resorted mostly to speaking English, as there just weren't words in the indigenous language for what he was attempting to describe. After much back and forth, the indigenous man pounded the wooden pole of his spear on the ground and stomped off in a huff.

Mark started to walk away, but Jason and Bill joined him.

"What was that all about?" asked Jason.

"He's upset," said Mark. "He thinks I'm abandoning him, leaving him to the Death Lord."

"That's unfair," offered Bill.

Mark shook his head. "No, it's not. I am abandoning them."

"There's nothing we can do for them," said Jason. "That's all there is to it. They don't have to like it."

"You said there's an armed security detail," said Mark. "They can help."

"They're just here for the ELT," said Jason. "Once they see we've retrieved it, they'll want to take off this God-forsaken island."

"They might feel differently if they know one of their own is massacring the native tribe," said Bill.

Jason sighed. "Well, if I know Susan, she's not going to care one lick."

"Your kind of gal," said Bill.

Jason arched an eyebrow. "What's that supposed to mean?"

"You know exactly what that's supposed to mean."

Mark slowed his pace, but the others didn't notice. "Guys, who's that?"

"No, I don't know what that's supposed to mean," said Jason, growing impatient. "Maybe you need to explain it to me."

Mark stopped. He was pointing over to a large thicket. "Guys, look."

Jason and Bill slowed to a stop and looked over at the thicket. Bill gasped. "That's a person!"

In the center of the vast thicket, hung up in branches in vines, was a woman. She was sagging, her head hanging off at an unnatural angle, as if her neck was limp spaghetti. Her black hair hung down at her side. Her legs were bloody, her pants and flesh shredded, and her entrails hung out of her split chest cavity.

Jason walked up to the edge of the thicket, but Mark grabbed him by the arm, stopping him. "Don't."

"That person needs help," said Jason.

"Those are poisonous thorns," explained Mark. "If they scratch your skin, you become paralyzed. Something got at her in there. She's dead."

Jason squinted to try and make out who it was. "Oh, man."

"What? You recognize her?" asked Bill. "Is she part of your group?"

"That's Susan. The team leader."

"Susan Kinney," gasped Mark. "Good God."

Bill looked panicked. "So, what does this mean?"

"It doesn't mean anything," said Jason.

"If she was your leader, then what does that mean?"

"There's the rest of our security detail and two helicopters at base camp. Once we get back, we're going to get off this island."

Bill pulled the ELT in tighter. "Well, don't get all sentimental on me, Jason."

"We don't have time for tears or eulogies," said Jason. "If we don't keep moving, we're going to run into some more of those nasty lizards or hungry zombie cannibals."

"She had a husband," said Mark, still gawking at his dead colleague. "They were having marital problems."

"TMI," said Jason. He consulted his compass and continued to walk in the direction of base camp.

"I have a wife," said Mark to Bill. "You married?"

Bill nodded.

They fell in behind Jason, who periodically checked the ground for tracks. Each time, he appeared satisfied the direction they were headed looked safe.

"Poor Susan," said Mark. "She sacrificed her marriage for this opportunity."

"She sacrificed a lot more than that," added Bill. "If I ever see my wife again, I'm going to hold her and never let her go."

Mark choked up. "My wife probably moved on without me."

Bill looked perplexed. "What are you talking about?"

"I've been here so long."

Bill shook his head. "It's only been a couple of months. Remember?"

Mark shook his head as if he was clearing out cobwebs. "Blows my mind. I can't believe it has only been that long. Feels like an eternity."

"I know what you mean. Hey, we're going to get off this island," said Bill. "Not if. When."

Mark smiled in appreciation. "Right. Not if. When."

Bill returned the smile. "Now you're talking."

* * *

Poseidon Tech
2 Months Prior

Mark Hong and Mike Deluca both stood up, and each shook Brenda Michaels' hand.

"Congratulations, you two," beamed Brenda. "Well-deserved."

"Thank you," said Mike.

Mark nodded, beaming.

As they left Brenda's office, Mike put his arm around Mark. "Ready to make history?"

Mark chuckled to himself. "We have a lot of work to do to prepare." As they strode down the hallway, they passed the coffee lounge. Mark's smiled faded as he saw Susan Kinney standing there. She was sipping a hot cup of coffee, but her expression was that of disappointment. Mark slowed down, pausing in front of the lounge. "Mike, I'll catch up with you later."

Mike looked over and saw Susan standing there, looking at Mark, expectant. "Okay. We'll meet after lunch, my office." He patted Mark on the back. He nodded to Susan, managing his most sincere smile, and he headed back to his office.

Susan waited for Mike to leave, and then she approached Mark, crestfallen. "Hey, Mark."

Mark smiled at Susan, looking sympathetic. "I take it you heard the news."

Susan nodded, cupping her coffee mug with both hands. "Yeah. I'm happy for you."

"Thank you, Susan."

"No, I really am…"

"I know," said Mark. "You were passed over. It sucks. You deserved this promotion."

Susan flashed him a conspiratorial glance and backed into the corner by the coffee maker. The lounge, at the moment, was otherwise unoccupied.

Mark, the dutiful friend, followed her. He knew what she was going to say. "I know, I know," he said in hushed tones. "*You* deserved to be project manager. You got screwed."

Susan looked around before speaking. "Mark, you know how many hours I've spent at the lab, compiling data. My models are the most accurate. We wouldn't be able to sustain the phase without my models. There'd be no island to explore."

"You were appointed lab director."

"Oh, come on. I didn't even get *your* position, assisting Mike Deluca. It's an insult. A damned insult."

"I-I don't know what to say."

"There's nothing you can say. It's not your fault. Do you know how many late hours and weekends I put in at the lab? My husband is ready to leave me. I haven't seen my kids in ages. In waltzes that sycophant, and takes it out from underneath me after doing a fraction of the work."

"You'll be closer to home," offered Mark, "instead of halfway around the world."

Susan raised the corner of her mouth. "You know this only means more long hours in the lab."

"It's a bump in pay."

"Yeah, but I needed *the* bump in pay. Mike's bump. It would've made all this worth it. At least I will have felt vindicated."

"He's not that bad, you know."

Susan chortled.

"He's not so bad. Really," insisted Mark. "He just knows how to get along."

Susan put her coffee mug down on the counter a little too hard. Some of her coffee splashed out onto the countertop. She placed her hands on her hips. "What's that supposed to mean?" She wasn't whispering any longer.

Mark gestured towards her with his hands. "*This* is what I mean." He quickly changed the subject. "How's your hubby these days?"

"Frustrated. Angry. Lonely."

"So, turn down the directorship. Take some time off. Be with him."

"Then I will have sacrificed all of this for nothing."

"Susan, I'm sure your husband will be happy to have you home. It'll be good for you guys."

Susan hesitated, biting her bottom lip. "You think so?"

"I know so. Your husband loves you. Take some time for the two of you. Go away somewhere on vacation."

"How about the South China Sea?" said Susan, her tone sardonic.

Mark cocked his head sideways, smirking. "Seriously?"

Susan looked as if she was pondering the option. "That might not be a bad idea after all, going on vacation. It would be good for us."

"Now you're talking."

Susan snapped her fingers. "I can tell Brenda that it's either Mike's position, or my current. No half-measures. It'll look like I'm playing hardball. I can use that later."

"See, that's the Susan Kinney I know. Never let a good crisis go to waste."

Susan ignored the backhanded compliment. "Let Brenda give lab director to Phil or Marcy. I'm going to take a good, long vacation."

"Good," said Mark. "Now I have to explain to Ellen that I'm going away to some undisclosed location for some undetermined amount of time. She's not going to be happy. You're not the only one who puts in long hours."

Susan arched an eyebrow. "Any time you want to trade…"

"You're going on vacation with your husband, remember?"

Susan shrugged, pretending to look sheepish. "I had to try." They shared a chuckle. "Just do me a favor…"

"Oh, God. This doesn't sound good."

"Make something happen to Mike, but make it look like an accident."

"Susan…"

"What? Maybe then Brenda will call me in, and you can work for me instead of that glad-handing sleazebag."

"I'll take my chances with Mike."

"What's that supposed to mean?"

"You know exactly what that's supposed to mean. I have a lot to do. Enjoy your vacation." Mark walked out of the lounge before Susan could reply.

CHAPTER 10

Peter checked his watch, which had stopped working at some point, likely due to the strange electromagnetic field on the island. When he looked up, he heard Torres' radio crackle.

"L-T. Go."

"Sir, there are three men approaching the perimeter. One is the hunter, another is holding an orange device, and a third is dressed in a Poseidon Tech uniform."

"Intercept and send them this way," said Torres. "Over and out."

Peter wasn't the only one who heard the message. The rest of the group came running over and surrounded Torres.

"What is it?" asked Allison, looking concerned.

"We found Jason," said Torres. "And, he has a couple of others with him."

The group buzzed. Tracey grabbed Peter's arm in anticipation, while Mary traded furtive glances with him.

Within minutes, Jason emerged out of the trees and strolled over to them, with two men following him. "Miss me?"

"Where the hell have you been?" demanded Allison, the protective mother.

Jason feigned blushing. "Why, Dr. McGary, I had no idea you cared."

"Yes, where have you been?" echoed Torres, only his inquiry had the hint of an accusation.

"Holy crap," said Tracey. She was looking at the shabby man holding the orange device. "Is that what I think it is?"

Torres approached the shabbily dressed man. "Is that the ELT from the plane?"

Bill nodded.

"Are you a survivor?"

"Yes. There was another. A woman..." Bill's voice trailed off. "One of the T. rexes got her."

"Yeah, well, they got our birds," said Torres. "Both of them. We're grounded."

"You've got to be kidding me," growled Jason.

"Unfortunately, I'm not. Did you see Susan Kinney out there?"

"She's dead," said Jason. "However, I found the original team leader." He gestured to Mark.

Mark stepped forward, extending a hand. "Hi. Mark Hong. I was Susan's predecessor."

"Original team leader? What are you talking about?"

Jason winked. "That's what I said when I found out."

"How did she die?"

"She got hung up in some poisonous thickets," said Bill. "Something took some bites out of her."

"Probably trying to flee from something," added Jason. "When we found her, she was dead."

"That coward ran away, leaving us to contend with two tyrannosaurs," snapped Mary.

"She was a complicated woman," said Mark.

"Aren't they all," quipped Jason, eliciting sneers from Mary and Tracey and eye rolls from Allison.

"She wasn't all bad," said Mark. "She was ambitious."

"That's one word for her," said Mary.

"So, why don't you explain to me everything that's happened since you've separated from the group?" said Torres.

Jason explained how he followed the tracks to find Bill, a survivor of the plane crash, being offered up by the indigenous people to a former Poseidon Tech employee and his underground cult of zombies with the ELT device. Bill shared his encounter with the tyrannosaurs and his scrape with the velociraptors in the cave, and Mark chimed in with Poseidon Tech's research and his experience with the indigenous tribe.

"So, let me get this straight," said Jason. "You're telling me that our only ways off this island are scrap metal."

"I'm afraid so," said Torres. "Any attempts to radio off the island have been met with intense electro-magnetic interference."

"It's the island phasing out of our reality," said Mark. "Poseidon Tech may be losing its grip on the island."

"Are you saying we're stuck here?" asked Peter.

"Not yet, but soon," said Mark.

"Oh, great," said Mary. "We're trapped on the island that time forgot."

"Not time," corrected Mark. "Spacetime."

She sucked her teeth. "Great. That makes me feel so much better."

Allison collapsed to the ground like a lump of jelly. "I'm never going to see my family again. My husband. My baby."

"There is a way off the island," said Mark. "The indigenous tribe that took me in described a series of tunnels under the temple where Jason found Bill and the ELT. The correct tunnel should lead to an opening in the side of a sheer cliff, hopefully close to sea level."

Everyone perked up.

"Really?" said Tracey. "That's great!"

"There's only one catch," said Mark.

"It's where your friend and his army of cannibals are hiding," said Torres, finishing his thought.

Mark nodded.

"We had a run-in with these things," said Jason. "They're nasty."

"That doesn't sound very safe," said Torres. "We'll find another way."

The group discussion degenerated into argument.

"Cannibals," said Allison. "I can't deal with cannibals."

Bill held up his index finger. "Zombies, technically." He withered at Jason's reproachful look.

"Oh, come on," said Peter. "If they don't get us, the carnivorous dinosaurs will. We have to do something, and those caves sound like our best bet."

"We don't even know where those caves will lead us," said Tracey. "Maybe it'll be nowhere near our ship."

"We might be able to signal them," said Mark. "I assume you still have portable com equipment?"

Torres nodded. "We do. But, as head of security detail, it's my job to keep you all safe."

"Hey, we're all in the same boat here," said Mary. "Who died and put you in charge?"

"Susan did," said Torres.

"Actually, we have a project manager," said Mary. Everyone looked at her, perplexed. She made a sweeping gesture to Mark. "We have the original project manager here. With Susan gone, he's in charge."

Mark cleared his throat. "Well, technically, even if she were still here with us, I would assume command of the operation. Her status was predicated on my being missing."

"I think that our priority is to get off the island and to safety," insisted Torres.

"I agree," said Mark. "I know how we can do it."

"I don't want to run into this Mike Deluca character and his army of possibly undead cannibals in a subterranean environment," said Torres. "*His* subterranean environment."

"This guy just wants to save his indigenous friends," said Jason, gesturing towards Mark. "I personally think it's dangerous and a waste of our time and resources."

"How else are we going to get off the island?" asked Peter. "We can't get any signal with the outside world."

"Outside dimension," corrected Mark.

Peter shot him a sharp glance. "You're not helping matters."

"Peter's right," said Tracey. "We have the ELT, which is what we came for. Let's get off this island before it phases out of our reality."

"How long would that take?" asked Allison, concerned. "We have time before that happens, right?"

All eyes were on Mark Hong. He shrugged. "Without communicating with the ship or HQ, there's no way of knowing. But, time is of the essence."

"Don't you mean spacetime?" quipped Jason.

Mary stepped in front of Mark. "So, maybe we should stop bickering and get moving on the only feasible plan we have."

There were nods of agreement almost all around.

"Well, if we're going to do it, let's do it," said Jason.

"The tribe will help us," said Mark. "They're tired of being attacked by Mike Deluca and his followers. They'll help us get to that cave down the side of the cliff."

"We just have to help them neutralize Mike Deluca and his army of cannibals," said Torres. "Okay, we're breaking base camp. Take only portable communications equipment and rations. My men will round up all the weapons we have left."

Everyone disbanded, scurrying like worker ants, spreading out to gather all the necessary equipment that could be carried.

Torres walked up to Mark, placing a hand on his shoulder. "I want to know everything there is about this Mike Deluca."

* * *

Approximately Three Weeks Ago in the Outside Reality
(A Longer, Undetermined Amount of Time Ago in Island Time)

Mark was helping the native tribe clean up after dinner, a fire-roasted wild beast garnished with local edible plants that resembled beets and potatoes. The men of the tribe sat back, bellies full, amused as he helped the women of the tribe clear the area.

Uneaten remnants of meat were fed to domesticated dogs, while the uneaten vegetables and tubers were thrown into a receptacle away from camp that looked to cultivate compost.

The women of the tribe had given up attempting to dissuade him from helping, as they had when he first joined their tribe as a guest. One tribal woman, who described herself as what sounded like Non Bak, took a shine to him, staying close as they cleaned up. She shot him stealthy glances, blushing and averting her gaze when she was caught in the act.

Lately, Mike Deluca had abided their pleas and took his place with the other men of the tribe, entertaining them with his lack of understanding of their language and customs. They appeared amused by his ignorance, but enjoyed his company. Yet, on this day, as Mark searched the area, Mike was nowhere to be found.

He excused himself from the women and walked around the village, searching inside and between the crude thatch huts. He called out for Mike a few times and questioned the natives as to his whereabouts, but without success.

Mike had been disappearing after dinner as of late. Rumor around the village was that he had been entering the temple outside of the village. The temple was a place of mystery, both revered and feared by the natives. To add to the element of danger, it was located off the plateau where the native village sat, which means it was out of the realm of relative safety, right in the middle of dinosaur territory.

As the evening passed, Mark was strolling the outskirts of the plateau, when he heard cries coming from the path leading down to the jungle. It sounded like a woman in distress.

Mark ran toward the cries, and he found Mike pressing Non Bak up against the rock wall, pawing at her like a depraved animal. Mark didn't know what to say, other than, "Hey! What's going on here?"

Mike, looking gaunt in the pale moonlight, turned his head slowly, still pressing Non Bak up against the rock with his hips. "Mark, this doesn't concern you. Turn around, and walk away." He turned back to Non Bak, kissing her neck as she tried, in vain, to wriggle away from him. She looked at Mark pleadingly, her eyes desperate.

Mark rooted his feet to the ground. "No, Mike. Leave her alone."

This time Mike released Non Bak and turned to face Mark. Non Bak circumvented Mike and ran to Mark, throwing her arms around him, sobbing.

A wicked grin crept across Mike's face, the shadows under his racoon eyes pronounced...or was it a trick of the moonlight? "So, there it is. She's sweet on you, it would seem."

Mark broke Non Bak's embrace, guiding her behind him. "She's terrified, Mike. You scared her half to death."

Mike laughed. It was a hollow, bitter sound. "I'm going to have to tell your wife about your little girlfriend, here." There was a strange glint in his eyes, like a cat's eyes reflecting the light.

"Where are your glasses, Mike?"

"Funny thing about this island...I don't need them anymore. In fact, all-in-all, I just feel capital."

"You think it's the island?"

Mike cocked his head to the side. "You mean you don't feel it? I feel it all over my body. I feel younger, stronger. It's as if the island speaks to me."

Mark frowned. "What've you been doing in that temple night after night?"

Mike cackled, a dry rattle and wheeze of his lungs. Although he claimed to feel power, he didn't sound very healthy. "Do you really want to know? I'll show you. We can go there right now."

There were the distant roars of tyrannosaurs in the jungle.

"Mike, I don't think that's such a good idea."

Mike's feral eyes reflected the moonlight. "Scared, Mark? Nothing ventured, nothing gained."

"If I go with you, will you leave her alone?"

Mike looked amused by the offer. "Always negotiating. Sure, Mark. I'll let her go. Whatever you say, buddy."

Non Bak, as if comprehending the discussion and its implications, clutched Mark's arm, pleading with him, shaking her head. Mark pried her off, reassuring her, gesturing for her to return to the village. She protested but ultimately ran off, crying.

"Enough screwing around," declared Mike, watching the whole scene with great enthusiasm. "Come with me. I have such sights to show you."

Mark knew he had to follow him. There was something qualitatively different about Mike. Once a pudgy computer nerd, he now looked lean and strong. And mean. He looked mean. But it wasn't just the threat of physical violence that spurred Mark on. He had to admit, he was curious. The scientist in him was curious to see what Mike was doing in the temple.

Mike turned and shambled down the narrow path, and Mark followed him. They descended the winding path together in silence, and as they drew closer to the jungle, Mark cringed at the thunderous footsteps that shook the ground.

As if reading his mind, Mike said without turning around, "Don't worry. As long as you're with me, you'll be fine."

"There are tyrannosaurs down here, Mike."

"I said, don't worry."

"You don't look well, Mike. In fact, you look horrible."

There was a chortle in the dark. "I've never felt better. You'll see."

"What've you been up to? What's in the temple?"

"I'll show you."

They made it to the jungle at the bottom of the path, and Mike meandered through the vegetation in the moonlight without the aid of torchlight. The native people rarely ventured out after dark, so they were alone, except for the ambling predators that haunted the jungle and the various ambient nocturnal fauna.

After a short while, they arrived at the temple. The opening was a dark, yawning entryway.

"We're here," declared Mike.

Mark stopped, looking around, but Mike continued inside, disappearing into the pitch-black void.

"Mike?"

A pair of glowing eyes flashed in the black. "Aren't you coming, Mark?"

Mark stood there, the small hairs standing up on the back of his neck. Suddenly, other pairs of eyes emerged in the dark. They didn't look human. They glinted red.

A hideous laughter rang out from the temple mouth, and Mark turned and ran. He ran as fast as his weary legs would carry him, but that laughter pursued him in the night, clawing at his back, ringing in his ears, as he dashed back to the village on the plateau.

* * *

Torres and the rest of the party burned most of the morning packing supplies for the trip to the indigenous village. After a rationed lunch, they set out into the jungle.

"So, you never saw what was in the temple?" asked Torres, wiping sweat from his brow. He led the trek to the native village with Mark Hong. They had already been hiking for a few hours.

"No," said Mark. "I was terrified."

"Those eyes, what did they belong to?" asked Tracey.

"I didn't want to find out," said Mark. "Could you blame me?"

"So, we're going into a subterranean lair, and we have no idea what we're up against," said Peter.

"Probably just men," said Jason. "Men who live underground and look feral."

"No," said Mark shaking his head. "There was something else."

Jason chuckled. "I think your imagination ran away with you. There's no such thing as monsters in the dark."

"Before this trip, you would've said the same about dinosaurs," said Bill, still clutching the ELT device. "As I would have."

Jason shook his head. "These are animals. Like Dr. Albanese said, they're technically not dinosaurs. What Mark is talking about is monsters…the supernatural."

"We're in another freaking dimension," said Mary. "That's not supernatural enough for you?"

"Technically, it's not supernatural," said Peter. "It still falls within the realm of science."

Mary shot him a look. "You're cute, but shut up right now." She winked at him.

Peter blushed and looked down at the ground.

A sharp look crossed Tracey's face, but quickly evaporated. Peter didn't notice, but Jason did. He chuckled, but the others thought it was over the discussion of supernatural vs preternatural.

"We're here," said Mark. He pointed up.

Everyone followed his finger, and they saw a tall, sheer rock cliff extending about fifty feet up.

"What's this?" asked Peter.

"The village is up on the plateau."

"Great. How do we get up there?" asked Allison.

Torres stepped in front, surveying the plateau. "There's a path, right?"

Mark nodded. "It's very narrow. Only about ten feet wide in some parts and as narrow as three in others."

"Smart," said Peter. "Too small for dinosaurs."

"Even the raptors?" asked Bill. "They're a bit smaller."

"There haven't been any in the village," said Mark. "Okay, follow me, single file. Watch your step."

PART III
SYNERGY

CHAPTER 11

When they reached the top, the ground opened up. In the distance sat small thatch huts and teepee like structures. Smoke rose into the air from small fire pits, and indigenous people clad in scant clothing strolled about.

"No guard detail," said Torres. "No wonder they're attacked by Mike and his ghouls."

"They don't come up the path," said Mark.

"How do they get up here?"

"They just appear. No one really knows how, and it's usually dark."

Jason laughed. "How's that possible? Is this guy a magician?"

Mark didn't answer him. Instead, he led them straight into the village. Women tanned animal hides and cooked over fires in the afternoon sun. Off to the left, a man covered in white powder sat, legs crossed, chipping away at a mostly hollowed out round stone.

"What's he doing?" asked Bill.

"He's making a bowl," said Mark.

"Native Americans did it, back in the day," said Mary. "They use certain stones to chip away flakes of stone. It's an art. Only a handful of artisans know how to do it now."

Peter regarded her with a look, impressed. She shrugged, blushing a bit.

Animals that looked like wild dogs ran around the camp. Mary called one over, making kissing sounds. When it came, upon closer inspection she saw it wasn't actually a dog, but some unknown kind of animal. Mary squatted down on her haunches.

"Careful," warned Allison, looking concerned.

"They're harmless," said Mark.

The creature approached Mary slowly, head hanging down. She reached out and pet its head, and it yelped and ran off.

"Amazing," gasped Bill.

"Would you look at that," said Allison, her voice trailing off at the end. She wandered off to where a few native women were tending to some kind of crop planted in rows.

Peter and Tracey startled when whooping and shouting erupted from behind them. Coming up the narrow path were a group of native men, their bodies and faces smeared with paint, carrying the corpses of what looked to be boar-like creatures and baskets. The entire village animated at their arrival. Women ran to greet husbands and sons, and children scurried to greet fathers, uncles, and older brothers. The youngsters poked at the slayed beasts, giggling and laughing as the hunters casually swatted them away. The women temporarily abandoned their various tasks to greet the men. Several produced hewn bowls, while others began to prepare a fire under a crude spit fashioned from tree branches.

Torres appeared unafraid, but his hand was on his rifle. Bill cowered behind him. Neither man forgot that this very tribe tried to sacrifice Bill to the horrors that now dwelled inside the temple. Mark smiled at their reaction, amused. "You have nothing to fear. The hunters have returned. It looks like we'll be eating well tonight."

A man emerged out front, his face and body paint the color indigo, whereas the others bore white. He was the tallest and well-muscled, but not the youngest. In fact, he appeared to be a well-preserved elder. The imposing man eyed the new guests, but when he saw Mark, he threw his arms out and rattled something off in his tongue.

"That's the chief," said Mark.

The man wrapped Mark in a hearty embrace, and the two men conversed a bit. Mark's enunciation was slow and labored compared to the chief's, but the chief appeared to comprehend him.

At last, Mark turned to Torres and the others. "I explained who you all were. He's pleased to have you as guests in his village, and he would be honored if you would join him for dinner with the tribe tonight. The hunters have caught more than enough game for everyone."

The chief watched their faces, expectantly. He seemed particularly interested in Tracey, which didn't exactly thrill Peter.

Torres managed a smile. "Tell him we'd be honored."

Mark said something to the chief, who then smiled and made sweeping motions with his arms. The village people cheered in response and scattered, making preparations.

Torres leaned in to Mark. "Tonight, at dinner, would be the perfect opportunity to discuss the subterranean cave system and how the hell we can get off this island."

Mark nodded. "Exactly. Leave it to me. I'll do all the talking."

Jason smirked. "Do we really have a choice?"

Mark shook his head. "Don't worry. I'm sure they'll agree to help, knowing that you intend to help them."

"Let's hope so," said Torres, shouldering his rifle. "We don't have much time."

As the village prepared for the feast, the members of the salvage team became absorbed in the various aspects of village life. Jason attempted to converse about the hunt with the hunters. They showed him their spears and appeared to be describing the hunt, pantomiming the movements of the animals and themselves, acting it all out.

Allison continued her study of the plants, pulling off leaves and clipping specimens when no one was looking, shoving them in specimen bags and slipping them into her pack. Tracey examined the tanned skins sitting in the waning sun and admired the elaborate basket weaving. Torres followed Mark around, asking questions.

Bill became fascinated with a group of toddlers waddling around, getting into everything. Their parents appeared to pay them no mind, but he was a parent and knew better. Unlike the modern parents of his native dimension, these parents didn't hover. Rather, they maintained a presence on the periphery, ready if needed but reticent to intercede. Bill watched in awe as the toddlers stumbled about like drunks, picking up sticks, sharing interesting stones, and chasing each other around the camp. When one would fall, no one rushed to pick the child up or offer comfort.

Bill thought of his wife and son back in Australia and wondered if he'd ever see them again. He looked over at the orange ELT device. The chief was examining it in great interest as Mark prattled on. Torres cast a watchful eye, never letting it out of his sight. It was their ticket off the island, and a promise of big bucks to the rest of the party. Everyone, except Bill. However, Bill didn't care.

He missed his family.

*

Peter stood by the cliff's edge, looking over the jungle.

"A penny for your thoughts," came a voice from behind him. Mary strolled up and stood beside him.

He flashed her a smile and continued to drink in the vista. "Isn't it amazing, how this was all sitting here, undetected? It's a part of an undiscovered world. Another dimension of existence."

Mary studied his face and pulled up the corner of her mouth. "You're disappointed."

Peter sighed. When he turned his head, their eyes met. "Is it that obvious?"

"You're disappointed that these aren't real dinosaurs."

"At first I thought a lot of questions were going to be answered," he said. "Now a whole other set of questions have arisen."

Mary elbowed his arm, her smile flirtatious. "Hey, you discovered another dimension's dinosaurs. I guess that makes you some kind of inter-dimensional paleontologist. You just created a new field."

Peter chuckled. "That's funny. Tracey would find that funny, too."

Mary's playful demeanor hardened a bit. "Why do you chase her around?"

Peter cleared his throat, as he was unprepared for such a remark. The jungle cooled a bit as twilight settled in, but his face became hot and he began to sweat anew. "Uh, um...what do you mean?"

"She's not worth it, you know."

"Now, that's not very fair."

"Isn't it? Look at you. You're a smart guy, kind of cute...you're even a hero. You saved Allison's life."

Peter stuttered and stammered, unsure of how to respond.

"What happened between you and Tracey, anyway?"

"Nothing," said Peter. "Absolutely nothing."

"You can cut the tension between the two of you with a knife."

"She's a bit upset with me."

"Why? What did you do?"

"A grad student kissed me once, at a university event no less. She walked in on it, and she's been weird ever since."

"She's not into you."

Mary's words were like a dagger in his heart. "Pardon? How do you know that?"

"How long have you been trying to win her over?"

"I haven't been..."

"In the jungles of New Guinea, there is a species of bird called the Black Sickle Bill. The male labors to create a perfectly clean area on the ground, free of any slight bit of debris. Then, after drawing the attention of a prospective female, it executes an elaborate dance, contorting itself into a variety of shapes using its wings, literally bending over backwards to impress her. Here's the rub...one misstep, one mistake, no matter how small, and the female rejects him."

Peter looked flummoxed. "So, you're saying I'm the male Black Sickle Bill?"

"Come on, Peter. How long has it been?"

"A while. It's like every time I get close, she pulls away."

Mary arched an eyebrow and leaned in to Peter, her expression conspiratorial. “Do you know how I know she’s not into you?”

“How?” His question was more of a challenge than a query.

“When she saw that grad student kiss you, it should’ve egged her on. Instead, it pushed her away even more.”

Peter crinkled his nose. “Well, if she didn’t care, why is she so upset?”

Mary shook her head. “Oh, I didn’t say she didn’t care.”

Peter scratched his head. “I don’t follow.”

“I know girls like her,” said Mary. “Hell, I *am* girls like her. It’s a game. She doesn’t want you, but she doesn’t necessarily want anyone else to have you either.”

“What? That’s…”

“Immature,” she said, completing his thought. “Now that I’ve heard myself say it, it does sound pretty sophomoric.”

“But, why? Why would she do that?”

“She’s a predator. She stalks her prey, marking it. It’s territorial behavior. You must know this after all of your study of theropod behavior.”

Peter blinked rapidly. “I’m her prey? I don’t want to be her prey.”

“Good, then don’t be.”

“How?”

“Stop chasing her and mark your own territory.”

“You want me to become a predator?”

Mary laughed.

Peter appeared deflated. “Oh, sure. Laugh at me now.”

“You’re…funny…in a nerdy kind of way.”

Peter turned away from Mary, his face flushed. “Oh, great. This is just great.”

Mary placed a hand on his shoulder and turned him back around to face her. “I think it’s adorable.”

Peter melted a bit. “Y-y-you…you do?”

Mary gazed into his eyes. He felt it penetrate his soul. “All my life I avoided guys like you. You were no challenge. No fun. But, truthfully, I’m bored of the mimbo’s. There’s nothing there. There’s no sport.”

Peter blushed. “Great, so now I can be your prey.”

Mary leaned in. “I don’t know many guys who would’ve risked their own neck against a freaking T. rex to save Allison.”

Their faces were only a few scant inches apart. Mary gazed at Peter with that ‘kiss me’ look that other guys knew so well. However, she bridged the gap and kissed him on the mouth. He tasted her and gave into it. He no longer felt awkward or nervous. Some primal instinct took over and he stepped forward, pressing his body against hers.

*

When the spoils of the hunt were properly roasted and the fruits and vegetables prepared, the chief was the first to sit on the ground under the stars in an area designated for meals. The others sat around him in a circle, and Mark went to collect the rest of his group.

The chief waited patiently until each member of the outsiders took their place in the circle, sitting on the ground, legs crossed like kindergartners. On either side of Mark sat Torres and Peter. Jason sat beside Mary, who sat beside Allison and Bill.

The chief looked around the large circle and made some kind of announcement. A few of the women passed around baskets filled with pieces of meat, fruits, and vegetables. A child, approximately ten or eleven years of age, walked around with a bladder filled with some kind of liquid and a crude ladle. He handed each person the ladle, and they took a drink.

The chief was the first to drink. When he finished his ladle-full, he wiped his mouth with the back of his hand and began to speak. All within the circle were quiet, except for Mark, who translated to Torres and Peter.

"He's thanking you all, as his honored guests, for attending this feast...he apologizes to Bill for offering him up as a sacrifice..."

Bill stirred uneasily as the chief made eye contact while speaking.

"Now he's talking about the tribe," continued Mark. "How they've existed in this jungle for generations, amongst the great lizards and the wild beasts...how they've made a home for themselves on this plateau, under the protection of the Light."

Torres frowned. "The Light?"

"It's their deity."

"Many ancient cultures worshipped the sun," whispered Peter.

The chief halted, asking Mark a question. Mark answered him and then said to Peter, "He wanted to know what you said, so I told him. He said that the Light doesn't refer to the sun. He said the Light exists in the ground, under the temple...."

The chief continued, as did Mark with his translation. "He said the Light was the source of all that was good...their bountiful hunts, their crops, their protection from the great lizards...but the Light has been corrupted by one of the Outsiders...the Strange Ones."

"Mike Deluca," said Peter.

Mark nodded.

"Tell him we wish his people no harm," said Torres. "We only want to get off the island, but we need his help. In return, we will help him with Mike Deluca…uh, the Death Lord."

Mark nodded and relayed the message. The chief listened intently, as a parent listens to a child clumsily speak, eager to glean the meaning of it. The chief shook his head and sat up straight. He spoke again.

"He said that the temple and the tunnels beneath it are now a dark and forbidden place, too dangerous to traverse."

Peter leaned in towards Mark. "Tell him that we, too, have a tribe that we miss terribly. We each have families…wives, children."

Bill and Allison both nodded.

"I have a baby," said Allison. "Tell him my baby needs me."

Mark nodded, organizing what he was going to say in his head, and he explained all of this to the chief. The chief listened intently to the explanation. When Mark was finished, he shook his head again and said a few words.

"What did he say?" asked Torres.

"Too dangerous," said Mark. "He wouldn't risk any of his people."

Torres unshouldered his rifle and laid it out in front of him. "Tell him we have weapons. Powerful weapons, like he's never seen."

The chief eyed the rifle with great curiosity and a hint of suspicion.

Mark opened his mouth to speak, but his words were drowned out in the cacophony of hoots and yells. Everyone turned around, and the chief blew a horn fashioned from what looked to be a triceratops horn, or something of the sort.

Confused, the outsiders watched the village erupt into violence as an undetermined number of people in white body paint raided the village. Eyes flashing red, they scrambled about, spearing villagers, setting fires to their thatch huts, and grabbing women and children.

Torres stood up, snatching his rifle. "What's going on?"

"It's Mike Deluca," said Mark, his eyes narrow, scanning the melee.

"Where'd he come from?" asked Jason, pulling his handgun.

Torres called to his men, one of whom had the ELT device beside him. "Guard the device!"

"What are we going to do?" Bill asked of Mark.

Mark clenched his jaw. "Fight for our lives."

Peter watched as the chief picked up a spear and joined the fray, leading his people in the defense of their plateau village.

The raiders reached where the outsiders congregated.

"Get behind me," ordered Torres, and he and his handful of men opened fire on the marauders. At first, it appeared as if they would hold the bandits back. However, they were quickly overwhelmed by sheer numbers.

"Where are they coming from?" cried out Torres, looking desperate.

Peter heard a woman's scream. He turned and saw Allison being grappled and dragged by two of the stark-white invaders, their expressions wild. "It's Allison!"

Bill was there first, exploding on the would-be captors with maximum violence. He threw wild punches at the attackers as Allison tried to wriggle free. Torres ran towards them, firing his rifle at any marauder in his way.

Mary and Tracey were fighting off a few cannibals, grabbing at their clothes with wild hands. Peter looked around, standing alone and at the moment untouched, searching for anyone to help. *Where did Jason go?*

He ran over to Tracey and Mary, throwing himself at one of their attackers. They collided, and both of them fell to the ground and rolled around in the dirt. The attacker's feral, red eyes and savage grunts caused Peter to cry out in fright as he grappled with him.

He caught a glimpse of one of the cannibals spearing Bill Gibson in his rib cage. Bill yelped, clutching the spear sticking out of his torso. A few seconds later, Torres was there. He shot the one who speared Bill at close range, hitting him in the temple, and the cannibal dropped like a rock.

However, Peter had his own hands full and was unable to see any more. The cannibal snapped his jaws at Peter's face, his breath hot and putrid. He laughed, drooling on Peter's face. Peter struggled to keep him away, pushing with both hands and kicking wildly with both feet.

*

Jason meandered through the crowd, conserving his ammo, only firing when one of the invaders got close. He dodged and weaved his way through, looking for their leader. His eyes scanned the tumult for anyone who would stand out.

Then, he saw him. In the middle of the fray, watching and completely ignored by everyone around him, stood a lithe man in a torn blue shirt and filthy, ragged khakis—Mike Deluca.

Jason flanked him, careful to stay out of his line of sight. The wraith-like man looked ahead, unaware of Jason's approach. He was unarmed. Jason crouched down, creeping through the commotion. A cannibal collided with him, grappling him. Jason had no choice but to fight.

He struggled, maintaining his balance, trying to free his gun hand, which the assailant had clutched in a vicelike grip by Jason's wrist. Jason turned his hips, careful of his footing, and threw the cannibal off-balance. The crazed attacker released his grip on Jason's wrist as he stumbled. Jason brought his gun around, pointed it at the man's temple, and pulled the trigger.

When Jason looked up, Mike Deluca was staring him down. His eyes burned with the hot glow of abject hatred. Jason, now only twenty or so feet away, aimed and pulled the trigger, but nothing happened. *Damn. Rookie mistake.* He ejected his clip and quickly slapped a fresh one into the handle of the gun, taking his eyes off Mike Deluca for only a moment. However, when he looked up, Mike Deluca was gone.

Mike slammed into him from the side, knocking the handgun out of Jason's hand with the sudden impact. Jason caught a glimpse of a light emanating from under Mike's shirt. He reached for his hunting knife and unsheathed it in one deft move. He brought the knife around, slashing Mike Deluca across the chest.

Mike backed away, laughing. He touched the gash across his chest, bringing away bloody fingertips. He licked them, streaking blood across his mouth, his eyes wild with savage fury.

Jason lunged at him with his knife, but Mike was suddenly behind him. Before Jason could process what had just happened, he felt a blunt strike to his back, and he fell forward to the ground. The wind knocked out of him, he struggled to breathe as he rolled onto his back.

Mike Deluca stood there, watching him. Then, just like that, he was gone. He had disappeared into the frenzy, like some kind of magician. Jason propped himself up on one elbow, his lungs burning.

*

Mark, turning his spear horizontally, shoved a cannibal off his feet. Mark speared another that was lunging at him, catching him in the throat. The man dropped to the ground, holding the spear jutting out of his neck. Mark turned it and pulled out, freeing the spear tip.

"Ah, a savage amongst savages," called a raspy voice from behind him.

He turned to find Mike Deluca, standing there, clapping his hands in mock applause.

"Why?" cried Mark. "Why do you butcher these people?"

Mike Deluca laughed. He looked different than Mark remembered, even from the last such raid on the village. He no longer wore glasses. He appeared even leaner, anorexic even, but he still appeared powerful.

"Why don't you join me, Mark? It would be so much better if you joined me."

"Those caves, underground…they've done something to you. I can help you, Mike. Let me help you."

Mike looked around the battle and flashed a wry grin. "Does it look like I need any help?"

"You're not well. This isn't you."

Mike Deluca's grin faded. "And this isn't our home. This island isn't supposed to be. These people, these creatures aren't supposed to be."

"It's what we've worked countless hours for," said Mark. "It's a new world to be discovered and studied."

"It's a fever dream," said Mike. "A nightmare, and I'm the Boogieman."

Mark's eyes narrowed. "Then you're no longer Mike Deluca." He raised his spear, pointing it at Mike.

Mike flashed a wicked smile and placed his arms out, palms up, like a demented Jesus, as if welcoming the strike. "Go on, Mark. Put me down. Put me out of my misery." His eyes narrowed, and he snarled like a wild dog. "Do it, or I'll rip your guts out!"

Mark lunged, but there was a loud pop, and Mike was gone. Vanished. Behind him, Jason stood, eyes bulging. The barrel of his handgun smoked. "No! I didn't…I'm sorry. I'm so sorry."

Mark looked down at his chest as blood poured out of a hole over his heart. He dropped to his knees, his head swam, and he felt his life slip away from him.

*

Peter had managed to roll on top of his attacker. Snatching a rock from the ground, he pounded the cannibal's skull with it repeatedly, caving in his face until he was no longer moving. He felt hands closing around his arm, and he turned, raising the rock, but it was Tracey. He dropped the rock, and she pulled him to standing. She sported a shiner under her right eye and a bloody lip.

"Where's Mary?"

Tracey snatched a spear off the ground. "She ran to help Allison."

"I saw Bill get speared," panted Peter. "I think he's hurt."

The gunshots and shouting began to die down, and the battle was over. Peter scanned the village, looking for his party. There were wounded everywhere. As he looked more closely, he saw dead bodies. More than a few. Bill Gibson was one of them.

He heard Torres shouting directions to his team. Women cradled their injured men, while others wailed for children carried away by the cannibals. The village chief, bloodied but alive, shouted instructions of his own.

Peter found Mary, crouched next to a woman's body. Blood obscured its face, but Peter knew it was one of them. His mind suddenly paralyzed with panic, as he avoided acknowledging who it was.

Mary looked up. "It's Allison. She's gone."

A wave of relief washed over him and was quickly replaced with guilt. He felt like a monster. He vacillated between shame and relief, just standing there, running his dirty hands through his sweaty hair.

Torres passed by him. "Are you all right?"

Peter nodded, beyond all capacity for words. His last coherent thought was that he was going into shock. He staggered, and someone caught him as his lost his footing. Then, the world went black.

CHAPTER 12

Peter opened his eyes. When his vision cleared, he noticed two eyes looking down at him.

"You're awake," said Mary. Tracey stood next to her. Her eyes were glassy, and there were wet streaks down her cheeks.

Peter struggled to sit up. "What happened?" The moon bathed the village in monochromatic light.

Torres walked over to him and squatted down. "You fainted."

Peter rubbed his eyes. "No, I know that. I mean what happened here?"

Torres sighed. "Mike Deluca happened. He killed a bunch of the natives and carried off others. Bill, Allison, and Mark are all dead. Mike Deluca took the ELT device."

"Damn," was all Peter could manage.

Tracey helped Peter to his feet. "The good news is the chief is sending us a guide and a few of the hunters to go down into the cave system. Or at least, that's what we think he said. Tough to know without Mark to translate."

"He was impressed by our weapons," said Torres. "You could tell he thought it was some kind of magic. At least, that's the impression I got."

"He's also desperate," said Jason. "He cannot afford to lose many more of his tribe."

Peter frowned, swatting a mosquito biting his neck. "What's the bad news?"

"We lost most of my men and a couple of the rifles are missing," said Torres.

"Great. Just great. Who's left?"

"You're looking at us," said Mary.

Peter looked over at Jason, who was standing apart from the group, sharpening his knife and avoiding eye contact. "What's with him?"

"He went toe to toe with Mike Deluca," said Torres. "He got his ass kicked. On top of that, he apparently shot and killed Mark by accident."

Peter gasped. "What?"

Torres looked over at Jason and frowned. "He thought he was getting the drop on Deluca. When he fired, Deluca had vanished and Mark was standing there. At least that's how he tells it."

Peter studied Jason. The man looked like he was in pain, and not the physical kind. "I believe him, if that's what he said."

"They had children," muttered Tracey. "Allison and Bill, I mean. They had families."

Torres drew in a breath, held it a heartbeat, and slowly exhaled. "Yeah, well, none of that matters now. We need to get the ELT and get off this island."

Peter put his hands on his hips. "You've got to be kidding."

Torres shot him a sharp look. "Do I sound like I'm kidding? Look, we go down into those caves, kill this Mike Deluca, get back the ELT, get off this island, and get paid."

"But what about Allison and Bill? What about Mark?" asked Peter.

"They're gone," said Torres. "Sitting around here and moping is only going to get us killed. We need to stay on-mission. Comprende?"

Peter shook his head. "No. No comprende."

Torres, obviously frustrated, walked off to check over whatever equipment and supplies were left.

"He's right, you know," said Mary.

"Baloney," snapped Tracey. "All he cares about is collecting his reward. People died. Women, children…our colleagues."

Mary squared off with Tracey. "Do you want to die, too? Huh? Do you? Because if you shut down now, that's exactly what's going to happen."

Tracey leveled her gaze at Mary. "I'm not quitting. I'm just showing respect for the dead, our colleagues on this crap salvage operation."

Peter turned to walk away from them, towards Jason.

Both women turned their heads. "Where are you going?" they both asked, almost in unison.

Peter threw his hands up. "I'm going to talk to Jason." When he reached Jason, the hunter was standing, sharpening his knife on a whetstone. Peter let out a heavy sigh. "Are you all right?"

"Am I all right? I got the drop on him…I had him in my sights…one minute he was there, the next he wasn't."

"It's not your fault, you know," said Peter.

"You should've seen the way he moved," continued Jason, ignoring Peter's consolation. "I've never seen any man move like that. He had this thing in his shirt…it glowed."

"What glowed?"

"How the hell do I know? I didn't get a good look at it."

"The Light," Peter muttered to himself.

"What's that you said?"

"The Light. Maybe what you saw was what the chief referred to as 'the Light.' You know, their deity."

"That's hocus pocus, mate. The primitive beliefs of a primitive man."

"Maybe not," said Peter. "Maybe whatever you saw was giving Mike Deluca his…powers."

"Now he's armed with some of our weapons."

"It's not your fault," insisted Peter. "Mark's death, I mean."

"How do you know?" snapped Jason. "You weren't there."

"I know you wouldn't have shot Mark on purpose."

Jason turned and met Peter's eyes. "Do you? Man, you don't know a thing about me. You have no idea what I'm capable of."

Peter smiled. It was patient and warm. "If you were capable of that, you wouldn't be so upset right now."

Jason turned away from him. "Who says I'm upset?"

Peter didn't dignify the question with an answer. There was no point. He turned to walk away.

"Thanks, mate," said Jason. "You're the only one who came over to check on me."

Peter stopped and smiled to himself. "Don't mention it. We're all in this together."

"She likes you, you know."

"I know," said Peter, turning to look at Jason.

Jason chuckled, obviously amused by the confidence of Peter's response. "Wow, look at you. Face off with one T. rex and suddenly you're James friggin' Bond."

"Mary kissed me before. She pretty much told me she was interested."

This made Jason laugh. "I'm not talking about Mary, you fool."

Peter squinted his eyes. "Who *are* you talking about?"

"Tracey. I'm talking about Tracey. Holy smokes, with all the bizarre shit going on, the most bizarre of all is that these two are both going for you…no offense."

Peter placed his hands up, palms out. "None taken. Mary told me Tracey wasn't interested."

"Bollocks."

"What?"

"Baloney, mate."

"What? She should know."

"Damned right she should know," agreed Jason. "That's why she's telling you the opposite." When he saw Peter wasn't following, he took his hat off his head and swatted his pants with it. "Man, for a college boy you ain't too bright. Tracey's her competition."

Peter stood there, continuing to look perplexed. Jason placed his hat back on his head, slapped Peter on the shoulder, and walked back towards the group, laughing to himself.

* * *

Some Undetermined Time Ago
Pre-Island

"Hello, Mike here…No, I have to step out for a moment…no, I brought my tablet…I don't know…It could be a half an hour, maybe more…Look, I'm doing the best I can here…Have I ever let you down before?...Yes, I'm aware of the deadline…Yes, I know…It'll get done…Okay…Okay…Bye." Mike Deluca ended the call as he pulled his silver luxury sedan in front of his mother's house.

He got out, strolled up her front path, and rang the doorbell. A woman answered the door. "Hello, Mr. Michael."

Mike stepped past her and into the house. "I hope this is a dire emergency, Ana."

"It is, Mr. Michael. The plumber is hiding upstairs, in the bathroom."

Mike released a heavy sigh.

"Come out, you damned thief!" he heard from upstairs, along with the pounding of fists on the wooden door. "You rat bastard! I know what you're up to!"

Mike exchanged looks with Ana. She shrugged, and he climbed the stairs. Ana followed behind him. When he reached the upstairs hallway, he found his mother standing outside the bathroom door in her robe, looking disheveled. Her blond/greyish hair was wild, but not as wild as her eyes.

"Ma! What's going on?"

She turned on him. "That son-of-a-bitch tried to rob me, Mike. I caught him red-handed."

"Mr. Deluca?" came a tentative voice from inside the bathroom.

"Shut up, you thief!" She began to pound on the door again.

Mike reached up, gently took her balled fists into his hands, and he gently guided them down to her sides. "Ma, that's the plumber. I called him. Remember?"

Her face was contorted with rage and confusion. "That's what he told you, but I know what's really going on here. He fooled you, Mike. He fooled us all."

Mike knew that he couldn't argue with her, not when she was like this. He spoke in a soft, measured way. "I'll take care of it. Why don't you go downstairs, and Ana can make you some tea?"

He looked over at Ana, who was half hiding behind him. She nodded, looking dubious. "Yes, Mrs. Deluca. I'll make you some hot tea. You can pick the flavor."

Mrs. Deluca hesitated, mulling over her alternatives.

"Ma, remember that big box of teas I got you?"

The confusion and rage faded for a moment, and a smile crept onto her face. "Yes. I do. I adore them. I try a different one each time."

Mike smiled. "Why don't you go pick one out for me as well? I'll join you in just a moment."

Mrs. Deluca pulled down the corners of her mouth. "You'll make sure he gives everything back?"

"I will, Ma. I'm sure he's learned his lesson. Everyone deserves a second chance."

"Even him?"

"Even him."

"Yes, I'm very sorry, Mrs. Deluca," came the voice from inside the bathroom. "I've learned my lesson. Thank you for setting me straight."

She placed her hands on her hips. "Well, that settles it then." She shoved past Ana and descended the stairs.

Ana looked sheepish. "Thank you, Mr. Michael."

He nodded and watched her go downstairs to tend to his mother. When the coast was clear, he knocked on the door. "It's safe to come out now."

The door opened, and a short, portly, middle-aged man in dirty jeans and a faded tee shirt stood there. He was sweating. "Thank you. I thought she was going to kill me."

"My mother has dementia. It's getting pretty bad now."

The plumber grabbed his bucket filled with his tools. "I fixed the leak. It should be good now."

Mike pulled his wallet out of his back pocket and pulled out five hundred-dollar bills, thrusting them out in front of him.

The plumber eyed the bills. "That's too much."

Mike smiled. “For your troubles.”

The plumber reached out and accepted the money. “Thank you.”

Mike smiled. “Come on. I’ll walk you out.”

As they descended the steps, Mike leading the way, he heard the clinking of mugs from inside the kitchen. His mother was chatting it up with Ana, who always listened patiently, chiming in only occasionally.

Mike opened the front door and saw the plumber out. When he closed the door and turned to the kitchen, Ana was making her way over to him, meeting him in the foyer. “I need to talk to you.”

Mike nodded and led her into the living room, where his mother was still within earshot. She was prattling on about something or other. He wasn’t sure if she thought she was speaking to someone or was just talking to herself.

“Mr. Michael, I don’t know if I can handle her anymore.”

He placed his hands up, palms out. “No one got hurt. The plumber fixed the leak.”

“She’s getting worse,” insisted Ana. “She’s going to hurt herself or me.”

“She’s never done anything to harm you.”

Ana shook her head. “That’s not true, sir. Just the other day, she threw a pan at me. Just missed my head.”

Mike crinkled his nose. “You never mentioned anything…”

“I am mentioning it now. She’s getting worse.”

Mike reached for his wallet. “Look, if it’s a raise you want, that’s no problem.”

She placed a hand on his arm. “No, it’s not the money.”

“Then what is it? This is the job. You knew that when you took the position.”

Ana gazed at him with a sorrowful expression, her eyes welling up. “I do my best, Mr. Michael.”

Mike paused to recollect himself. He closed his eyes, took a deep breath, and opened them again. “I’m sorry, Ana. I didn’t mean to yell at you. I know you’re doing your best.”

His softening of demeanor appeared to embolden her. “Perhaps it’s time to think about a nursing home.”

Those words hung out there in the air. They were an inevitability that he had anticipated for some time now. Mike plopped himself down on the couch like a dead weight. He slouched, looking defeated. “I-I just can’t handle all this on my own. I have a senile mother, a wife who’s battling cancer, and I’m working my ass off to pay for my kids’ college tuition. My boss is demanding. She doesn’t even know the full extent of it. She doesn’t know about Barbara being sick.”

Ana wrung her hands in sympathy. "Why don't you tell her about it? Maybe you can take some time off."

Mike shook his head. "We're on the cusp of something big. A major breakthrough. I can't back out now. It'd be the end of my career."

Ana sat next to him on the couch and placed a hand on his. It felt warm. It reminded him of his mother's touch when he was a child. "When I first came to this country, I was in a lot of trouble. My husband was murdered, and I had my baby daughter." She paused a moment, making sure he was listening. His eyes met hers.

They heard Mrs. Deluca jabber-jawing in the kitchen, paying no mind to the drama unfolding in her living room. "Getting here was hard enough. Once I was here, I had to get a job. To survive. I didn't speak good English, only what I knew from soap shows. When I found a job, I had no one to take care of my daughter for me. I worked in a garment shop, sewing and making dresses. I snuck my daughter into the shop, placing her in a basket and covering her with fabric so the boss wouldn't see. The other workers looked the other way…"

Her voice trailed off as her eyes drifted away from Mike. "Except for one. She told on me, and I was fired. I went from job to job, carrying my daughter with me, hiding her."

"That's terrible," said Mike. "Didn't they understand? What could you do?"

Ana met his eyes and nodded. "Some did understand, but the places I worked in were no place for a baby. When she was old enough for school, it gave me freedom, at least for six hours a day. I tried to find jobs close to her school so I could pick her up on a break."

Mike shook his head in disbelief. "What did you do with her after school?"

"I made a few friends. We would try to have different days off to watch each other's children. Other times…" Her voice trailed off again.

Mike didn't probe. He knew, from her expression, that she had to do things that she now regretted. It was all over her face. "I'm so sorry, Ana. I had no idea."

"Just like your boss has no idea," she said. "But I know why you never told her. I understand."

Just then, the tea kettle whistled in the kitchen. "Tea's on!" announced Mrs. Deluca, her voice cheery.

Ana jumped up from the couch, straightened her outfit, and shuffled into the kitchen. Mike followed her.

When he stepped into the kitchen, his mother was already sitting at the table, picking through the large wooden crate of teas he bought her for her birthday. It had a glass door on top. Ana grabbed the kettle off the stove.

Mrs. Deluca was fingering through the envelopes of tea. "What kind of tea do you want?"

Weary, Mike sat down at the kitchen table, his limbs feeling like lead. "Orange spice, if you have it."

His mother's face lit up. "Ah, yes. That was always your favorite."

Ana poured his mother a mug full of hot water, then Mike.

"Why don't you join us?" said Mike.

Ana flashed him a warm smile. Something was different between them. An understanding had been reached. Intimate secrets had been shared, and they had something in common with each other, more than they realized.

Mrs. Deluca shoved an envelope into his hand. He looked down, and he saw the word "Peppermint" in red and white striped lettering. His mother had forgotten he wanted orange spice. She had forgotten there had even been a plumber there. Her mind, her experience, was like a slate wiped clean, leaving no residue of memory or emotion.

Mike pondered if it made things easier or worse for her.

*

Mike had to work late to make up for the time spent with his mother, so when he got home, he felt grateful. His exchange with Ana gave him a new kind of appreciation for his life, namely his family. He just wanted to sit and watch television with Barbara and talk about anything but work. He considered telling her about Ana, but he decided against it. What passed between them was private, and he respected that.

He grabbed his briefcase and dragged his sorry carcass to his front door. He let himself inside and tossed his keys into the bowl on the small table by the entrance. The house was dark, except for the flickering light of the television in the living room. He heard the soft murmur of a show, but he was unable to make it out.

He figured Barbara had fallen asleep on the couch in the living room. The chemotherapy had tired her out on many an occasion. She fought through it like the strong woman she was. She was fighting for her life, and he was going to fight for his. On the commute home, he had decided that he was going to take a leave of absence to sort things out.

He turned on the light, and Barbara was on the couch, covered in a blanket. He sat down next to her, placing his hand on the curve of her hip. Something was wrong. She didn't feel right.

"Barbara?" He moved his hand up to her side, peeling back her blanket. She was still. He placed his hands on her ribs, waiting to feel the ebb and flow of her breath as her chest heaved, only there was nothing but stillness. "Barbara?" He placed his face by hers, searching her face for a twitch or the flutter of eyelids. There was nothing.

"Barbara! Honey, wake up!" He shook her. There was nothing. He shook her again and again, repeating her name. Barbara was gone.

A week later, after the burial, his mother had passed. He felt dead inside, as if a great emptiness had crept into his soul and nested there, draining his will. He cried with his son and daughter. Family and friends largely absent during Barbara's illness suddenly called, offering empty platitudes. A handful even dropped by the house. Hopes and prayers. Might as well have been unicorns and leprechauns.

Mike took a brief leave of absence and returned to Poseidon Tech renewed, driven. His children returned to college, and his house had become an unbearable empty nest. Ana dropped by a couple of times, and they had coffee or tea together. Now *he* scurried about the kitchen, procuring treats and refreshments for her, as she was no longer his employee; she was his guest. He treasured her visits, as she felt like the only genuine friend in his life who understood his predicament.

Barbara was gone. His mother was gone. His past and future were wiped out, all in the same week. There was nothing now but the present. Work was all he had left in his life, and he was going to devote himself entirely to it.

And, just in time…Poseidon Tech had just discovered an uncharted island in the South China Sea.

CHAPTER 13

The native chief gesticulated wildly, trying to bridge the communication gap with Torres, who was growing impatient.

"I don't understand," said Torres.

The chief paused and then began to speak slower.

Torres threw his hands up. "I still don't understand. Speaking slower doesn't help." Yet, he realized that he was speaking slower himself. "This isn't working."

Comprehending Torres' remark, the chief walked off, disappearing into the crowd.

"Looks like we're on our own," said Jason.

Torres nodded. "We're better off."

Tracey put her hands on her hips. "How are we better off? We're going up against a self-proclaimed Death Lord who controls a tribe of cannibals, or zombies, or whatever the heck they are."

"We have guns," said Torres.

Jason shook his head. "It's not going to help. Not the way this guy moves."

"Maybe we can sneak past him," offered Peter.

"How are we going to do that?" asked Mary. "That's his realm. He knows those caves."

"Not only that," said Jason, "I think he can control them."

Torres raised his eyebrows. "What? The caves?"

Jason nodded. "You saw it. You all saw it. One minute there was a tunnel, where Mike Deluca and his cannibals came from, and the next minute it was gone."

Torres stood in front of Jason, leveling his gaze at him. "What are you suggesting? This guy knows magic?"

Peter looked at Jason. "Tell him about what you saw."

Torres looked confused. "What? What did you see?"

Jason sighed. "This whole thing sounds bonkers…but here goes…When I went at Our Death Lord friend, I saw something glowing under his shirt."

Tracey crinkled her nose. "Glowing? What do you mean?"

"I mean glowing. Like an orb or an amulet, or something."

"Maybe that's the source of whatever power he wields," said Peter.

"Dinosaurs, cannibals, and now a magical orb," said Mary. "Great. The hits just keep on coming."

"It could've been an amulet," said Peter, but he withered under the look Mary shot him.

The crowd of natives anxiously watching the exchange between these strange outsiders parted, and the chief returned with six hunters. He said something no one in the party understood. He gestured towards the hunters, and then gestured towards Torres.

"I think he's giving us these hunters," said Peter.

"Six hunters," said Torres. "That's all he can spare?"

"That's six more people than we had before," said Tracey.

"Great," muttered Torres. "We leave shortly. Gather up whatever supplies you think we'll need."

"What about Allison and Bill?" asked Mary.

Torres looked as if he was about to lose his patience. "What about them?"

"We have to bring their bodies back with us."

"The hell we do."

"They have families," said Tracey. "We owe it to them. Poseidon Tech owes it to them."

"The bodies will only slow us down," said Torres, turning away, as if it were end of discussion.

Mary and Tracey pursued him.

"You're a representative of Poseidon Tech, right?" said Tracey. "So, imagine if you return without members of the salvage party, no bodies, no rational explanation."

"It's going to be a political mess," added Mary. "There'll be lawsuits. You'll be made an example of. You'll be lucky if you just lose your job."

Torres stopped and turned back around to face them. "I'm a consultant, not an employee of Poseidon Tech. This is on them."

Peter stepped forward. "Try telling that to the brass when you return without half of their employees that left with you. You were responsible for their safety. You *are* responsible for our safety…and try getting another private security gig after this mess."

Torres sighed and looked down at the bodies of Allison and Bill, wrapped up in large leaves interwoven into a lattice, the natives' handiwork. He made a sweeping gesture. "How are we going to transport them?"

The chief, listening intently, called over one of the hunters and muttered something in his ear. The hunter nodded and walked off.

"We can carry them," offered Peter.

Torres shook his head. "Do you know how heavy a body is? It would take two people per body, and it's going to slow us down."

The hunter came back dragging two poles lashed together with a netting in between. The chief gestured at it, saying something.

"What's that?" asked Torres.

"It's a travois," said Peter.

Torres looked perplexed. "A what?"

"A travois," repeated Tracey. "It's something Native Americans used to drag loads."

"It's what the hunters used to bring back their bounty," added Jason.

"That could work," said Peter.

"It will work," said Jason. "I've used them up in Alaska to drag supplies and such through the snow."

"Two of the hunters can shoulder them," said Peter.

"No way," said Torres. "I'll need every warrior I can use. This is your idea. You guys will manage it."

Peter, Tracey, and Mary all traded looks. "You've got to be kidding me," said Mary.

"Make it work," said Torres. "We leave in fifteen."

Peter strode up to Torres. "We'll handle the bodies, but don't you think we should rest a bit first? Everyone's banged up and tired."

Torres shot Peter a sharp look. "I'm growing tired of your constant questioning my decisions."

Peter shrugged. "You're in charge. I'm just thinking out loud."

Torres leaned in. "If we wait, that provides another opportunity for attack. We can't sustain another attack. This village can't sustain another attack."

"Maybe it'd be better to do this during daylight," said Peter. "You heard Mark. The attacks tend to be at night. This was the attack for tonight. I doubt they'll return."

"We don't know that," said Torres.

Peter scratched the top of his head. "In fact, I think Mike Deluca pretty much knows we're coming to him."

"How's that?"

Peter looked Torres dead in the eye. "Because he has the ELT."

"It's useless to him."

"Is it? He knows it's of value to us. Maybe he wants to use it to get off the island."

Torres scratched the stubble on his chin. "If he can get a signal out, he'll lead our ships right to him."

Peter nodded. "That's right."

"Then time is of the essence," said Torres. He paused for a moment, considering his options. He turned to the others. "Brief rest. Make it count. We leave in two hours."

*

It was still dark when the party set out to enter the temple. They descended the narrow path, negotiating the rocks and boulders. Peter and Tracey each dragged a body behind them. Peter dragged Bill, and Tracey dragged Allison. Tracey was having a better time of it, as she was in better physical shape. Peter huffed and puffed, sweating profusely and grunting under the burden.

Torres sent his two remaining men up front to take point, while the hunters armed with spears followed him. Peter, Tracey, and Mary brought up the rear.

Mary looked at Tracey. "Let me know when you want to switch off." Tracey nodded and trudged along.

They reached the temple without incident. The yawning entrance was pitch black.

"I still don't think this is a great idea to go at night," said Peter.

"Down in the caves, it's always dark," said Torres. "What difference does it make?"

"He has a point," said Jason.

Torres and his men produced flashlights. Torres shined his light into the temple entrance. "Well, it's now or never. Stay close together and try to keep up, and for God's sake, be careful."

"That's your job, isn't it?" said Peter, but Torres didn't dignify the remark with a response. A combination of sleep deprivation and the heat was making them testy.

Peter noticed the edges of the entrance had teeth carved around it, and above there were two carved eyes. The carvings appeared eerie bathed in monochromatic moonlight.

Torres turned and addressed the group. "Okay. My two men will take point, followed by the natives, and then us. Stay close together. Try not to fall behind. We have no idea what to expect inside. Any questions?"

"Can we turn around and go back to the village?" asked Peter, only half in jest.

Torres nodded to his two men, and they switched on the lights mounted on their assault rifles. They dashed forward in formation, entering the dark opening and vanishing, as if swallowed whole by the dark. Torres nodded to the tribesmen, who entered and were also swallowed whole.

"Ok," said Torres. "Stay close. We're going in."

Peter nearly jumped out of his skin when he felt Mary slide her hand into his. She squeezed it, and he squeezed back. Jason snickered and walked around them, following Torres and hefting his own rifle. Mary let go of Peter's hand, allowing him to drag Bill's body. She let Tracey pass, dragging Allison's body, and she brought up the rear.

Peter grunted as he followed Torres, the beams of flashlight shining on the stone walls of the temple. He was happy to leave the ambient sounds and distant roars of the living jungle behind him, but he was terrified to face whatever lurked in these caves.

They trekked down a long tunnel that felt like it was sloping down, as if the tunnel was going subterranean. It was cool and dark, and there was a vague dripping sound coming from somewhere ahead. Torres' radio crackled, a report from his two men up front. Peter thought he heard something about a door.

"What is it?" asked Mary.

"They've found a door," said Torres.

When they caught up with the two scouts and the tribesmen, they stood before a six-foot stone door that didn't appear to have a handle or hinge. In fact, in the darkness, it was difficult to even make out the outline of the door's outer edges. It almost looked like part of the wall.

The men shined their lights on it.

"There's a picture," said Jason. "Some sort of cave painting."

Depicted on the large stone door was a large white face with black eyes sunken into their sockets. It wore a black, toothy grin that made Peter uncomfortable. Its nose was barely distinguishable.

"Is this what they worship?" asked Jason.

Shouldering his rifle, Torres scanned the seam around the door, tracing its outline with his finger. "How do we get this door open?"

As if they comprehended the question, two of the tribesmen pressed the door. One placed his palms flat against the figure's eyes, the other against its mouth, and they shoved. The bottom of the stone door grinded against a stone floor as the door opened inward.

"Help them," ordered Torres. His men put their backs into it, and the door opened quickly. Torres shined his light into the next room.

The mercenaries and native warriors blocked Peter's view of the next room. "What is it?"

"It's another room," said Jason, shining his own light inside.

"What's in it?" asked Tracey.

Torres shined his light around the next room. "It's a larger room…it looks like there's no floor…"

Peter and Tracey exchanged anxious looks.

"No, there's a floor," said Jason, craning his neck to get a good look. "But it's…spiral shaped."

Mary looked perplexed. "What?"

"Maybe we should check for traps," said Peter to Tracey.

"What?" This time it was Tracey who was confused.

"Traps," repeated Peter. "Just in case."

Jason snickered. "He thinks it's one of his role-playing games."

"He's probably right," said Tracey. "You don't think Mike Deluca, Death Lord extraordinaire, is going to let us just waltz into his domain, do you?"

Jason pulled the corners of his mouth down and nodded. "She has a point."

Torres looked at his men. "Okay, be careful."

The tribesmen stirred, trading worried glances.

"What are they all nervous about?" asked Jason.

Torres turned to them. "Is it dangerous in there?" No response, only blank stares. "Dan-ger-ous?"

"They don't understand you," said Peter. "Speaking slowly doesn't help. Remember?"

"A lot of good they are," said Torres.

His two men re-emerged out of the room. One of them leaned in to Torres. "It's a large room with two stone doors on either side, and one on the far side. The floor drops off, and there's a set of narrow paths reaching across to the other side."

Torres looked at Peter. "Satisfied?"

Peter shrugged. "Not really."

Torres nodded. "Okay, we're going in. Everyone, stay close, and stay away from the edge." He led the way into the room, followed by his men, then the tribal hunters, then the rest. When inside the cavern, Peter dropped his heavy load for a moment and stepped forward.

Torres jutted out an arm, barring him from going forward. "Careful."

Peter smiled at the chief security officer. "I'm touched. I'll be fine." The floor extended approximately twenty feet from the door, and then it dropped off. He peered over the edge and into the dark chasm below, kicking a pebble over the edge. It dropped, and Peter strained to listen, but he never heard it hit the bottom.

"What's he doing?" asked Torres.

Tracey smiled and winked. "Checking for traps."

Torres rolled his eyes.

Peter pointed to the paths. "Shine your lights on the walkways." Torres and his two men abided, and Peter studied the paths reaching across the chasm. They were checkered, and they intertwined, looking like a giant crossword puzzle. "The paths are tiled, and the tiles are different colors—black, white, and red."

Tracey and Jason stepped next to Peter to take a look.

"I'll be damned," said Jason. "He's right. They seem to alternate."

"So what?" said Torres. "What does it mean?"

Peter stroked his chin, staring at the tiles. "I don't know." A cold draft emanated from the dark void below, giving Peter goose pimples.

"Well, that's handy," snapped Torres. He turned to the tribal hunters, sweeping across the cavern with his hand and backing away, shining his flashlight on the narrow walkway. "Why don't you go first?"

They stared, eyes bulging, but they did not budge.

Torres gestured towards the paths again. "Go ahead."

"Why don't *you* go ahead?" said Mary.

Torres dressed the hunters down with looks of condescension. "The tribe's bravest. A lot of good they are."

Peter was eyeing the doors on either side of the cavern. A path led up to each from the center. Then he looked at the open doorway on the opposite side of the chasm. "Maybe they know something we don't. Why is the door open on the other side, and the two side doors closed?"

Torres addressed his two men. "Okay, I'll go first. Molina, follow me and watch my six. Hausman, stay here and pass out glow sticks from your pack. And for God's sake, cover me. Keep an eye on those side doors."

They both nodded. Hausman unshouldered his pack and unzipped the opening. He reached inside and produced several glowsticks. "Here, take these. Crack 'em and shake." He passed them around to Peter, Mary, and Tracey, who cracked the sticks and shook them as instructed. A blue light emanated from the sticks. Jason declined, as he had his own flashlight. Torres produced a handful of his own glow sticks from his pack. He looked at Molina. "You too. Just in case I run out." Molina nodded, shouldered his rifle, and grabbed a handful from his pack.

The indigenous hunters startled at the strange blue light, gasping and whispering to each other. They huddled together, clutching their spears close to their bodies.

Jason slapped Torres on the back. "Be careful, mate."

Torres nodded. He shouldered his rifle, swallowed hard, and stepped out onto the first black checkered square of the path in front of him. The tile depressed, sinking an inch into the ground. Torres froze, his body rigid, as a grinding sound came from the doorway behind them. A round stone door rolled from inside the wall across the doorway, barring it.

The group stirred. Tracey, startled, jumped back, dropping her load, backing into the cold cave wall. Mary tried to shout a warning, but the grinding of the rolling stone door drowned out her cry. The hunters hoisted their spears, scanning the cavern.

Torres looked down at his foot. "Right," he said to himself. "Search for traps." Then to the group, "Is everyone all right?"

"Yeah, we're okay," said Tracey. "But we're trapped in this room now."

"No, we're not," said Torres. He pointed to the open door on the opposite side of the cavern. "That's the way out."

"By design," added Peter. "That's where someone wants us to go." In table-top role-playing it was called *railroading*.

"Maybe try to be a little more careful," said Jason.

Embarrassed, Torres muttered to himself and turned back around. He stepped with great caution now, careful not to place his full weight on each tile, testing. He stepped on a white tile, another black tile. The path was a few tiles wide, and he zig zagged his path a bit, cracking, shaking, and dropping glow sticks from his pack to light the way for the others. Molina followed in his exact footsteps. From where the others were standing, it looked as if they were playing hop scotch.

Torres stepped on a red tile, feeling more confident now, and there was a crack and a snap. Torres's right leg dropped through the path, and he nearly fell off. Molina grabbed him just in time.

The others gasped and cried out. "Are you all right?" Peter called out.

Molina steadied his CO. Torres turned to address the others on the platform, his face even hotter with embarrassment. "Don't step on the red tiles! They're a trap!"

"How do we know that?" said Peter. "Maybe it was just that one?"

Torres turned back to the path, huffing in exasperation, and carefully stepped forward until he came next to another red tile. He shoved the uncracked glowsticks in his pocket, unshouldered his rifle, turned it in his hands, and brought the stock down on the red tile, smashing it with ease. "Hypothesis tested!" shouted Torres. "As I said, avoid stepping on the red tiles!"

Peter snapped his fingers, as if hit by a sudden epiphany. "That's it! The face on the door outside only had two colors—black and white. There wasn't any red."

"What are you babbling on about?" chortled Jason.

Tracey nodded. "In role-playing games, there are rules to the dungeons."

"This isn't a game," said Jason.

"Come on," said Peter, now himself exasperated. "Before today we didn't believe in dinosaurs and Death Lords and such…"

Jason put his hands up. "Okay, okay. I get it. So, tell me about these rules."

Peter waved his hands, gesticulating as he explained. "Each dungeon has its own rules and puzzles. You need to know the rules to solve the puzzles and get through safely."

Jason frowned. "Okay, are there any other rules we need to be aware of?"

Peter glanced at the two side doors. "Something bothers me about those doors."

"What?"

"They're there for a reason."

"What reason?" asked Mary.

"I don't know yet."

Torres cupped his hand on the side of his mouth to amplify his voice. "Okay, I want you all to start to come across, single file. Don't step on the red tiles."

Tracey looked down at Allison's body. "What about the bodies. How are we going to avoid the red tiles?"

"You'll have to leave them behind," said Jason. "You can't endanger the group."

"We can't just leave theme here," protested Mary.

Peter mulled it over. He called out to Torres. "Are there any groupings of red tiles that you can see, or are they isolated?"

Torres looked around at his feet. "They appear to be isolated! I don't see any groupings!"

"Do you hear that?" asked Jason, looking around the cavern.

"No," said Tracey. "What?"

"There's no echo."

"So, what?"

"There should be an echo," said Jason, his eyes darting around the cavern. "Why isn't there a bloody echo?"

Peter put his hand on Tracey's arm. "We're going to be dragging the bodies across, distributing the weight across multiple tiles. We're not focusing all of our body weight on one foot. We should be fine."

Tracey and Mary exchanged looks and nodded.

"Okay," said Peter. "Let's go."

The tribal hunters had already stepped onto the path and were gaining on Torres and Molina. Molina had taken over dropping glow sticks onto the path. As they drew close, Molina pointed to the red tiles, shook his head emphatically, and made gestures with his hands like a baseball umpire declaring a runner 'safe.' They appeared to understand and stepped around the red tiles.

Jason stepped in front of Peter, Mary, and Tracey. "You have your hands full. I'll go first. Step where I step."

Mary placed a hand on Tracey's shoulder. "My turn to pull Allison."

They all nodded in agreement, and Jason stepped onto the first black square of the path. Then he stepped to another, and another, calling out the tiles he was using. Peter followed, dragging Bill's body behind him, and Mary followed, each echoing the tiles Jason was calling out. Tracey followed behind Mary, and Hausman brought up the rear.

Peter looked up ahead, rather than look down, and saw Torres and Molina meandering, the path snaking left and then right, convoluting and folding back on itself.

"Hey!" It was Mary.

Peter turned around. "What's wrong?"

"You're knocking the glow sticks off the path. I can't see the tiles."

"Pardon?" Then he realized what had happened. Bill's body was dragging over the glow sticks, dragging them along or pushing them off the path. "Oh, sorry."

Mary released her load for a moment. She reached inside her pocket, pulled out a handful of glowsticks and began to crack and shake them. "I'm holding on to mine to use as I go."

Peter nodded. "Good idea." He followed suit.

Tracey was already cracking and shaking hers.

Peter realized that this meant he had to hold the glow sticks in one hand to illuminate the walkway and drag Bill's body with the other. He adjusted his stance, turning sideways. He'd have to sidestep. He looked back and saw Mary was doing the same. He heard Jason mutter something about bringing the bodies along as having been a mistake.

Peter shot a glance at the void below, and his anxiety spiked. He lost his footing and stepped with his left foot on a square that Jason had not called out. His right foot was on an identified square. Both of his feet sank about an inch. "Guys? Guys!"

Everyone stopped and looked at Peter.

"Peter, what is it?" cried Tracey from behind him.

There were more grinding sounds as the stone doors to their left and right rolled away, revealing a passageway behind each.

"What did you do?" snapped Torres from ahead.

"I stepped on the wrong tile," said Peter.

"You stepped on two adjacent tiles simultaneously," noted Mary.

Peter nodded. "Okay, don't step on two adjacent tiles simultaneously!"

Jason smirked. "Another rule?"

"We don't know if this is bad," said Tracey.

Peter chuckled. "It probably isn't good."

There were scratching sounds coming from the newly opened passageway on the left. Everyone froze, listening. Torres and Molina trained their rifles on the left passageway. Scratching sounds then came from the right passageway. Jason trained his rifle on that one.

Peter looked at the hunters on the path in front of him, gripping their spears. His attention was drawn to the snorting and croaking sounds now coming from each side passageway. The head of a velociraptor appeared in one and then the other, sniffing the air.

"Oh, crap," said Peter.

The velociraptors stepped into the doorways, hunched over, claws reaching out, eyes on the fresh meat navigating the labyrinthine crossing.

Torres looked horrified. "Everybody, let's move!" He and Molina dropped their glowsticks, picked up the pace, and stepped with a little less caution. Peter dragged his load, following Jason, who kept an eye on the two velociraptors. Tracey reached down and grabbed Allison's feet, helping Mary.

Sensing the panic of frantic prey, the velociraptors each stepped out onto the path. After a few careful steps, testing the path, their claws clicking on the hard tiles, they began to venture out, moving faster and faster.

"They're coming!" cried Tracey.

Everyone picked up their pace, following the meandering path, careful not to step on the red tiles. As Peter dragged Bill's body behind him, he saw Torres stumble up ahead. The paths of the humans and the raptors meandered and turned, at times bringing them close to each other. Torres and Molina fired shots at the predators, who snapped their jaws at them in passing. There was a point where one of the raptor's paths was merely ten feet away, and the razor-sharp teeth came dangerously close to Molina's head.

"Holy hell, this is like some kind of maze," shouted Jason, taking some choice shots of his own at the raptor on the right.

"Let's hope these paths don't intersect at some point," said Peter, watching his step.

Torres, losing focus on the tiles, stumbled and nearly fell through the path up ahead. "There're more red tiles up here!"

Peter looked behind him and saw Tracey and Mary hefting Allison's body. Mary held out her left hand clutching the glow sticks, dragging Allison's body with her right. She looked up and met Peter's eyes. "We're okay. Don't stop for us." Her features were spooky in the blue light.

The native hunters were doing their best to maintain balance on the narrowing path. One threw his spear at a raptor during a brief, close encounter. The spear hit its mark, but the raptor seized it in its teeth, pulled it out of its haunch, and snapped it like a toothpick in it jaws.

"Oh shit!" It was Torres. He had stopped and was looking down. "There's an intersection here."

"Then stop talking and haul ass," shouted Jason from behind.

The raptors wound their way around on each side, and they made their way toward where Torres stood only a moment ago.

"Hurry!" cried Peter, grunting under the weight of his burden. His knees buckled, and he wished he had found more time for exercise in his life. He also began to regret bringing the bodies along.

As the native hunters reached the intersection, one of the raptors drew close on the left. Sensing its prey, it picked up speed, its claws skidding, sending pebbles down into the black abyss below.

The hunters panicked and began shoving each other. One lost his balance and fell, his screams extinguished as he was swallowed by the black void. The raptor hunched over, contracting its leg muscles. In an explosive movement, it sprang across and grabbed one of the tribal hunters in its clawed feet, pinning him to the ground on the path to the right of the intersection. The man screamed in terror as the raptor reached down and crushed his skull in its jaws. His screams turned to gurgles as it clamped down on his neck and he choked on his own blood.

Peter halted, catching his breath, as Mary collided with Bill's body, nearly knocking him off the narrow path. However, Bill's weight on the tiled ground allowed him to steady himself.

"What are you doing?" cried Mary, annoyed. "Why did you stop?"

Peter pointed ahead. "Look!"

The remaining four hunters thrust their spears at the raptor, the sharpened tips finding purchase. The raptor thrashed about in pain, swinging its tail, as blood oozed out of its back and side. Its tail took the legs out from under one of the hunters, and the native fell backwards off the path like a scuba diver falling backwards off the edge of the boat and into the ocean. Clutching his spear and holding on, another native was thrown around like a rag doll, as the raptor spun around, trying to bite him.

Up ahead, Jason took aim with his rifle and shot the raptor in its left eye. The raptor lost its footing and fell off, taking the clinging tribal warrior with him. The remaining two pressed forward with great urgency.

"Let's go!" Peter crossed the intersection, as did Mary and Tracey with Allison.

"Hurry up!" boomed Jason. "The other raptor is coming!"

Preoccupied with following Tracey in the rear, Hausman didn't notice the other raptor flanking him on the right. He raised his weapon, but the raptor lunged, turning its head sideways, and sunk its teeth into his torso. Hausman let out a cry that waned under the pressure of the bite, like an accordion given one long squeeze.

Peter looked up ahead to find Torres and Molina had already made it to the other side.

"Hurry up!" shouted Torres as he and Molina took aim at the raptor, pausing as the two remaining indigenous made it to the other side, crossing their lines of fire.

Peter's lungs burned as he pumped his legs, careful to maintain his balance. Bill's body rolled to the left and then the right, like wheeled luggage falling off balance, as he crossed over the red tiles that Torres and Molina crushed. He turned around and struggled to keep the load centered on the narrow path.

At last, Peter made it to the other side. He dropped his load and his glowsticks, and he returned to the end of the path in time to catch Mary as she lost her footing. He grabbed her around the waist and pulled her off the path and onto the ledge. He stumbled, falling backward, and Mary fell on top of him. They lay face-to-face, panting, eye-to-eye, surrounded by Mary's scattered glow sticks. Tracey, now on the other side as well, side-stepped them, dropping Allison's feet to the hard ground.

Torres and Molina opened fire on the raptor, which had now ripped Hausman's rib cage open and tore chunks of flesh off with its teeth, holding his body down with its clawed foot. The horrific scene was illuminated in strobe by muzzle flashes and flashlight beams.

Mary, her mouth a couple of inches from Peter's, smiled. "You saved me." She was breathy, and her voice was thick. "My hero."

Tracey held out a hand, offering it to Mary. Mary grabbed it and allowed herself to be pulled up. Peter sat up to see the raptor fall over the edge of the path, leaving part of Hausman behind.

Mary and Tracey each offered Peter a hand and helped him up. He brushed himself off as Torres took stock of the survivors. "Hausman's gone. He was a good man." He turned to Peter. "Search for traps, huh? Every dungeon has its rules?"

Peter traded dubious expressions with Tracey.

Torres pointed at the two of them. "You two play these games together?"

They both nodded in unison.

"Good. The natives will drag the bodies. I want you two taking point."

CHAPTER 14

Peter and Tracey peeked through the doorway and into the next cavern, shining flashlights provided by Torres and Molina. It was dimly lit. Peter looked up and saw that the ceiling of the cavern had fallen in some time ago. This room was a cenote of sorts.

"What do you see?" asked Torres, standing right behind them.

Peter and Tracey shone their flashlights around the room. Tracey turned to Torres. "Plants everywhere. Big, lush, tropical plants."

Peter shined his light on the cenote walls. They were shiny and wet. "Lots of moisture in here."

"Any traps?" asked Torres.

Peter and Tracey looked around.

"Hard to tell," said Peter.

"And our botanist is dead," added Tracey. "So, we can't account for the flora."

"Look around," directed Torres. "Do you see anything strange or out of place?"

Peter and Tracey scanned the cenote. It was lush with vegetation, so they were unable to see much in front of them.

Peter shined his light on the ground in front of him. "I don't think so."

"Okay, we're coming in."

Peter and Tracey stepped forward, allowing the others to come inside. Peter stepped forward on what looked like a path, swiping large leaves and fronds away from his face.

"Be careful what you touch," warned Tracey.

He swept the ground with his flashlight as he took a few steps, but he stopped dead in his tracks. "I found something!"

Tracey was at his side in a flash. “What is it?”

Peter pointed at the ground. “Look.”

Tracey looked down and saw a five-foot hole in the ground. Down below was another cavern. Tracey squatted, shining her light down below.

“Careful,” warned Peter.

“There’s another cavern,” said Tracey, squinting her eyes to try and make out what was below.

Mary and Torres walked up to Peter.

“What is it?” asked Torres.

“There’s a cavern beneath us,” said Tracey. “It looks like there are more plants down there. They’re very large…and open at the top.”

Mary pushed past Peter and Torres. “Let me see.” She squatted next to Tracey and looked into the hole. She got down on her hands and knees and lowered her head over the hole.

“Careful,” said Peter, shifting nervously on his feet.

Mary pulled her head out of the hole. “I’m no botanist, but those appear to be some kind of carnivorous plant. Like a pitcher plant, but gigantic. Rows and rows of them.”

Torres helped her up. “Pitcher plant? What the hell is a pitcher plant?”

Tracey now stuck her head in the hole, shining her flashlight down on the plants to get a better look.

“It’s like a Venus Flytrap,” said Mary, “only it doesn’t grab. Prey falls into the ‘pitcher’ part and gets slowly digested by fluids held inside the ‘pitcher.’”

Peter shined his light on the ground in front of them, sweeping his beam from side-to-side across and up the path. “There are other holes.”

Torres placed his hands on his hips. “Okay, I think we can make it across. I’ll take point, everyone else follow in my footsteps. Be careful of the holes.” He paused. “Do you guys see anything else?”

Jason was up ahead, squatting, probing the ground with his index finger. “I found tracks.”

Torres looked at him. “What kind of tracks?”

Jason ignored him, studying the tracks.

“It makes sense,” said Peter.

“What makes sense?” snapped Torres. “Will somebody tell me what the hell is going on here?”

“This setup is all wrong,” said Peter. “The holes aren’t enough to sustain such a proliferation of carnivorous plants. Something is helping them.”

“What? What’s helping them?” asked Molina.

Mary brushed dirt off her legs. “In nature, there are frequently symbiotic relationships. A species of pitcher plants known as Nepenthes lowii attract tree shrews, who feed on the nectar. In return, the tree shrews defecate into the pitcher, providing valuable nutrients.”

Torres shifted his feet. “What does any of this have to do with what we have here?”

“The placement of these holes,” said Peter. “They’re meaningful. They serve a purpose.”

Jason stood up and approached them. “The tracks are dinosaur.”

“Let me see,” said Tracey.

Jason led her over to the tracks, and they both squatted, examining them together. Tracey looked up. “It’s a theropod…dilophosaurus, I think.”

“Which one is that?” asked Molina. “I’ve never heard of that one.”

Peter frowned. “Remember that movie, where the dinosaur spat venom at the guy, disabling him?”

“Oh, Christ,” muttered Torres.

“Exactly,” said Peter. “However, they don’t spit venom. That’s only in the movies.”

Torres smirked. “That’s comforting. How big?”

“Seven meters long. Strong legs. Big, clawed feet.”

Torres looked at Jason. “You come with me and keep an eye on those tracks. I’ll watch out for holes.” He turned to Molina. “You take right flank.” He addressed the rest of the group. “The rest of you, follow me. Stay close.” Torres instructed the two remaining indigenous to drag the bodies.

They pushed into the cenote, moving silently. Torres identified the locations of holes leading to the cavern below, and Jason followed the tracks on the ground.

“They’re all over,” said Jason. “The tracks cross each other. It’s difficult to tell their numbers.”

Peter, Tracey, and Mary followed behind Torres and Jason, and the hunters brought up the rear.

There was a rustling in the vegetation off to the left of where the natives walked single-file. “Shhhh…” Jason stopped and scanned the bush, training his rifle. “There’s something out there.”

Everyone froze in place. Torres also trained his rifle on the bush where the noise was coming from. There was the whistle of a snout and more rustling. The moon above cast everything in gentle monochromatic light, causing everything to blend into everything else.

There was a cry from the right flank. Everyone turned to look. Plants shook violently. Thrashing sounds and the grunts and growls of a predator came from within the vegetation.

"Molina!" Torres turned and trained his rifle on where he heard his man cry out. "Molina, report!" The staccato pops of gunfire drowned out the growls.

The natives behind them started shouting as the brush to their left rustled. Strange sounds filled the jungle around them, a combination of high-pitched whistles and what sounded like goose honking. The hunters clutched their faces and stumbled around blindly, nearly falling into nearby holes.

The face of a dinosaur popped out of the brush in front of Torres. Its head bore two crests, and it rattled at him.

"Jesus!" He raised his rifle, but the thing's mouth spat a large glob of mucus at his face. He clawed at his face. At first, it burned like the collective stings of an entire colony of fire ants. Then, it went numb. He stumbled backwards. Peter reached out to grab him, but he wasn't quick enough. Torres fell into a hole.

Jason shot at the dilophosaurus, and it vanished into the bush. "Move! Double-time!"

He dashed forward, dividing his attention between the holes in the ground and the noises in the vegetation around him.

Peter struggled to follow him, as the seasoned hunter bobbed and weaved through the cenote. He heard Mary and Tracey panting behind him. Tracey sprinted past him, and he felt Mary's hand slip into his, pulling him along.

Because he was watching Mary instead of the ground, he tripped on a tree branch and wobbled sideways…

*

Mary felt Peter tug on her hand sideways, nearly pulling her off-balance. Palms sweaty, he slipped out of her grip. She turned in time to see Peter tackled by a dilophosaurus.

"Wait!" she screamed at Tracey and Jason. Jason stopped, Tracey running into his back. He turned and saw what Mary was pointing at. He turned to Tracey. "Get the hell out of here!"

She turned and saw Peter pinned down under the carnivore. "But…"

"I've got this," said Jason. "Keep running!"

Mary stood there, not knowing what to do.

Jason stepped forward and raised his rifle. "Get out of the way!"

Mary stepped aside and Jason took a shot, hitting the dilophosaurus in its chest. It looked up at him and hissed, rattling, its crests flaring. It launched a wad of venom in Jason's direction, but he dodged it. Out of ammunition, Jason threw down his rifle and drew his handgun. He fired at the theropod, hitting it in the chest and head. The dilophosaurus staggered, unsteady, and fell into the hole, still clutching Peter in its clawed feet. Peter was gone.

"No!" cried Mary.

Jason grabbed her by the arm. "We have to go! Now!" They took off in the direction opposite where they entered. They burst into a small clearing and through a small opening in the rock wall on the other side.

Tracey was there, waiting for them. "Thank God you're all right!" As Jason and Mary struggled to catch their breath, Tracey looked around, frantic. "Where's Peter?"

Jason shook his head.

Tracey didn't initially comprehend what the head shake meant. "Is he still out there? You said you'd get him." Her eyes pleaded with Jason.

"He's gone," said Mary.

Tracey's eyes welled up. "What happened?"

Mary looked Tracey dead in the eye, still panting. "A dilophosaurus...pulled him into...a hole. He's gone."

"What?" Tracey was incredulous. "How?"

"I thought...he said...those things don't...spit venom..." said Jason, catching his breath.

Mary frowned. "It doesn't matter now, does it?"

"Where are the tribal hunters?" asked Tracey.

Jason ejected his empty clip and slapped in a fresh one. "They're gone, and so are the bodies. It was a bad idea to drag them along."

"What do we do now?" asked Mary.

"We press on," said Jason. "We can't go back."

A man burst through the narrow doorway, colliding with Jason, knocking him to the ground. The man fell on top of him.

Jason rolled him off. "What the hell?"

It was Molina. He rolled onto his stomach. Weary from fighting for his life, he stood up. He offered a hand to Jason.

Jason took it, and Molina pulled him up. Jason brushed himself off. "Where the hell were you all this time?" His question was clearly an accusation.

"We thought you were dead," said Tracey.

"I almost was," said Molina. "I barely got out of there with my life." He looked around. "Where's everyone else?"

"They didn't make it," said Mary.

"But we're happy to see you, mate," said Jason. "How much ammo do you have left?"

Molina tapped his handgun in his holster on his right hip. "Just one more clip. You?"

"Same."

"We have to keep moving," said Molina.

"What do we do when we find Mike Deluca?" asked Tracey.

Mary sighed. "Do you really think we can take him? It's only the four of us now."

Jason looked at Molina, who said, "Not in a straight up fight. Not with this few people. We're going to have to surprise him."

Jason nodded, agreeing. "He moves too fast. One minute he's there, the next he's somewhere else. It's that glowing thing in his chest, whatever it is. It has to be."

Molina shook his head. "Great. Dinosaurs, pitcher plants, and magic."

Jason shined his flashlight down a narrow corridor. "We have to press on. We don't have much time until the island phases out."

"For all we know, it already has," said Molina.

Tracey looked panicked. "Then what?"

Jason met her eyes with his. His look was fierce. "If we're stuck on this island, then we have to kill Mike Deluca anyway, or he'll eventually get us. Either way, the 'Death Lord' must die."

"How do we know if we can even kill him?" asked Mary.

"If we can get that glowing amulet, or whatever it is, away from him, he can be killed," explained Tracey. When everyone looked at her, dubious, she said, "Dungeons have rules, remember?"

There was a collective moment of somber silence for Peter.

"He was a smart man," offered Jason. "Okay, let's go."

* * *

Peter plunged into the cavern below, riding the dilophosaurus. They crashed onto the top edge of a pitcher plant, and the dinosaur beneath him slid into it. Peter struggled to stand up, pushing the dinosaur down with his feet, struggling not to slide in himself. Disoriented from the fall and weak from multiple gunshot wounds, the reptile waved its four-fingered arms about in a futile gesture as it slid under the pool of digestive fluids.

Peter kicked off the dilophosaurus and grabbed onto the rim of the pitcher. He pulled himself up, the rim sturdy under his weight. He hoisted himself up, onto the edge and rolled over, falling to the ground below.

The soil was soft and cool on his face. He stood up, clutching his side where the dilophosaurus had gripped his body. There were two wet spots on his shirt, stained dark. However, the stains were small. Peter pulled up his shirt and touched the two puncture wounds. Fortunately, they weren't deep, and the bleeding had almost stopped.

He looked around. There were pitchers everywhere, each one about twenty feet tall, a few feet apart. He turned his body sideways and slipped in between two of them. He looked up at the cavern ceiling. Moonlight shone through the holes in the ceiling. He pondered which direction to walk in, but he had no idea where he was going, or if there even was an exit.

He picked a direction and slipped between the pitcher plants, making his way to one of the walls of the cavern. Finally, he reached a stone wall. He pressed his palms to the wall. It was cool and damp. He heard dripping sounds coming from somewhere, which meant there was water. He followed the wall to the right, tracing his path on the cool rock with his left hand.

After walking for a bit along the perimeter of the cavern, his fingers became wet as a thin stream of water trickled over them. He tasted his fingers; there was no trace of salt. It was fresh water. He placed his mouth to the wall and licked at the trickle of water. It was cool and refreshing.

As he reveled in the hydration, he looked around the cavern, and something bothered him. He looked up at the holes in the ceiling, which from this vantage point didn't look so haphazard. He looked at the neat rows of pitcher plants. Someone designed this and was maintaining it.

He continued to follow the wall until it wrapped around, and there was an opening about twenty feet high and ten feet wide. It was dark. He placed his hand on the edge of the door and felt a raised edge that traced the cave entrance. It was carved into the stone.

Peter looked up and gasped at what he saw. He backed away until his back hit the side wall of one of the pitcher plants and placed a hand over his gaping mouth. The opening itself was carved into a gaping mouth. Two nose slits were carved into the rock above the opening, and above them sat two large, dark stones for eyes set into the wall. They were oval in shape. It was a big face.

Peter produced his flashlight and shined it on the carvings, and the onyx eyes reflected the light in an uncanny effect. The stone around the face was carved in a rough fashion, giving the indication of scales.

Of course, Peter chastised himself. *Why wouldn't there be another race on the island? One that would exist in symbiosis with the dilophosaurus colony above. One that designed and kept these pitcher plants.*

He whirled around as he heard skittering and crunching sounds from behind him. There was something moving amongst the tall pitcher plants. He turned to look back at the dark entrance behind him, weighing his options. He didn't know what was inside the dark cavern. Then again, he didn't know what was chittering amongst the pitcher plants either.

He backed towards the dark portal, almost inside it, but keeping his eye on the pitcher plants in front of him. The skittering grew closer. Peter braced himself for whatever was coming.

A large, ant-like insect ambled around the outer edge of the pitchers, dragging the corpse of a smaller insect. The larger insect was the size of a rhinoceros, and the smaller insect was the size of an adult human. On its back, the larger insect donned the bodies of other insects as a kind of armor.

Peter watched as the larger insect hefted the smaller carcass onto its back, maneuvering it until it remained in place, an extra link in the exoskeleton chain mail of sorts. It turned and regarded Peter with large, black eyes, and then proceeded back around the outer edge of the pitcher plants, vanishing from whence it came.

Peter let out a deep sigh of relief, wiping the sweat off his brow. His skin itched from the humidity and the myriad of bug bites on his back and shoulders. He turned to face the darkened portal again. He shined his flashlight and decided to step through.

*

He emerged on the other side, his body becoming rigid when he saw his flashlight bean bounce off of several tall figures standing in the dark. They appeared to be seven feet tall and humanoid, and they stared at Peter.

He waited, grimacing in the dark, bracing for an attack, but none came. When he allowed himself a look at the figures in the dark, he realized they were motionless, statuesque even. He tentatively crept towards the closest one and shined his light on it. He reached out, touching the surface. Stone. They were statues. He let out a sigh of relief and shined his light on the others. They were all statues, arranged haphazardly, or so it appeared.

He stepped forward, through them, shining his light on the back of the cavern. However, instead of seeing a back wall, the cavern opened up into a much larger space. He passed through the statues and saw a great city of ruins below. Shining his light on the ground, he saw the floor drop off, and he stopped short before nearly stepping off the edge. The drop appeared to be about a hundred feet. He strained his eyes and ears for any sign of life, friendly or hostile.

The massive cavern was silent as a tomb, and Peter figured this wasn't too far off from being one. He saw a set of stairs descending to his right. He decided to descend them, one step at a time, exercising extreme caution. *Checking for traps*, he mused to himself. There was no railing, and the staircase was open, so he switched his flashlight to his right hand and traced the stone cylinder that rose up through the center of the spiraled staircase as he went. It was cold and hard, the stone smooth. His footsteps echoed in the room, and Peter prayed he wasn't alerting anyone to his presence.

However, upon closer inspection of the steps, he saw a thick layer of dust. As if by mere suggestion, Peter let out a roaring sneeze, startling himself and the bats hanging off the ceiling. Some took flight, their leather-like wings beating the still air. These steps hadn't been climbed for an eternity, and he had the feeling the same went for the ruins below.

When he reached the bottom, he stirred up more dust on the cavern floor. His nostrils itched and his nasal passages burned, but he stifled a sneeze. He looked down at the ground, casting his light upon it. The floor was stone, but smooth and flat, not rough like the caverns above. He swept the ground and the space in front of him. He was surrounded by buildings. But there was something else.

There was something down here…a presence of some kind, and it was calling to him.

He walked down one of the streets, shining his light on all of the defunct buildings he passed, which were not only empty but in a state of ruin. Crumbling walls, caved-in roofs, the city must've been ancient, even by the island's standards. In intersections stood statues of towering humanoid forms, acting as sentinels. Peter wondered if they were effigies of prominent figures in whatever civilization this once was.

He approached one, shining his light up its body and on its face. It initially appeared to don armor, some kind of chain mail. However, upon closer scrutiny, he realized the figure was covered in scales. When he saw its head, he realized that he was looking at a representation of a reptilian man. The statue bore no other markings. There appeared no evidence of any kind of written language.

Startled, he quickly turned his head, as he thought he heard something. His skin went cold, and goose bumps rose on his skin. The sound wasn't from somewhere nearby in the city. It was inside his head. It was a language-less, wordless voice that called to him, as if it knew him.

He followed it, meandering through foreign streets with an uncanny certainty of where he was going. The voice led him to a large building made of white stone, like marble but without the striations. The building appeared to be intact, and the entrance in the façade was framed by two massive white pillars of stone. When he shined his light on the steps and floor by the front entrance, he saw a single set of footprints. Whatever was calling to him was doing so from inside. Yet, by all indications, the building appeared to be completely abandoned.

Peter swept his light across the front steps and the entryway, his ears pricked for any slightest sound. "Hello," he decided to call out, but he was only answered by his own echo. He looked around, and the surrounding streets and buildings were silent. He steeled himself, drawing in a deep breath, and climbed the steps. He placed his foot inside one of the footprints in the layer of dust, and it was slightly bigger than his foot. *What size shoe do you wear, Mike Deluca?* Peter smiled and entered the temple.

Inside, the room appeared to brighten, but it had nothing to do with Peter's flashlight. In the center of the room sat a floating onyx orb the size of a Gypsy crystal ball, and it appeared to provide a faint illumination to the room. The walls of the temple were unadorned, as was the ceiling. When he inspected the floor, Peter noticed the footprints leading up to the orb and then at right angles, off to the left and right.

Peter retraced the footsteps, careful not to trigger any traps. As he reached the orb, it appeared to brighten the room. When he reached it, the room was well-lit. Peter traced the other trail of footprints off to the left to a stone box that appeared opened, as if several overlapping stones had slid away from the top. From where he stood, the box appeared to be empty. Then, he traced the footprints going off to the right. There was another stone box, unopened.

Peter studied the orb in front of him, stooping to get a closer look at its surface. The dust had been disturbed on the surface. Peter reached out, grimacing as he prepared for a jolt of pain, and lay his right hand on the orb. However, no pain came. Instead, the wordless voice inside his head grew louder and the walls and ceiling of the room evaporated into the air.

A series of images flashed before him in rapid succession, narrated by the alien voice. Although he didn't comprehend the voice, he somehow understood what was being explained. Some time long ago, there existed a civilization of reptilian humanoids that shared a common ancestry with what Peter understood to be dinosaurs. They had evolved over centuries, developing civilization, laws, and government. Lacking a written language in the traditional sense, information was recorded for posterity within these onyx orbs.

Peter, his head hurting from the strain of decoding these mental representations, released the orb. The immersive images immediately ceased, and the walls and ceiling of the temple rematerialized. Peter rubbed his temples, grunting. As his vision stabilized, he wondered if the walls and ceiling really had dematerialized, or if it was an illusion created by the orb.

He looked down at his watch and was struck by a question. How much time had elapsed during his 'visions?' He felt as if he had viewed a multi-hour documentary in his mind's eye, but he was unsure how much time had initially elapsed.

As his disorientation faded, Peter wondered if Mike Deluca's condition was the result of repeatedly accessing this orb. Perhaps repetitious use had induced his madness. Peter questioned whether or not he should proceed. While what he had learned explained the presence of the city, it didn't explain its current condition. More importantly, it didn't explain Mike Deluca's current condition.

He knew sooner or later he'd have to deal with Mike Deluca. As he considered that notion, the wordless voice called to him, this time seeming more familiar. The familiarity appeared to draw its power from his interaction with the mysterious orb, and it felt to him as if the orb was a two-way corridor. He accessed the history of this ancient civilization, yet it also felt as if the orb had accessed something of Peter's history. It was as if it knew him like an old friend, and now the unopened stone box to his right called to him, tugging on the most intimate parts of his psyche, digging deep and anchoring itself onto his memories.

He wondered if Mike Deluca received such a calling in his time down here. Was it the stone box to the left that called to him? Peter shook his head to clear it, but the voice only became stronger, as if in reaction to his consideration of the opened stone box. Extending its tendrils into his mind, it drew him over to the unopened box, as if his mind and body hungered for what was inside and was repulsed by what once lay in the opened receptacle to the left.

When he reached the stone vessel, he looked down and saw symbols on its surface, a dead lexicon as alien to him as the island itself. The symbols called out to him, reading his thoughts and feelings, and he reached his hand out over them.

He felt his hand drawn to the surface like a magnet, and there was a grinding sound from within the box.

CHAPTER 15

The long, winding tunnel seemed interminable.

"How far does this passage go?" asked Mary.

"It feels like the ground is moving," said Tracey.

"The walls and ceiling, too," added Jason. "The whole damned tunnel is shifting."

"That's impossible," said Molina.

Jason shot him a look.

"Okay, okay," conceded Molina. "Assuming this tunnel is moving, what does that mean?"

Tracey sighed. "It means he knows we're coming."

"She's right," said Jason. "Remember how that tunnel appeared in the middle of the village?"

Molina nodded. "Yeah, and then just like that, it vanished."

Jason waved a hand, gesturing. "I think Mike Deluca can control these tunnels."

"He's leading us right to him," gasped Mary.

Tracey stopped dead in her tracks. "Then we should turn around, go back." Everyone else stopped trudging down the tunnel for a moment.

Jason shook his head. "He'll lead us right back to him."

"We're being railroaded," said Tracey.

Jason frowned. "He's tiring us out, making us walk for a long time. Meanwhile, he's waiting for us, all rested and ready."

"So, what's the plan?" asked Molina.

Jason scratched the stubble on his chin. "We can't beat him in a straight up fight. I say we try and get the drop on him. It's the only way."

Molina held up his Glock. "I've got a full thirty rounds left."

Jason tapped his Baretta. "And I a full twenty."

"How do we get the drop on him?" asked Mary.

"Not *we*," corrected Jason. "*I*. I can hunt. I'm used to moving undetected, stalking game."

"What about me?" asked Molina.

Jason grinned. "You're going to hit him head-on, draw his attention. The ladies, here, will try and make their way to the exit to the cliff."

"I don't like this plan," said Molina.

Jason shrugged. "Do you have any better ideas, mate? Now would be the time."

Molina looked at the hunter. "Are you as good as you think you are?"

Jason nodded. "I'll get him."

The group of four continued to walk on. At last, the tunnel opened up into a large cavern. Molina stopped them just before entering. Inside the cavern, there were the scattered ruins of what looked like a now defunct civilization. The ground was littered with broken foundations, battered walls, and horizontal stone pillars.

"What's that noise?" asked Tracey.

"Shh." Molina placed a hand out to silence her. "Those are voices," he whispered.

"Lots of voices," added Jason.

Chanting echoed off the massive cavern walls, many voices in unison.

"We stay hidden," muttered Molina. "Follow me. Stay close. We'll use the ruins as cover." He turned to Jason. "Turn down your radio." Both men turned their radios down.

Jason started to creep off to the right, away from the group. Molina grabbed his arm. "Where are *you* going?"

Jason winked. "Let me do my thing, mate."

Molina released him, and Jason skulked off, disappearing into the ruins.

"That man is deeply nuts," whispered Tracey. No one argued.

Molina led the way, crouching behind fragments of walls and fallen pillars. Tracey and Mary followed closely behind him, staying low. The cavern was dark, except for some flickering torchlight emanating from some unknown sources. Molina followed the light.

As they meandered to the center of the subterranean cavern, the ruins gave way to a large clearing. Within the clearing stood a large crowd of the cannibals, covered in white paint, huddled together. They faced away from Molina, Tracey, and Mary, all looking at something or someone. Molina noticed that in between the chants of the crowd, there were the chants of a man, and Molina would've bet a thousand dollars who that man was. Ducking behind a large fallen pillar that must've been at least ten feet thick, he scanned his surroundings.

To his right stood a building that had a semi-intact second floor. The remnants of a staircase led up to a floor that was half demolished. A triangle of floor remained between two mostly intact, adjacent walls. The entire back of the building was gone.

Molina scanned left. There was an exit past the crowd and several more buildings, and it was illuminated. He turned towards Tracey and Mary. "I'm going to go over to that building and get a better vantage point from the second floor." He pointed to the half-building. Then, he pointed to the exit all the way to the left. "When I signal you, you'll both make your way to the exit."

Mary shook her head. "What about you?"

Molina smiled. "I'm going to try and get the drop on our Death Lord friend. Even if I miss, it'll draw attention away from you two. Get out, try to find the outside. Signal the ship."

Tracey swallowed hard. "Once you fire, they'll know where you are and come for you."

Molina glanced around the cavern. "I'm hoping Jason is out there, doing his thing. When they come for me, he'll make his move, and I'll back his play as long as I can."

"You don't have to do this," pleaded Mary.

Molina nodded. "I do. Wait for my signal."

The two women nodded.

Molina crept off to the right, careful to stay low, staying in the shadows.

*

As Molina slinked around the ruins, keeping a watchful eye on the chanting throng, he made his way to the building. He slipped inside, taking soft footsteps. Rubble was strewn about the hard floor, and he was careful not to kick or crunch it, for the smallest sound would carry with these acoustics. Fortunately, the racket from outside served as ambient camouflage, and he only moved during the chanting, which was rhythmic and predictable.

He ascended the stone staircase and stole over to a primitive window, an open frame devoid of glass. He snuck a peek and saw the cannibals arranged in a semicircle around Mike Deluca. Cast in torchlight from sconces behind him, the project manager stood, wraithlike, his eyes cast in the shadows of raised sockets, his cheekbones angular and sharp. A glow emanated from under his shirt, waxing with each chant from the crowd and waning in between. It looked as if his very heartbeat was illuminated.

Molina had a clear shot at him from up there. However, the muzzle flash would give away his position. He had thirty shots, but each one had to count. He considered his possibilities. He would have to take a shot at Mike Deluca first. If he missed, he pondered his next moves. The cannibals would surely come after him, swarming the building.

Molina looked over at the stone staircase. It was narrow. They would only be able to climb up in single file, possibly two abreast at most. He looked back out the window. He figured he had up to three shots at Mike. That left him twenty-seven for the rest. He hastily counted heads. There were easily forty cannibals down there, possibly more. He could hit them as they came up, leaving around ten or so when he'd run out of ammunition. When that happened, he'd have to fight hand-to-hand. He fingered his hunting knife in its sheath. It was possible, or at least that was what Molina was trying to convince himself of.

He scanned the surrounding ruins. This had once been a thriving metropolis, but not for eons. There were statues of lizard men posted at intersections, with broad snouts, tails, and all. Molina wondered what the hell Mike Deluca got mixed up in down here.

*

Mike Deluca stood before his followers, feeling his power pulsate through him.

"Soon we will be released from this prison," said a beautiful woman, standing next to him. "We will be home, together again."

Mike looked over at Barbara. She looked as beautiful as the day they met. She appeared young, radiant, like she was before the cancer had begun to consume her, piece by piece.

She looked at him, her eyes ethereal. "They will try to stop you. You know what you have to do…for me…for us."

Mike nodded slowly, his eyes drunk with the sight of his beloved. "They're already here."

*

Molina searched the cavern for any sign of Jason. *You'd better be here.* The thought did cross his mind that Jason may have bugged out, but Molina didn't think it likely. Jason had lost to Mike Deluca, and he was the kind of man who didn't like to lose. Worse yet, Mike caused him to kill one of their team. There was no way Jason had split. He had unfinished business.

Molina crept to the left wall and peered around at Tracey and Mary. Tracey watched the cannibals, but Mary looked up at him. When Mary saw him, she tapped Tracey on her shoulder, and they both looked up at him. He waved them to the exit on the far left. They nodded and began to sneak around in that direction.

Molina returned to the window and looked down. No one had apparently seen Tracey and Mary's exit. Molina took a deep breath. "Jason, I hope you're out there, ready to make your move," he whispered to himself in silent prayer.

Just then, he heard a soft clicking sound. It was his radio. The clicking was in Morse Code. "In position," it read.

Molina felt better, knowing he wasn't alone. He had no idea where Jason hid, but he was out there, ready. Molina knelt on one knee and placed his left forearm out horizontally in front of him. He rested his pistol hand on his left wrist, steadying it, sliding it over his left wrist until it caught in the crook under his left hand.

He sighted Mike Deluca, who was still looking ahead at his congregation, his eyes still hidden in the recesses of his sockets. Molina squeezed the trigger.

In the middle of squeezing the trigger, one of the cannibals leapt in front of Mike Deluca, shielding him with his body. It happened so fast that Molina didn't have time to react. The bullet left his gun and hit the human shield. He fired again, and the bullet was stopped by another human shield. The third also blocked.

"Crap."

The throng of cannibals turned and looked up at Molina's window, their faces contorted with rage. Mike Deluca was pointing at him with a long, gaunt finger, like a grim reaper. His followers ran towards the building Molina perched in, swarming it.

Molina turned and placed his back to the wall, breathing heavy, trying to stifle his panic. He heard shouting from the floor below him as they flooded the bottom level of the building. He trained his gun at the top of the staircase, where it met his floor.

He reminded himself that he had to control his shots, making each one count. Bald, white heads with fierce eyes appeared above the floor, and he fired once, then twice. Both shots found their targets, and the bodies were shoved aside by those clamoring up the stairs behind them.

He fired at the bodies as they appeared, but with each successive wave, the marauders inched closer. It would be a matter of moments before Molina was swarmed.

*

Tracey and Mary both heard the gunshots from behind them, off to the right as they crept towards the exit. They looked over their shoulders to see the cannibals dashing to where Molina sat, his position revealed.

Tracey pushed Mary from behind. “Come on. Let’s move.”

They picked up their pace, no longer crouching. They were fifty or so feet from the exit, and Mike Deluca’s attention was fixed on Molina.

Two shadows appeared in the exit, blocking their path. Mary skidded to a stop on the smooth, hard floor, and Tracey ran straight into her, nearly shoving her to the ground.

“What is it?” asked Tracey. She looked in front of them and saw.

The silhouettes stood there, watching silently.

“Let us pass,” ordered Mary.

The two forms stepped out of the shadows. Bill and Allison looked pale, their clothes ragged, and they gazed upon Tracey and Mary with raccoon eyes. They trained rifles on the two women…the rifles stolen from the village.

“No way,” gasped Mary.

“This just keeps getting better and better,” said Tracey.

*

Jason sat in the shadows, behind a large pile of rubble. The half wall in front of him cast a shadow from the torchlight, concealing his position. He had Mike Deluca’s back.

He saw the muzzle flashes from the second-floor window off to the left, and he watched as the cannibals swarmed the building. At last, Deluca was alone, and Jason had the advantage of surprise.

Jason raised his Beretta, aiming for Deluca’s center of mass, and squeezed the trigger. At the sound of the shot, Mike Deluca dodged the bullet without even turning around. Jason fired again and again, trying to lead his target, but Deluca was always a half a step ahead. His reflexes were unnatural.

The Death Lord turned to face Jason, dodging another bullet, and another. Jason held his fire. Plan A wasn’t working. He had fifteen shots left. It was time for Plan B. Jason ducked backwards into the shadows. He shifted from cover to cover, receding into the ruins. If he couldn’t reach Mike Deluca, he’d bring Mike Deluca to him.

“Come out, come out, wherever you are,” he heard Mike sing. “Ollie ollie oxen free.”

Jason retreated in a zigzag, trying to cover his tracks. He knew he had to get Mike Deluca into closed quarters, keeping it tight, leaving him less room to dodge. It was the only way.

He backed into a collapsed ruin of a building. The walls and ceiling had caved in, creating a small cave-like cubby hole. Jason backed into it, scurrying further and further back until he could go no further. There was one way in, and one way out. If Mike Deluca came for him, he'd have to enter through the one opening, and there was no room to dodge.

He heard Deluca's voice draw nearer and nearer. He wheezed when he spoke, his voice sounding like an off-tune set of bagpipes. Jason hadn't experienced fear like this since he had been cornered by the wolves in Alaska, trapped and completely at their mercy. He had anticipated his demise in that moment, and he anticipated it again, in this moment.

*

Mike Deluca paused outside the small cavity where his hunter prey hid as a disconcerting sensation washed over him. He turned on his heel and faced the cavern. He watched as his half-dead minions cornered the man with the gun on the second floor of the dilapidated building. His eyes moved past them, and his mind reached out into adjoining caverns until he felt the rush of the awakening of an antagonistic energy that sickened him to his core.

The apparition of his wife turned to him, her eyes aflame with a cold, blue light. "There's another who has found the sacred chamber. The Orb has deemed him worthy."

Mike Deluca nodded, understanding the implications of what she said. He reached out with his mind, the illumination under his shirt growing in intensity, and commanded his cannibals to flood the tunnels and rush the sacred chamber, destroying whomever stood in it.

*

Bracing himself for death, Molina closed his eyes, waiting for the first thrust of a spear to penetrate his body. However, none came. When he opened his eyes, he saw the cannibals rushing off with some great urgency. Suspicious, he slowly rose to his feet and peered out the back of the partially collapsed building. The cannibals were swarming out of the cavern.

When Molina turned to look out the window, he saw Mike Deluca casually strolling out into the open street.

"My minions have something urgent to attend to," boomed Mike Deluca. "You'll have to be content with dealing with me. Come out, both of you, and face your judgement."

Molina wasn't sure who else Mike Deluca was referring to, but as he scanned the ruins, he saw Jason creeping amongst them. Tracey and Mary were being led at gunpoint to where Mike stood. He screwed his eyes and gasped when he recognized their captors to be Bill and Allison. They looked haggard, and they had the rifles stolen from the plateau village.

Molina decided to descend the stairs and face Mike Deluca. Perhaps, if he could distract him enough, Jason would get the drop on him. He unsheathed his hunting knife and crept out of the building and onto the street, where the Death Lord waited for him.

"Ah, at last we meet, face-to-face," grinned Mike. His eyes appeared sunken in dark sockets, his face wan and angular. "Tell your comrade to come out. He won't get the drop on me."

Reflexively, Molina looked behind Mike, and Jason emerged from the ruins. He had his pistol trained on Mike, but he shot a glance at Molina. "Are you all right?"

"For the moment," said Molina. He turned to Mike. "Where'd your zombies run off to in such a hurry?"

"It's no matter," said Mike, waving a dismissive hand. His fingers were pale, long, and bony, the knuckles knobby. He looked like death warmed over.

"Oh, see, I think it does matter," said Molina. "Something's wrong."

For a moment, Mike looked to his left, as if someone was standing there. He even nodded to no one before answering Molina. "I'll have just enough time to dispense with you and the hunter, here."

"You're worried about something," pressed Jason, slowly approaching Mike from the rear. "I know fear when I see it."

Mike turned to face Jason. "Yes, you know fear…fear of being eaten alive by a wolf pack. Fear of the hunter becoming the prey in a quick moment where the tables are turned. You know what it feels like to underestimate your prey. That moment of bitter regret. The embarrassment. The shame. To die with shame is the worst way to go, don't you think?"

"Careful," warned Molina. "He's trying to get inside your head."

"It's too late," said Jason, pointing his gun at Mike Deluca's face. "How do you want to play this?"

Molina raised his large knife, brandishing it. "We take him together."

"He moves fast. Real fast," said Jason.

"You cover me," said Molina.

Mike Deluca stood there silently, smirking, amused, as if any attack they would levy would be futile and ridiculous. Tracey and Mary stood at gunpoint, watching, helpless.

Molina lunged at Mike, bringing his knife down. He narrowly missed Mike as the Death Lord sidestepped the attack, as if he had anticipated it. The wraith moved in a blur, dodging each swing of Molina's knife.

Jason trained his gun on Mike, trying to choose his shot. He had already killed one of their party by accident.

Mike Deluca reached out, placing his hands on Molina's shoulders, and spun him around so that Molina faced away from him. In one deft motion, Mike grabbed Molina's head and snapped it sideways, breaking his neck. He then released the mercenary, allowing his body to drop like a stone, lifeless.

Tracey screamed as Mary cried.

Mike turned to face Jason, who was now trembling, and slowly stepped toward him. "You hesitated, and your comrade died. You killed him with your failure to act."

Jason slowly backtracked as the monster approached, tears streaming down his face. He shook his head. "No. You did it. You did it."

"*We* did it," said Mike. "We're both killers. We both exert a dominion over death, extinguishing life as we see fit."

Jason stumbled on rubble as he blindly stepped backwards, maintaining his distance from Mike Deluca. He managed to keep his balance. "What if I see fit to extinguish you, mate?"

Mike stopped and shrugged his shoulders. "Well, then it comes down to your dominion over death versus mine. In this, I'm afraid you are horribly outmatched. Mate."

Jason raised his gun, his finger over the trigger. He wanted so badly to squeeze and silence this delusional piece of garbage, but he knew if he did, the man would just dodge it. There had to be another angle. "You weren't always like this. Something is driving you."

Mike paused, amused at the change of strategy. "The island? Of course, you idiot."

Jason shook his head, sniffling. "No. Something before the island. Like with me. I lost my brother, which led to me becoming who I am today. I hunt for revenge, because I cannot bring him back."

Mike's face quickly changed expression. It was like a tell in poker, transient and almost unnoticeable, a micro-flash of emotion. However, he quickly regained his composure. He briefly looked off to his left into thin air and then back at Jason. "You are a fool. It was amusing toying with you, but I'm afraid I must kill you now." He advanced upon Jason.

Jason stood his ground. Now *he* was grinning. "That's it, isn't it? I hit the nail on the head. You keep looking at something. Something that haunts you. A ghost from your past?"

Mike swept over to Jason, getting in his face. His eyes burned with an icy rage as he met the hunter's gaze. "You are a fool. You know nothing about me."

Jason didn't budge. He remained practically nose-to-nose with Mike. "You lost someone dear to you. That's why you're messing around with this magic. You want to bring this person back, yet you don't understand this power."

Mike seized him by the front of his shirt and drew him in close. His breath reeked of death and rot. His teeth were yellow and his gums black. "*You* don't understand it! You're not *worthy* to wield it. *I* was deemed worthy. *Me*! Not you!"

Jason glanced down and saw the illumination under Mike Deluca's shirt. It was glowing bright, surging with Mike's hatred. However, that wasn't what was foremost on Jason's mind. He squeezed the trigger, again and again, pumping Mike full of lead.

Mike, distracted by his grief and rage, looked down as crimson welled-up under his filthy shirt. He released Jason and stumbled backwards, clutching his chest. He reached his long fingers under his shirt, probing the bullet holes with his fingertips. He looked at Jason, stunned.

Jason merely looked on, hopeful and horrified, not knowing what to expect next. He turned and saw Tracey and Mary looking at Mike, then Jason, and then Mike again.

Mike closed his eyes and focused, and as he did so, the glow from under his shirt grew brighter. Mike's features shifted, his facial bones becoming cartoonish in their proportions, his eyes more sunken, his body increasingly lithe. His skin took on the pallor of a corpse. When he opened his eyes, they were glassy and lifeless.

Jason turned to Tracey and Mary. "This can't be good."

Mike Deluca lunged at him, and Jason fired his handgun, getting off a couple of rounds before he was seized. Mike lifted him off the ground and threw him backwards. Jason landed on his back and slid until he came to rest against the remnant of a stone wall, unconscious.

"You monster!" cried Mary.

Mike wheeled around and drifted over to the two ladies. His racoon eyes burned in their sunken sockets. "I haven't forgotten about you."

Mary met his gaze, her eyes narrowed. "If you're going to kill us, get it over with."

Mike wagged a long, bony phalange. "I have another purpose for you."

CHAPTER 16

The grinding of stone emanated from inside the box as the top and side panels slid away, revealing a smaller, glowing orb inside. Peter reached out to touch the orb. On contact, it linked with him, reading his thoughts and his desires. He gleaned from it that it possessed power over life itself.

The room darkened, as if someone or something else controlled the illumination. Peter nearly jumped out of his skin when he saw the silhouettes in the shadows that he recognized to be the humanoid reptilian statues from outside. His blood chilled when he realized they moved. They shuffled towards him, slow and deliberate, their skin sallow and even ashen, their eyes glossy in the dim light. Some crept, hunched over, while others slithered along the ground, dragging necrotic limbs and tails in their wake.

He knew they were dead. Normally, he'd soil his pants in a situation like this. Yet, he was unafraid. Perhaps it was all the role-playing games he'd played, with stories much like what he was experiencing on this bizarre island. He knew this was meant to happen.

They surrounded him, looming in the darkness, making no further move. He had garnered an audience with a defunct race, but to what purpose he was unclear. One reptilian figure, adorned in elaborate armor, stepped forward, eying the glowing orb that Peter held in his hands. It reached out its three-clawed hands and began to push the orb towards Peter.

In reaction, Peter raised the orb to chest height, but he didn't push back. That wordless voice inside his head calmed him, instructing him to let it happen. As the voice bade him, he allowed the orb to be pushed against his chest. However, to his surprise, the orb passed through his chest and into his body. He felt a sudden rush of warmth and what he could only describe as inner light, and the cavern around him felt so much colder. Yet, he didn't shiver, like one would do with a fever. It was because the difference wasn't based on actual temperature. He was imbued with the well of life, and the death around him felt cold and empty by comparison. Peter looked down and saw the orb glowing in his chest through his shirt.

The well-armored reptilian figure extended an arm and pointed out of the temple, in a particular direction. Peter knew who lay in wait in that direction, and he knew what he needed to do. He also sensed his friends—some of them, anyway. Two of them, Bill and Allison, felt colder than the others, but not as cold as these humanoid reptiles standing before him.

He knew Mike Deluca was there. He knew Mike was in possession of the other orb, which imbued him with powers diametrically opposite to Peter's. He also knew that Mike had Tracey and Mary as hostages. He sensed Jason's inner light, but it was fading, and Molina's had been newly extinguished. Peter knew it was time to face the Death Lord.

With that realization, the room illuminated and the reptilian warriors vanished. Peter was unsure of how his powers matched up against Mike's, but he was emboldened with a confidence he hadn't felt before.

As he reached the entrance of the temple, he heard a commotion outside—raised voices, grunting, and growling. When he stepped outside, unafraid, he was surrounded by scores of cannibals. He felt their light, which was dark, like a blacklight. They felt somewhere between the reptilian men and his friends. In fact, they felt exactly like Bill and Allison.

The cannibals in their white war paint snarled at him, brandishing spears and snapping their jaws, but they did not approach. Did they sense his change?

Peter closed his eyes, and the light emanating from his chest burned in intensity. The light reached out, brightening the vast, outer cavern.

The cannibals shrunk back in apparent fear. Some dropped to their knees, as if in reverence and contrition to the great light. Peter opened his eyes when he heard them wailing. As he looked around, he saw them thrashing and writhing on the ground, crying out and gnashing their teeth. Their pallor gave way as their flesh renewed. Peter felt the blood course through their vessels as their temperatures rose and their bloodlust abated.

Their transformation complete, Peter stepped amongst them, and they parted, gawking. He passed through them and left them behind to sort themselves out. He had bigger fish to fry. He was coming for Mike Deluca.

*

When Peter had reached the cavern containing the ruins, he felt the presences and their varying 'temperatures.' It was like a paper he had read on space travel some time ago, that mentioned the cloaking of vessels was impossible in the cold, dark void of space. Any vessel would disperse even the smallest amount of heat, placing a spotlight on it. That was what Peter felt. He felt the others as if they had been highlighted.

As he moved between the crumbled buildings and rubble, that wordless voice inside his mind recognized each structure. He passed a merchant's shop, which once sold armor and various weapons. He passed a bank, a governmental building; a library that once contained orbs like the one inside his chest, only they were lesser orbs crafted for record keeping.

At last, he reached a clearing where a pale wraith waited for him. Behind the figure, stood Tracey and Mary, held at gunpoint by Bill and Allison.

"Pete, go back!" cried Tracey.

"It's a trap!" added Mary.

Peter looked, and Jason was lying on the ground off to the left, his vital signs fading quickly. On the ground, in front of the pale wraith, lay Molina's body, its head twisted in an unnatural direction.

"Mike Deluca, I presume." Peter's voice was unnaturally calm and matter-of-fact, as if he were calling the sky blue or water wet.

Mike Deluca grinned, his lips pulling back over yellow, rotten teeth. "You must be from Poseidon Tech. Come to survey the island you've phased into existence?"

Peter shook his head and stepped forward, pausing twenty feet in front of the Death Lord. "I'm more of a consultant. A paleontologist, actually. Why don't you let the others go?" More than a question, it was an implied threat.

Mike laughed. It was an empty, wheezing sound. "A paleontologist? How interesting. Well, paleontologist, if an accomplished hunter and an ex-military mercenary couldn't fight me, what makes you think *you* can?"

Peter noticed Tracey and Mary looking at him. More specifically, they were staring at the glow in his chest.

"Pete?" was all Tracey could manage. That simple word and its inflection was pregnant with so many questions. 'Are you all right?' 'What are you doing?' 'Are you going to help us?'

Peter waved her off and returned his attention to Mike Deluca. "I'm not going to fight you."

Mike bellowed, the harsh sounds echoing off the cavern walls and ceiling. "Then you won't get your friends back."

Peter grinned. "We'll see about that."

Mike feigned a shocked expression. "Oooh, tough talk. Tell me...Pete...I have the death orb, which controls death and destruction. You obviously have the life orb. You can heal and harness the power of life itself. Tell me, which do you think will win?"

Peter's grin widened. "For you to know that, you must've tried to go for the life orb, but it wouldn't let you control it, am I right?"

Mike's smug expression faded, and he nodded. "Yes, you're right about that, but you still haven't answered my question."

Peter closed his eyes. He heard Tracey and Mary gasp. He felt the warmth well up inside him as he reached out, not to Mike, but to Bill and Allison. He felt their chill, their dim inner light. He turned their bodies, washing over their cells, rejuvenating them, until their light grew inside them.

When Peter opened his eyes, Bill and Allison had dropped their weapons and released Tracey and Mary. They appeared stunned, confused as to where they were and what was happening. Tracey and Mary hugged them, telling them they were all right.

Mike Deluca looked amused. "Nice trick. Why don't you try that on me?" His eyes narrowed. "I double doggie dare you."

Peter closed his eyes, and the light inside him burned like a flame. He reached out to Mike Deluca, who stood before him, and extended his warmth. However, Mike's essence felt frigid to the touch. Something bolstered Mike's power. Peter's warmth receded, shrinking away from the coldness of death. Peter focused harder, stoking the flames of life welling up inside of him, reaching out with all his might, pressing against Mike Deluca's icy barrier. Frustrated, Peter grunted as his warmth refused to penetrate Mike's shield.

Spent, he opened his eyes and staggered, almost losing his balance. He looked over at the others. "Get out of here. Now."

Tracey's eyes were pleading. "We're not leaving without you."

Peter appealed to Mary. "Get them out of here."

Mary nodded, reluctant, but she grabbed Tracey by the arm and addressed the others. "Come on, let's go."

Confused, the others followed her lead, and they crossed the cavern to the exit on the other side.

Mike let them go. "They won't get far. So, still feeling confident?"

Peter wiped spittle from the corner of his mouth. "You wanted the life orb to bring your wife back. She was sick with cancer. But the orb wouldn't let you. So, you thought you could bring her back by controlling death."

Mike looked startled. "There was no way for you to know that. I kept you out."

Peter took a few steps forward. "The only problem is, controlling death doesn't create life."

Mike jutted out a long index finger, pointing at Peter. "I see you, Pete. I see what you are doing, and I see what you can't do."

Now, Peter was taken off guard. He squinted his eyes. "What's that?"

Mike grinned wickedly, looking more monster than man. "You can control life, but you cannot inflict death. So, if you can't turn me, how exactly do you plan to take me out?"

Peter cursed himself silently. He hadn't considered this. Suddenly, Mike exploded in a blur of movement, closing the distance between them in the blink of an eye. Peter felt intense pain as Mike hit him with an upper cut, forcing Peter to bite into his own tongue.

Hot blood welled-up inside his mouth, and Peter was knocked supine. His head rang from percussion with the hard, rock floor. The room spun as he heard Mike's hollow laughter fill the cavern.

Peter sat up, grimacing, and tried to push himself to standing. However, the ground began to move beneath him. He looked up and saw Mike Deluca waving his hands about like a magician. Peter lost his balance and fell on his side. Mike strode up to him and kicked him in the ribs. Peter clutched his side and curled up into a ball as Mike rained down more punches and kicks.

*

Jason lay there, watching his comrade get the stuffing knocked out of him, too weak and powerless to intercede. *Fight, damn you. Fight back.* However, Peter just lay on the ground, the blows causing him to writhe in the dirt in agony.

"Leave him alone, you bastard," was all Jason could muster. Saying that much took whatever reserve of energy he had left.

Mike Deluca stepped back, surveying the damage. Peter lay on the ground, breathing heavily, blood mixing with drool and dangling from his split mouth.

Mike pointed at Jason. "Yes, you'll watch him die, and then I'll finish you. Then, I'll bring you both back to serve me."

Peter grunted as he strained, but it wasn't to get up. His chest began to glow, and when the light dimmed once more, he was sitting up. Jason didn't believe his eyes. Peter wiped the blood and spittle from his face, and his face appeared undamaged.

Mike turned to face Peter, as the paleontologist stood up again. "Ha! Nice trick! I'll have to try harder."

The Death Lord rushed Peter, punching and kicking in a streak of violence. Jason was unsure if Mike was indeed moving that fast, or if it was the concussion he had sustained.

Peter took each and every blow, weathering the storm of ferocity, doing little to resist or fight back. The light in his chest burned its radiance, increasing in intensity as he took more and more damage. *Fight back, dammit*, thought Jason to himself. Mike grabbed Peter's head and twisted. Peter's eyes went vacant, his expression slack, and Mike released him. Peter crumpled to the ground in a bloody heap.

Jason, however, noticed that Peter's light had not extinguished. It hadn't even dimmed. He gasped as he saw Peter sit up, his head jutting off at an odd angle from his body, his neck clearly broken. Slowly, Peter's head turned, as if on its own, his neck straightening as bones cracked and mended. Peter stood up, once again, and faced his adversary.

Mike huffed in exasperation. "Stubborn SOB, aren't you?"

*

Peter wiped his mouth on the back of his arm, cracked his neck, and smiled at Mike. "Looks like we have a bit of a stalemate."

Mike shook his head. "No, I'm just going to have to facilitate things a bit." He lunged forward in a blur and seized Peter. His grip was unnaturally strong. Peter attempted to wriggle free, but it was no use. Mike Deluca was too strong.

Mike went nose-to-nose with Peter as he gazed into his eyes. Mike's eyes glowed like hot embers in dark sockets. "I'll turn you, like I've turned the others. You'll be my slave."

Peter felt Mike reaching out, touching his soul, the sensation like frost. Peter summoned his own inner strength, reaching out.

"You cannot stop me," hissed Mike Deluca. "You're too weak." His eyes burned brighter, the illumination white-washing Peter's vision. However, Peter didn't need to see. He only needed to feel. He lashed out with his bright energy, finding its target, and it quickly faded. Peter was spent.

Mike Deluca's eyes burned. "See! I told you! You are too weak! Death always extinguishes life!"

There was a loud thump, and Mike's eyes dimmed for a moment. He released Peter, who dropped to his knees, and reached wildly behind him. As Peter's vision cleared, he saw Jason standing behind Mike, his face straining with effort. He pulled out his large hunting knife and drove it into Mike's back again.

Mike Deluca yelped and jerked his body away. He whirled around, stunned, to face his assailant. "But you…you were dying."

Jason winked at Peter. "All I needed was a little boost from my mate." He plunged the knife into Mike Deluca's cold heart and left it in his chest.

Mike staggered backwards and dropped to his knees, clutching the knife's handle protruding from his chest. He hunched over, wheezing.

Peter and Jason watched. Peter looked horrified, but Jason was grinning, vindicated. Their expressions, however, faded as Mike's wheezing morphed into dry laughter.

"Come on," protested Jason. "Why won't he just die?"

Mike looked up and gazed upon the hunter. "You cannot kill what is already dead."

*

Tracey, Mary, Allison, and Bill dashed down the long, winding tunnel hewn into the cliff.

"Where are we going?" panted Bill. "Do we even know?"

"There has to be an opening to the outside," said Mary. "Mike Deluca was trying to keep us away from here, so it must be close."

As they rounded a bend, the dark tunnel began to brighten. "Look," said Bill, pointing ahead.

"Is that daylight?" cried Allison.

"I think so," said Tracey, but it was more of a hope than a confirmation of fact.

"Only one way to find out," said Mary.

They ran down the tunnel, and the light grew brighter until they saw the bright, white daylight from a breach to the outside. They ran to the mouth of the cave and skidded to a halt at the edge, knocking a few stones and pebbles off the edge to the ocean below.

"Look, it's our ship," pointed Tracey. A helicopter circled around.

Allison shoved her way to the front and began waving her arms. "Over here! Over here!"

Tracey and Mary exchanged looks, shrugged, and began waving their arms and crying out, too. Bill joined them. "Over here! Help!"

However, after some time, the helicopter or the ship gave no indication that their cries had been heard. "Okay, this isn't working," said Tracey.

Mary looked down. "We'll have to jump."

"Jump? I'm not jumping," said Allison.

Mary arched an eyebrow. "You want off this island, don't you?"

Allison shook her head, panicking, her hair blowing in the ocean breeze. "There has to be another way."

Mary shook her head. "There is no other way. If we go back, it means death."

Tracey looked down. "That's what, maybe fifty feet down?"

Bill looked over the edge, holding Mary's shoulders to steady himself. "Maybe. Tough to tell."

Allison looked at Tracey, her eyes pleading. "We're not really going to jump, are we?"

Bill placed a gentle hand on her shoulder. "I want to see my wife and boys again. Don't you want to see your family? They're waiting for us, but we're going to have to jump."

"I'll help you," offered Mary.

"You can do it," added Tracey.

Allison balled her hands at her sides and drew her shoulders up to her ears. "Ooooooh, this is a really bad idea."

"It's our only idea," insisted Mary.

Bill and Tracey stood at the edge, looking down. "Okay, we go first," said Bill. "On three."

Tracey nodded, her body tightening out of fear, bracing herself for the plunge.

"I don't think I can do this," muttered Allison.

"We'll watch them go first," said Mary. "If they make it, then we'll jump."

Tracey looked back at Mary, incredulous. "Oh, great. So, we're the canaries in the mineshaft, now?"

Mary shrugged her shoulders.

Tracey took Bill by the hand and squeezed it. "I'm ready."

"We have to jump so that we clear the cliff, okay?"

"Got it," said Tracey. "What about those waves? They'll slam us against the rock cliffside."

"When we go under, swim out, away from the cliff. When we come up, we take a deep breath and go under the waves, swimming away further and further, like a surfer swimming under the waves to go out further."

Tracey clenched her free hand into a fist. "Okay, that should work. In theory. On paper."

Bill nodded and began the count. "One…two…THREE."

Holding hands, they jumped off the ledge. Allison gasped and covered her eyes. Mary watched them fall until they disappeared into the ocean. She watched, waiting for them to resurface. The image of the ocean outside began to flicker, and there was a glitching sound of static.

Allison uncovered her face. "Did they make it?" She saw the flickering image of the outside. "What's that? What's happening?"

"The island is probably phasing out of our dimension," said Mary, grabbing Allison by the hand. "We have to jump now."

Allison yanked her hand away and stepped back, away from the drop. "No way. I can't. It's too high."

Mary stood in front of her, her eyes meeting Allison's. "We have to go now, or we'll be stuck here. Your husband and baby are waiting for you. If you stay here, you'll be lost forever."

Allison paused, weighing the options. She swallowed hard and nodded. "Okay. You're right."

Mary smiled. "Good. We're going to do it together, just like Bill and Tracey."

Allison nodded, looking dubious.

Mary stood at the edge as the image of the ocean, their ship, and the helicopter outside glitched with increasing frequency. She held out her hand, and Allison took it. Mary led Allison next to her. "Okay, on three. Right?"

Allison nodded.

Mary looked forward. "Here we go. One…two…" Before Allison's body could tense up and become rigid, Mary let go of Allison's hand and shoved her off the edge. Allison cried out as she fell face forward and dropped, disappearing into the crashing waves below.

*

Mike Deluca laughed again, the blade of Jason's hunting knife rattling inside his hollow chest. He looked to his right and saw his wife standing there. She, too, was laughing with him, a bitter sound.

She looked at the others and then him. "Gather your strength and finish them both. Then you will possess both orbs and have complete dominion over life and death. You can go back to your world and raise me, bring me back."

Mike's enthusiasm faded. She looked at him, disappointed at his lack of expression or response. "What? What is wrong?"

"You mean *our* world," said Mike.

"Yes, that's what I said," said his wife.

"No, it's not," said Mike.

"What difference does it make?" snapped his wife. "This is no time to quibble over words."

"You're not Barbara," said Mike, a cold tear streaming down his cheek. "You never were."

His wife shook a fist at him. "I gave you power. I gave you perpetuity. Finish this and take your place as master of life and death. Bring me back." Her expression softened. "I miss you so much, honey. We're so close. We can be together again."

It didn't matter anymore. Nothing mattered anymore, except getting her back. Cancer had taken her away from him, but he was going to remove its power. He was going to take her away from cancer.

He stood up, but the paleontologist stepped in front of him, his chest glowing. To Mike's surprise, the man embraced him, careful to avoid the protruding knife handle, gripping him tightly.

Mike felt a warmth emanate from the paleontologist named Peter. It thawed the edges of his icy façade and pushed its way in, towards his core. His faith momentarily shaken in what purported to be his wife, he was too weak to fight back. Deep down, he knew it wasn't really Barbara, and he dropped his defenses, allowing the paleontologist in. Before his eyes, Barbara transformed into a horrid apparition of tight skin drawn over bone, its mouth open in a silent scream, and it vanished before his eyes.

The man embracing him strained with focus as his inner light pored over Mike. Pete invoked such power that the cavern itself rumbled and shook, causing one hell of an earthquake. The ground began to open up and ruins crumbled once more, as did the ice that had walled-in Mike's heart.

His flesh began to thaw, blood recirculated through his veins, and Mike's heart beat once more. However, the heart tissue around the blade could not close, and blood pooled out of the wound and into his chest. Red trickled and then streamed from around the knife handle jutting out of his chest.

How ironic that this Peter had killed him by bringing him back to life.

*

Peter felt the entire cavern shake as he strained to imbue the last dead cells of Mike Deluca with life. It had taken all he had in him, and the orb within his chest felt as if it was going to explode, but he had done it. Feeling spent, he opened his eyes to find Mike lying on the ground on his side, thick blood pooling around him, eyes vacant. The Death Lord was dead.

Jason came over to Peter and placed a hand on his shoulder. “You okay, mate?”

Peter nodded, the simple action making him feel woozy. “I think so.”

Jason grinned. “You clever man, you did it. I would’ve never thought of that. And, thanks for bringing me back.” He stretched and bounced on the balls of his feet. “I’m feeling pretty damned good. Fit as a fiddle, in fact.”

By contrast, Peter’s entire body felt sore, and he had one hell of a headache. “I think I overreached.”

“What do you mean?”

“It’s hard to describe…when I was trying to reach him, I had to unleash. It was as if a nuclear bomb had detonated.”

Jason shrugged. “I figured you caused that earthquake. What happened to all of those cannibals? Where’d they go?”

“Home. I turned them, too.”

Jason looked at Peter in genuine admiration. “Holy smokes. Out of all of us, *you* were the damned hero all along.”

Peter smiled. “You kind of helped by getting the drop on him.”

Jason returned the smile. “A little bit.”

“Yeah, just a little, but I did most of it.” Peter laughed.

Jason looked around the cavern. “Do you think the others made it?”

Suddenly, Mike’s chest began to glow. Peter and Jason jumped back, fearing the worst. However, Mike Deluca didn’t move. The orb within his chest passed out of his body and rose into the air, pulsating its icy blue light.

Jason pointed at Peter’s chest. “Look.”

Peter looked down to find his orb pulsating in unison with the other orb. “That’s weird.”

“Be careful, mate.” Jason backed away slowly, as if the other orb could turn on him at any moment.

Peter stepped forward and reached out.

Jason jutted a hand out. “What are you doing?”

“I know what I’m doing.”

“Be careful.”

Peter reached out, grabbed the orb, and brought it to his chest. It passed into his body, just as the other orb had, and melded with the other orb. There was a sharp sensation of pain, and Peter let out a yelp.

Jason stepped forward, looking unsure of what to do. "Are you okay? Peter, talk to me, man."

Peter grimaced as he felt all kinds of strange sensations pass through his body. "I can feel it."

"Feel what?"

"The pulse of the island. The entire island. I can feel the people and the animals…there are other tribes on this island, other dinosaurs that we haven't seen yet."

"What about the others?" asked Jason. "Did Tracey, Mary, Allison, and Bill make it off the island?"

Peter closed his eyes and reached out. "I can no longer feel them…except for Mary. She's still on the island. She's walking back towards us."

"That's strange."

Something stirred in the ruins.

"There's something else…"

Jason looked around, scanning his surroundings. "There's movement in the shadows. Take cover."

Peter placed a hand up. "No, it's okay…I think."

Jason's eyes darted around the cavern. "That doesn't sound very convincing now, does it?"

Silhouettes crept in the shadows, emitting hisses. They closed in on Peter and Jason, surrounding them.

Jason started to panic. He spun around, assessing the threat. "Okay, what now? There's got to be hundreds of them. Do something. Use your powers, or something."

"I already have. That's what caused this."

"What?"

"Remember when I said it was like a nuclear bomb going off? Well, I think I kind of woke something up."

"What? What did you do?"

The figures stepped into Peter's illumination. They appeared humanoid, but with reptilian features. Peter recognized them from the statues in the other cavern and his vision in the temple. However, these creatures looked quite alive and quite healthy. He had the strong suspicion that it was his doing.

"Relax," Peter told Jason. "I don't think they're going to hurt us."

Jason stepped closer to Peter. "How do you know that?"

One of the reptilian figures stepped in front of Peter and crouched over, looking at the bright glow in his chest with large, black eyes. It hissed, but softly. It didn't appear to be an aggressive or defensive response. It stepped closer, holding a clawed, three-fingered hand over the orbs, as if warming its hands over a fire.

Jason inched closer to Peter, standing behind him. "Careful."

In a sudden movement, the reptilian figure genuflected in front of Peter. In response, all of the other lizard men took a knee, bowing their heads.

Peter looked up and saw…no, felt, Mary enter the cavern on the far side. She was okay. She had, for some reason, come back. He knew she came back for him. He also knew the island had phased out and they were no longer in their home dimension.

There'd be time to discuss it with her at length, but right now there were other pressing matters. He, a misfit, from his own spacetime, awkward and meek, had run the gauntlet of dinosaurs, cannibals, and a Death Lord. Lost in spacetime, he had gained dominion over the powers of life and death, freed a tribe besieged by a power-hungry project manager, and awoken a lost race that now appeared to worship him as a god. Oh, and it looked like he was going to get the girl. Not the girl he thought he wanted, but life had a funny way of throwing a curveball at the most opportune times, like a lost island from another dimension filled with dinosaurs, lizard men, and magic.

The corners of Peter's mouth curled up into a grin.

* * *

Allison kicked her legs with all of her might and breached the surface, filling her lungs with much needed air. As she bobbed up and down in the surf, she saw Bill and Tracey waving their arms and calling out to her.

Allison looked around, but she didn't see Mary. In fact, she didn't even see the sheer cliff of the island behind her. The island had vanished.

She turned back to see the helicopter approaching. The pilot must've spotted them. She was going home.

CHAPTER 17

One Year Later

The doorbell rang as Tracey was eating cereal at her parents' kitchen table. Her father got up, placed a gentle hand on her shoulder, and went to answer the front door. Her mother sat across from her, regarding her with pity and concern, as Tracey sipped some hot coffee. She loved her mother's coffee.

Her father returned to the kitchen. "Tracey, honey, there's a man here to see you. He says his name is David Lennox."

Tracey's skin went cold at the mention of that name. She swallowed a mouthful of cereal and wiped the milk off her lips with a napkin.

"Is he someone from the university?" asked her mother.

"No. He's a recruiter."

Her mother's expression lightened. She leaned forward. "That's great, honey! It's been too long…" She paused, switching gears. "Did you know he was coming? You have to get dressed."

Tracey put a hand up to silence her. "It's fine." She stood up and turned to her father. "Can I speak with him in the study?"

Her father, looking puzzled, smiled. "Sure, honey. Are you sure you're ready for this?"

Tracey nodded. She was ready, but not for what her father thought. She left the kitchen and padded in her bare feet into the living room where David Lennox stood, waiting patiently. He was in his usual designer suit, his hair slicked back, perfectly coiffed.

"Hello, Tracey. Is there somewhere private we can talk?"

Tracey nodded and guided David into the study. She stepped inside, closing the door behind her. She gestured to the couch. "Please, have a seat."

David did as he was told, and sat at the far end of the leather couch, regarding the bookcases lining the walls.

Tracey decided to remain standing. "What do you want?"

David plastered his best endearing grin on his face. "I wanted to see how you're doing."

"Baloney."

"If you don't mind me saying, you look terrible. You've lost weight, and you look tired. I heard you resigned from your position at the university. Why?"

"You know why."

He shook his head. "Actually, I don't. You went to all those years of school to become a paleontologist, you even got to see dinosaurs first-hand, and then you resigned."

"You might say I've lost my taste for the subject matter."

David managed an awkward chuckle. "I have to admit, that seems odd."

"It is odd. Everything that happened was odd."

David leaned forward, his expression suddenly grave. "Tracey, our labs have re-established contact with an island…we believe *that* island."

"I'm not interested."

"Why not? You still have a close friend and colleague on that island."

"That island ruined my life."

"Ruined your life? How? You survived. Your colleagues in the party, according to your own account, all survived, even the ones you thought died. You witnessed dinosaurs firsthand. You got to observe and interact. Isn't that every paleontologist's dream?"

"I haven't been the same since."

"I still don't follow."

Tracey met his eyes with hers. "I found out things about myself on that island, things I didn't like."

"You're harboring guilt," said David. He looked down at the floor and sighed. "I know things happened on that island. Strange things. People died and somehow came back. I know you blame yourself for some of what happened."

"You have no idea," she said in sharp reply.

David stood up and walked over to Tracey. "You say the island ruined your life. Yet, when you returned home, you readily accepted your stipend, and you honored the non-disclosure clause. You told no one outside of Poseidon Tech what happened."

"I honored your gag order. So what?"

"Tracey, do you think that mission was ever about the ELT device? We had breached spacetime and phased an island from another dimension into our reality, and now we've done it again. This is your chance to find Peter. To bring him back and make things right."

"I'm not interested. Find someone else."

"We tried. Allison McGary and Bill Gibson both declined."

"I said I'm not interested."

"Baloney," said David.

She narrowed her eyes. "Excuse me?"

"Come on, now. You resigned from your position at the university as soon as you returned. You haven't done anything resembling employment since."

"What's your point, Mr. Lennox?"

"You're lost, Tracey. You've been lost ever since you returned. Find Peter. Bring him back. Rid yourself of this burden of guilt that you lug around with you."

Tracey looked him in the eye. "You want to talk baloney. Okay. Let's talk baloney. You want me to go because I've already been there. I know what to expect, and let's face it, paleontologists don't exactly grow on trees. You also want me to go because it wouldn't serve Poseidon Tech well to have too many paleontologists know about your dirty little secret. The fewer people that know about it, the better, because even with all the gag orders in the world, if enough people know, somehow it'll get out."

David's earnest expression gave way to a sly grin. "Yes, those points are all valid. Let's help each other out. You help us continue to explore another dimension, and we'll help you rescue Peter and get that monkey off your back."

"What's the endgame in all this?" asked Tracey. "Why not go public?"

"We can't right now."

"Why not?"

"It's too soon."

"What are you after? Something tells me it's not for the sake of *exploration*."

"Why does it matter to you?"

"Because it does. I don't want to help you create a weapon or threaten the safety of this dimension. What if those things get off the island?"

"We wouldn't allow it to happen."

"If you bring an island from another reality into ours, what makes you think no one else would notice—Russia, North Korea?"

"We've taken precautions. Frankly, that's all above your paygrade."

"What are you looking for, Mr. Lennox?"

"I'm looking to recruit you back onto the team."

"That's not what I meant. What's Poseidon Tech looking for?"

David smiled. It was his best and only defense. He produced a silver business card holder out of his breast pocket and opened it. He slid a single card out, walked over to the desk, and placed the card on it. "Here's my card. Think it over. We haven't even discussed remittance yet."

"I don't need your money."

"That may be so, but I still think we can help each other out."

"Peter is dead. There's no bringing him back."

David now produced his cell phone and toggled through menus to call up a picture. He handed the phone to Tracey.

Her skin went cold. She accepted the phone and looked at the picture. "What's this?"

"Not what. Who."

"This is impossible."

"Why? Bill survived on that island for months by himself. As you can see from that pic, Peter's not alone."

She handed the phone back to David, who slipped it back into his pocket. "This doesn't change anything."

David walked past Tracey and opened the door to the study. He paused in the doorway. "Think it over. We'll need your answer in forty-eight hours. Take care, Tracey." That being said, he left.

Tracey chewed on the fingernails of her right hand as her mind raced. *Was the picture authentic? Was it really Peter in the picture? What were those other figures around him? Why was he glowing?*

She walked over to her father's desk and picked up the business card, bending it between her fingers. Her father poked his head into the study. "Everything okay? How did it go?"

Tracey turned, lost in thought. "I'm not sure."

THE END

facebook.com/severedpress
twitter.com/severedpress

CHECK OUT OTHER GREAT DINOSAUR BOOKS

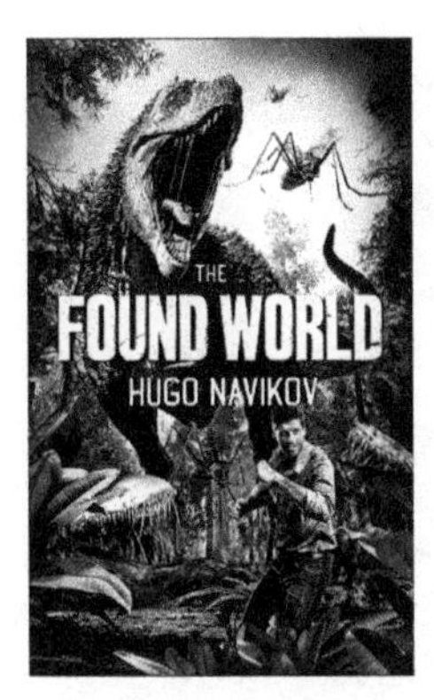

THE FOUND WORLD
by Hugo Navikov

A powerful global cabal wants adventurer Brett Russell to retrieve a superweapon stolen by the scientist who built it. To entice him to travel underneath one of the most dangerous volcanoes on Earth to find the scientist, this shadowy organization will pay him the only thing he cares about: information that will allow him to avenge his family's murder.

But before he can get paid, he and his team must enter an underground hellscape of killer plants, giant insects, terrifying dinosaurs, and an army of other predators never previously seen by man.

At the end of this journey awaits a revelation that could alter the fate of mankind ... if they can make it back from this horrifying found world.

HOUSE OF THE GODS
by Davide Mana

High above the steamy jungle of the Amazon basin, rise the flat plateaus known as the Tepui, the House of the Gods. Lost worlds of unknown beauty, a naturalistic wonder, each an ecology onto itself, shunned by the local tribes for centuries. The House of the Gods was not made for men.

But now, the crew and passengers of a small charter plane are about to find what was hidden for sixty million years.

Lost on an island in the clouds 10.000 feet above the jungle, surrounded by dinosaurs, hunted by mysterious mercenaries, the survivors of Sligo Air flight 001 will quickly learn the only rule of life on Earth: Extinction.

facebook.com/severedpress
twitter.com/severedpress

CHECK OUT OTHER GREAT DINOSAUR BOOKS

FLIPSIDE
by JAKE BIBLE

The year is 2046 and dinosaurs are real.

Time bubbles across the world, many as large as one hundred square miles, turn like clockwork, revealing prehistoric landscapes from the Cretaceous Period.

They reveal the Flipside.

Now, thirty years after the first Turn, the clockwork is breaking down as one of the world's powers has decided to exploit the phenomenon for their own gain, possibly destroying everything then and now in the process.

A MAN OUT OF TIME
by Christopher Laflan

Five years after the Chinese Axis detonated an unknown weapon of mass destruction off the southern coast of the United States, Special Ops Sergeant John Crider and the members of Shadow Company have finally captured what they all hope will lead to the end of the war. Unfortunately, the population within the United States is no longer sustainable. In an effort to stabilize the economy, the government enacts the Cryonics Act. One hundred years in suspended animation, all debt forgiven, and a chance at a less crowded future are too good to pass up for John and his young daughter.

Except not everything always goes as planned as Sergeant John Crider finds himself pitted against a land of prehistoric monsters genetically resurrected from the fossil record, murderous inhabitants, and a future he never wanted.

CHECK OUT OTHER GREAT DINOSAUR BOOKS

PRIMORDIA
by Greig Beck

Ben Cartwright, former soldier, home to mourn the loss of his father stumbles upon cryptic letters from the past between the author, Arthur Conan Doyle and his great, great grandfather who vanished while exploring the Amazon jungle in 1908.

Amazingly, these letters lead Ben to believe that his ancestor's expedition was the basis for Doyle's fantastical tale of a lost world inhabited by long extinct creatures. As Ben digs some more he finds clues to the whereabouts of a lost notebook that might contain a map to a place that is home to creatures that would rewrite everything known about history, biology and evolution.

But other parties now know about the notebook, and will do anything to obtain it. For Ben and his friends, it becomes a race against time and against ruthless rivals.

In the remotest corners of Venezuela, along winding river trails known only to lost tribes, and through near impenetrable jungle, Ben and his novice team find a forbidden place more terrifying and dangerous than anything they could ever have imagined.

PANGAEA EXILES
by Jeff Brackett

Tried and convicted for his crimes, Sean Barrow is sent into temporal exile—banished to a time so far before recorded history that there is no chance that he, or any other criminal sent back, has any chance of altering history.

Now Sean must find a way to survive more than 200 million years in the past, in a world populated by monstrous creatures that would rend him limb from limb if they got the chance. And that's just his fellow prisoners.

The dinosaurs are almost as bad.

CPSIA information can be obtained
at www.ICGtesting.com
Printed in the USA
LVHW042316250623
750763LV00005B/283